Black Butterfly

Katie L. Carroll

To all the unreliable narrators out there

THIS STORY CONTAINS scenes that depict
death, violence, terrorist attacks,
and psychological and physical torture.
The main character experiences
memory loss due to a head injury,
thoughts of self-harm, and suicidal ideation.
Please read with care.

Thin arms wrap around me, cutting through the heat of flames and betrayal, and lift me in a feat of impossible strength. The smell of burning is everywhere. Phantom screams fill my head, and the stench of charred flesh stings my nose.

Just a memory.

My only memory.

A bubble of panic boils in my stomach, but before it overwhelms me, my instincts take over and I pull in a fresh gulp of air. Eyes closed, I focus on my body, feel the air fill my nose and reach my lungs until the frantic beat of my heart settles.

My eyelids flutter open to a sky of ash. Floating through the air. Covering the ground. Coating my tongue with a chalky paste. It's like looking at the world through a screen.

An eerie quiet presses against me. I squeeze my eyes shut against the dull gray sky that feels all too bright and wonder why I'm outside, but that thought quickly falls away to more pressing ones. I search for something about myself to hold on to, but all I get is a throbbing pain pushing against my skull. My hands clench, nails digging into the raw, red skin of my palms.

A pallor of dread hangs over me, like a leftover feeling upon waking from a dream that is immediately forgotten. Only this isn't a dream I've lost; it's my life.

"Hello. Are you awake?" asks a deep voice. The person's warm breath brushes my cheek.

Instantly my muscles tighten—poised, as if anticipating an attack—but my pulse remains steady, calm. I feign sleep. The cold sensation at my sore back tells me I'm lying on metal. A potential weapon. Though I don't need a weapon to kill a man.

A less disturbing thought than it should be, but it's not the time to linger over such things.

I sense the person hovering above me and wait until I hear them move away, sense a little space between us. Then I whip open my eyes and jump off what turns out to be a gurney on wheels. It crashes onto its side. I shove it between me and the threat and duck behind it like a child hiding from a thunderstorm.

My brain screams for me to stay hidden. Yet my body is primed to fight, itching to take down the threat. Being frightened should make sense, but the fighter instinct fits like a second skin. My beige hands, nails caked with grime under my French manicure, shake while my mind and body wage a war over what to do next.

The person stays on the other side of the gurney where I can't see them, which I don't like. Still, I stay out of sight and soak in my surroundings, hungry for information. I'm in a service station parking lot. A six-lane highway stretches out in front of me; it's completely empty, not a single car in sight. Which is odd, right? It's hard to trust my mind when I have no concrete memories of my life.

A digital sign that is supposed to display the price of

gas is dark. A large white tent is set up near the signpost. Ten sheets cover body-shaped figures on the ground. It takes mere seconds for me to take in the scene, as if I'm practiced at assessing my environment. But what I'm seeing doesn't make sense.

I swallow through a lump in my throat, tasting ash. My vision blurs, turning as scattered as my thoughts. A splitting headache tap dances a frantic rhythm in my head. The pain starts at the base of my neck, snakes up the back of my skull, and wraps around to my temples.

I peek over the side of the gurney and note the person is younger than I expected, more an overlarge boy than a man. Probably late teens, 6'2", a wiry 150 pounds. It's like he's an item in a catalogue and I'm able to size him up in a single glance. A handy skill, but it's unnerving not to understand why I can do this.

I hazard a question, though it's not the one I really want to know. "Who are you?"

The question ends on a tremble that sets off a spike of emotion in my gut. Anger maybe. Like I'm angry at myself for showing vulnerability, though that is the rawest, most visceral feeling I have right now. Why should I hide that?

"I'm Elijah Aarons," he says.

It occurs to me that if I don't know who I am, then I might know him and not remember, but that doesn't seem to be the case as he shows no hint of being surprised by my inquiry.

He holds his hands out in an offer to help me stand. As if I need help.

"You were injured fleeing the city after the attacks." His last word hisses in my brain—attacks, attacks, attacks.

I shake my head, worsening the headache. "What city?" My mouth is dry, so licking my chapped lips does nothing to soothe them.

He moves closer, his footsteps muffled by the ash, and I duck lower behind the gurney. "New York."

I can picture the skyline in my head—the streets full of cabs and buses, the sidewalks teeming with people—but not my place among them.

"What's your name?" he asks, the voice closer than I expect.

Albany, Annapolis, Atlanta, Augusta…no, no, no. I shake my head to clear away the list of names that aren't mine. Washington, Adams, Jefferson, Madison, Monroe… fuck! What is wrong with me?

My vision blurs again, and I pull in a sharp breath as pain shoots through my head. A pit of dread settles in my stomach, but I can't trace the source of the feeling. My emotions are untethered, disturbing without memories tied to them.

My own name. I don't know my own name.

I rub my fingertips along my forehead, trying to force out any scrap of useful information. Then Elijah is kneeling in front of me, his brown eyes wide in a warm face I don't trust. A bead of sweat drips from his russet-colored hair. He reaches out to touch my shoulder.

My body snaps into action. I grab his shoulders, pivot on my feet, and force him on his back in one swift motion. My right knee stabs him in the chest as I pin him to the asphalt. I clasp his wrists above his head and hold them tight enough for my knuckles to turn white. Our noses are inches apart.

I do this on pure instinct.

His chest heaves, and his breath comes in puffs strong enough to blow my long, black hair away from his face. My own breath is calm, measured. An elbow to the right place on this guy's temple will kill him. I won't do it, not unless I have to.

What the fuck is wrong with me?

I scramble off Elijah and scoot away in horror.

A woman emerges from an old VW van on the side of the tent I couldn't see while hiding behind the gurney. She's mid 30s, 5'4", and a much softer 150 pounds than Elijah. I'm getting used to this clinical assessment of people. It seems to be a part of my past life that has stuck around, and it's useful. Her flowing orange dress is garish in the gray, muted world, and it reminds me of something I can't quite name. Am I supposed to know her?

Bright orange flames dance through debris, pirouetting their way to my trapped body. Hot asphalt burns my hands as I try to push off a heavy object that pins me down. Smoke fills my lungs. I cough, an anemic expulsion, the weight on my back constricting my chest against the ground. My arms and legs are too weak to free me of this nightmare. There is no escape.

A memory.

I'm leaning heavily on the overturned gurney when my senses return. A rolling nausea seizes me. Shaking arms barely support me. Elijah sits, staring at me in shocked wonder, and his features swim in and out of focus. Blinding pain sears my temples. I fall to the side and retch, bile stinging my throat.

Even with the racket I'm making, I hear the woman's feet shuffle up next to me, too close for comfort. I'm too wrecked to move away. A small, warm hand rubs my back and another holds my hair away from my face. I fight the instinct to tackle her. I'm not sure I could take her right now. I'm not sure why I feel the need to protect myself from this woman.

My body shudders one final time. Those warm hands roll me on my back. The woman cradles my head in her lap and rubs sticky sweat from my brow.

The gray sky is oddly bright. I try to squint away the throbbing and wince when my left hip stings.

"Elijah, what did you do to her?" the woman scolds. She clearly didn't see what I did.

"Nothing," he whispers.

My eyelids flutter and close. The woman hums a soft tune in rhythm with the rubbing. A wave of emotions rolls through me. The thought of exposing such raw feelings in front of strangers—I really don't think I know them—physically hurts my chest. I force it down, deep into my gut.

Questions dart through my brain, infiltrating the sense of detachment. What kind of person can't remember her name? What kind of person finds comfort in having a young man's life in her hands? Because that's what I felt when I was on top of Elijah, a sick surging power and relief to be in control.

Now all I feel is sick…and scared.

"I'm sorry, I'm sorry," I whisper over and over again.

"It's okay, honey," the woman says. "We'll take care of you." She rubs my sweaty head.

The floodgates open. I recoil from her touch and fold my legs tight to my chest, my face hidden in my arms. The sobs come in great, heaving gasps. I can't stem the avalanche of feelings bleeding out of me. She rubs my back until the sobs subside to a trickle.

"Imah, will she be okay?" asks Elijah.

"Hush," Imah says. "She'll be as fine as the rest of us in a couple of days."

I don't believe her on that count. Nothing about this is okay.

Imah hums a tune I don't recognize. I search for a word to describe the touch of her hands on my back. My brain examines the hidden reservoir of my past and comes up dry. Then a word I dare not trust surfaces. My heart constricts and I shudder.

A hint of its power comes from those hands. How can a woman who doesn't know me exude this word? I fall into unconsciousness as the promise of it tingles my scalp.

Hope.

2

A rough surface scrapes my hand and wakes me from a quiet, black sleep. The sky is a darker gray than before, the ground dusted with a light layer of ash. Cinders snow down. I lift my hand to find a smear of blood where the asphalt rubbed the already raw skin. No nightmares. A deep sigh of relief escapes and quickly fades as I realize I'm in motion.

A low, wooden cart shakes under me as it's pulled down the road. I try to sit but can't. I'm pinned down by a strap at my chest and another at my thighs. My heart rate accelerates as I fumble to undo the bindings, but a wave of dizziness threatens to knock me out cold.

I rest my head back on the cart and focus on steadying my breathing until I can think of a way out. I'd rather my mind give me something about my past—like why I attacked Elijah. Not that it did me any good, given I'm now tied up. It was foolish to hope Elijah and Imah would take care of me...or care for me.

The cart lurches to a stop. A shadow looms overhead.

"Let me help you," says the deep voice of Elijah. He loosens the straps and slips them off. "Didn't want you to fall."

Or he didn't want me to attack him again.

He averts his gaze but offers a hand. Reddish purple bruises circle his wrists. No doubt from me. I take the hand and sit. My heart calms to a steady pace.

He sits next to me but not too close. With steady vision and only a slight headache, I once again assess my surroundings. We're on a giant highway of four sections, three lanes each. A blue sign a little way down reads Service Area 1 Mile.

A caravan of people, some with pets, shuffle past, gazes cast to the ground. They pull or push their belongings on wagons, carts, even wheelbarrows. The mood is somber, all hushed tones and pensive expressions. No cars or trucks. The road itself suggests it's the 21st century, but the people and their primitive transportation don't. Nothing makes sense with what I thought I knew of the world.

"Where are all the cars?" I don't recognize the scratchy voice that comes out.

A tickling sensation builds in my throat and a coughing fit seizes me. I double over, tears stinging my eyes. Every cough fills my aching head with a pulse of fresh pain. The fit lasts maybe a minute, but it feels a lot longer.

When I'm recovered, a thin film of sweat coats my skin and my hair sticks to the back of my neck. I straighten up to find Elijah holding out a small metal flask.

"It's water," he says. "It's clean."

I wouldn't care if it was a dirty container full of piss. I gulp it down in several long draughts. I wipe my mouth with my sleeve and hand the flask back to him.

"It's because of the travel ban," he says. "That's why there's no cars."

I have no idea what he's talking about. Despite an effort to conceal my confusion, it must show on my face. Is it safe to let him know I've lost my memory? It's hard to trust anyone when I don't trust myself.

"All major transportation systems are closed," he says as if reciting from a book. "Civilian transportation has been banned since the attacks. No one's allowed to drive except military and essential government officials."

That word again. "Attacks?"

"Imah said you might not remember." His deep timbre has turned quiet, and he rubs the soles of his worn-out sneakers on the road, avoiding eye contact. "Terrorist attacks. Yesterday morning. New York and a bunch of other cities. The president spoke earlier today. The entire nation's in a state of emergency."

He doesn't offer any more information. My body sags. The country is as much of a mess as my brain.

"When you say attacks…?"

His voice takes on the reciting tone again. "Large-spread cyber attacks and also physical attacks targeting infrastructure in major cities."

"Physical attacks?"

"Like explosives and stuff." He shrugs, gaze still pinned to his shoes. "Reports are still coming in."

"What about…?"

"Casualties?"

He finally glances at me as I nod. I was going to say "deaths" but found the word stuck in my throat.

"Not sure yet. Probably a lot." His voice is deadpan, but the shine of his eyes reveals a flood of emotions.

I let that sink in, an ache rising in my chest. A lot dead, but I made it out of the city alive. Alive, but with a blank spot in my memory the size of the Empire State Building, not entirely whole. It's hard to think about, to process, anything else.

"Are you hungry?" he asks.

"Yeah." The lie comes too easily, like I'm practiced at it. My stomach is a churning riot and the last thing I want is food. I tell myself I lied because I know I should eat, even if I don't want to.

He digs around in his backpack and comes up with an apple. He rubs it on the inside of his t-shirt before handing it over. I bite through the crisp skin to the sweet flesh, flavor bursting through the ash in my mouth. The apple scratches my throat as I swallow, but I think I've never tasted anything so wonderful in my life. I guess I *was* hungry.

While I devour the fruit, we sit in a silence that is more comfortable than not and watch the people parade past.

A little girl, maybe two years old, passes by in a stroller pushed by a wearied woman. The girl stares at me with deep brown eyes framed by frizzy black curls. Her round cheeks are covered in soot, except for two tracks on either side of her nose streaked clean from old tears. The light pink of her dress shows through the grime. If not for the soot, she could be a doll with her delicate features. Her hands, covered in thick bandages, awkwardly grasp a stuffed animal too dirty and beat up for me to identify. It falls to the ground, but the mother doesn't notice.

I rush to pick it up and hand it to the girl. The corners of my mouth twitch with the hint of a smile, but my brain messes it up and I end up in a grimace. Her face scrunches up, and she lets out a loud cry. Fresh tears stream down her face. I back away slowly as the woman takes the girl from the stroller and cradles her.

"Shh, shh, shh," the woman says. "It's okay. Momma's here."

The child screams louder.

"I know it hurts, baby," the mother says. "It's okay, it's okay." She repeats this as she rocks back and forth until the child's cries calm. The woman's shoulders slump in exhaustion, but she doesn't put the child down. She simply props the girl on her hip and uses her other hand to push the stroller.

I wonder what the child has lost in the attacks. Her home? It appears to be just the two of them. Did she lose the rest of her family?

From her mother's shoulder, the child stares at me with doleful eyes. The stuffed animal, awkwardly held with a bandaged hand, bumps against the mother's back with each step. The child nestles into her mother's neck and buries her nose in hair. Whatever else she has lost, that child has her mother and a ratty stuffed animal to comfort her. As young as she is, she probably has a favorite food, a favorite toy, a favorite TV show. A whole list of likes and dislikes.

I have no list for myself. At two, this girl has a better sense of herself than I have at...whatever age I am. I sniffle and blink back tears.

"We should get moving," Elijah says. I wonder how long he has been standing next to me, staring at me with his head cocked to the side. "Everyone else is walking until dark and then setting up camp on the side of the road. Might be able to catch them if we walk fast."

I tuck my sadness away and force a tiny smile. I don't have the energy to ask who "everyone else" is; I'm not sure I care.

Elijah grabs the cart handles and heads down the road at a brisk pace. With no one else in the world to follow, I catch up and walk beside him.

3

As I walk with Elijah, he remains silent. It means I don't have to try and think of something to talk about, but it also allows me too much time to be in my own blank head. I can't stop thinking about the family I might be leaving behind. Did my mother once comfort me as a child?

Love as a concept feels foreign to me, but maybe that's because I don't remember anyone to love...or miss. Did my friends and family all die in the attacks? Who will mourn them if I don't?

A wave of dizziness stops me in my tracks. I fall to my knees as my vision darkens.

"He touched me!" I scream. I hug a ratty stuffed bunny. I'm too old for a lovey, but I clutch it to the very chest I'm accusing this man—my mother's boyfriend—of touching. "He came to my room after I showered..."

My voice breaks. It doesn't take much to blink tears from my eyes. I've fake cried before, almost as many times as I've cried for real.

"George, is that true?" my mother asks in a thick southern accent I've work very hard not to acquire.

He holds his hands up and waves them frantically as he backs into the wall, almost cowering in the face of my accusation. "No. No, no."

"He did!" I scream. "Ask him. Ask him what my birthmark looks like." I touch the spot just above my left breast, near my heart, where there is a small birthmark in an irregular C-shape.

"A butterfly wing," he whispers. I've never thought of it that way, but I like the description. He saw it one night when I was rummaging in a bottom cabinet, my low-cut shirt hanging open to my braless chest. It was only a peek, but I caught him, and he couldn't even be bothered to look embarrassed. A guy like that should be punished.

The gears in my mother's brain turn as she looks from my tear-stained face to George's stammering mouth. She'll tolerate her boyfriends hitting me now and then, but touching me is new territory. I'm betting on the fact that her jealousy will be strong enough for her to throw him out.

My mother slaps him. "How could ya? She's only thirteen. A child."

Behind her back, I flash a smirk at George to mask the fear that makes my heart pound so hard I'm afraid he'll see it. He takes one last, pleading look at my mother before she shoves him out the door.

Then she turns, slaps me in the face, and says, "Don't you ever prance around half-naked in front of my boyfriend again, you little whore."

I run to my room, the fake tears turned real.

I gasp, a fish out of water, unable to breathe.

"You okay?" Elijah asks. The ringing in my ears makes his voice seem far away. The shock of suddenly being entrenched in such a vivid, fucked up memory has rendered me speechless. Deep in my quivering core, I know it's a real moment from my past. "Black Butterfly?"

The nickname clicks in my brain and jolts me back

into the present. Something about it feels right. I press my hand to my heart where my birthmark is.

"What did you say?" My voice trails off weakly, but my stare is as intense as the headache building at my temples.

He blushes and stammers. "B...b...black Butterfly. I, uh, saw the tattoo. When Imah—my sister—dressed the wound." He points to my hip.

I slip my fingertips under my waistband and find the skin there covered with gauze. Underneath it on my left hip is a slightly distorted tattoo. It's intact enough for me to see it's a black butterfly, wings spread wide. My skin prickles with the remembrance of the needle, but my brain doesn't inform me when or under what circumstances I got the tattoo.

"Is that what I'm called?" I murmur.

"What?" he asks. He raises a hand like he wants to pat my arm but pulls back, probably recalling the last time he reached for me and I pinned him to the ground.

Now I almost stammer. Almost, but not quite. "Black Butterfly," I say a little too loudly. "That's what my friends call me."

I think of my 13-year-old self and wonder if she had friends. I have no idea what they would've called me. Somehow, to my present self, the idea of friendship—like love—feels foreign, an old pair of boots that never quite fit right. And now I know my mother doesn't love me like that mother loves the child with the ratty stuffed animal. Maybe my friends did, though, and maybe they are missing me...if they're still alive. I take deep breaths to try and still my shaking hands.

Elijah hovers nervously. "You okay to keep going?"

"Yes." I stand and find my legs are steady. Elijah

begins to pull the cart again. "Wait!"

He immediately stops and turns around. The sense of pleasure I get out of his obedience twists my stomach. I can't unpack all these feelings right now and press on with my original thought. "You and Imah, you rescued me?"

"No. We found you."

"Where?" I whisper, my voice still raw. "How long ago?"

"On the Jersey side of the Holland Tunnel. Yesterday, a few hours after the attacks."

The phantom stink of fire fills my nostrils. I try to rub it out but can't.

"You were unconscious," he explains, and then hangs his head. "We weren't able to save anyone else."

At 13 I was in a trailer with my mom, presumably somewhere in the south. Yesterday I was in New York City and barely escaped with my life. Then I was unconscious for less than a day and forgot who I was. How did I go from there to here? What happened in the years between? There are too many gaps to fill. I wince with the pounding of my head.

Elijah looks to the darkening sky, the sun hidden behind clouds and ash. "We'll meet up with the others soon. You can talk to my sister. She's a doctor."

He searches my face with as many questions in his expression as I have swirling in my brain. What was I doing in the city on the day of the attacks? How did I get out? Why was I one of the lucky ones? Or is lucky the wrong word? I don't know if any of the questions are the right ones.

He looks away, and then reaches into his pocket and pulls out a small object, which he holds tight in his big hand so I can't see what it is.

"I think you should have this." He opens his fingers to reveal a small pocketknife, the blade tucked neatly into the handle. "It might get dangerous. If supplies get low, there could be riots."

I hesitate and flex my hands at my side; they are practically twitching to snatch up the weapon. I stare at him, but he won't meet my gaze. Disbelief floods me that this young man who was on the receiving end of my violent attack would offer to arm me. The weapon is puny, but dangerous all the same. He must truly believe I will have a need for it...and he must trust that I won't use it on him.

I hold out my hand and he places the knife there, careful not to make contact with my skin. The pocketknife is warm from his touch. I squeeze it, feel the solidness of it in my palm, before placing it into one of the roomy pockets in my black, non-descript pants. A feeling rises above the initial eagerness to possess the knife, one that is rusty with disuse but deeply ingrained. Confidence. I know how to use this weapon. I can take care of myself in a fight.

"Thank you..." I trail off, too confused with my conflicting feelings to say more.

He fills the silence by holding out his hand. "Nice to meet you—" He waits for me to fill in my real name.

"B is fine." Short for Black Butterfly, the closest thing I have to a name.

His expression is serious but not unfriendly as his offered hand waits in the air. I take it and squeeze with a firm shake, hoping I have at least one friend now.

4

Elijah and I find the others as the sky changes from gray to deep indigo. They are settled in a small clearing a little way off the highway. A fire blazes in the center and dinner is ready. Baked beans and canned corn. A "dinner of champions" Elijah calls it, a wry grin on his face. It's the first time I've seen him smile, and it makes him look younger, boyish even.

Including Elijah and his sister, there are 14 people in the group…if I count myself, 15. Among the ones I don't know are eight women and four men, all older than me and Elijah. I dared to ask him a few questions while we walked and one of the things I learned is that Elijah is 19. I don't know my exact age, but it feels like we're around the same.

I keep a little distance from everyone while we eat, until Imah insists she take a look at me. Aside from the wound where my tattoo is, I've only a few minor cuts and burns. The rest of my body is unscathed. Inside my head is a whole different story.

It's terrifically dark out here with power out in

most places and the sky obscured by clouds and smoke, so we sit close to the fire despite the warmth of the air. During my careful prying, Elijah informed me it's late May, but it feels more like a warm, humid July. Perhaps an after-effect of the cloud of ash from the attacks or climate change in general, it's hard to know for sure.

It's strange how I know about things like climate change and have expectations about what the weather should be like this time of year, but I know nothing about what to expect of myself. My behavior is as foreign to me as a new language. Thinking about languages sets off a conversation in my head, in Mandarin of all languages. It's in a man's voice, and one-sided like he's on the phone. And I understand every word of it!

The distraction of this latest revelation, keeps me from wincing while Imah works on cleaning and spreading antibiotic on my wounds. She's been chatting about how everyone in the group resides in a small community in upstate New York. They live almost totally off-grid, growing much of their own food and using solar and wind power for electricity and heat. I try to pay attention to her instead of the noise in my head.

"It makes us better equipped to deal with disasters like this," she explains. "We have our own supplies that can travel with us." She gestures to the backpacks full of food and medical kits spread around the fire.

"Did you come to the city to try and help after you

heard about the attacks?" I ask.

"No." Her lips are pursed in a displeasure that seems to stem from more than the shitty situation we're all in. "We were in the area already." She doesn't elaborate and her face closes off behind a mask of indifference.

I'm hungry to know what's behind the change in her mood, but I sense it's not the time to press too hard, so I keep my mouth shut.

Imah holds onto my hands, though she's done tending to them. "It's a miracle."

"What is?" I ask.

"You, here and alive."

"Mmmm," is all I say and turn my gaze to the fire.

"Things are likely to get worse before they get better, but we'll endure," she says, her lips pursed with determination. "Elijah says you're experiencing memory loss. How much do you remember?" She shines a flashlight in my eyes, staring deeper into them than I'm comfortable with.

"Nothing of the attacks," I admit in a pained whisper. "And there are still gaps in my recent memory." A total understatement, but I'm not about to admit I can only remember a few snatches of my past.

"Head trauma, likely only temporary." Her diagnosis sounds very official, and I wonder who this unpresumptuous woman really is. What secrets is she hiding? She merely pats my hand affectionately and smiles, her eyes crinkling at the edges. "We'll take good care of that head and before you know it, you'll be reciting the bedtime stories your mom used to tell you."

She putters off to the other side of the fire. I'm left thinking about the memory of my mother and George. Aside from the snatches of the inferno in my nightmares, it's my only memory and I should want to hold on to it with every bit of my deadly grip—the deadly aspect a fact I'm not ready to think about too closely. I'm torn between wanting to remember it all and wanting to banish the few memories I have to the place where the rest of my past is.

I remain on the outskirts of the group, not really belonging here...or anywhere. Being around this many people who all know each other is overwhelming. Besides Imah and Elijah, only one, Tony—5' 6" and 180 pounds—spares me a glance, more a glare really. He mentioned earlier, his voice filled with contempt, how most of the people traveling on the highway gathered at a rest area for the night. He called them "indoor, power-dependent people."

The thick air is oppressive, the lingering stench of stale fire mixing with the scent of the fire the off-gridders set up. I run my fingertips in the grass, but the ashy texture feels all wrong. How much of the world is covered in ash? I sigh so quietly I'm not sure it makes a noise.

I'm still a little weak on my feet, but the headache has subsided. I could slink away and escape into the darkness if I wanted to, try and find someone or somewhere I know. I have a feeling I'd have no trouble taking care of myself, so long as I don't pass out again. But where would I go? From what I've overheard, New York City is a mess, nothing to go back to there.

Nervous energy crackles around the others like embers popping in the flames. Firelight dances on their features as I eavesdrop in plain sight. Tony is fiddling with an old shortwave radio. My gaze flits to Elijah and lingers. My almost friend. He smiles when he notices, and I quickly glance away.

He comes and sits next to me, heat radiating off his body. It warms my skin, but not my insides. He remains quiet, but it's an amicable silence. I concentrate on his soft breathing instead of the conversations around the fire. Unintentionally, I've matched my breathing to his, making it indistinguishable to anyone who might be listening for it. I marvel at the things my body does by instinct, how at odds they feel with what a girl my age—late teens I've decided, though I'm not positive about that—should be doing.

"They should be sadder," he mumbles.

I keep silent. I'm not the kind of girl who needs to fill the empty spaces with chatter, a little piece I have learned about myself. You can learn a lot by letting people talk. A laugh from nearby stabs our solitude.

"So much destruction," he whispers.

"I know," I whisper back. "What *are* they so happy about?" I jerk my chin toward the others.

Elijah's intense gaze indicates there's a lot more going on in his head than he's telling me. Like with Imah, I don't press him. We're all entitled to our secrets, even the ones we keep from ourselves.

He rubs his hands together, like I make him nervous. I should make him nervous.

"The president," he finally says. "He's speaking again tonight. Tony's trying to find it on the shortwave."

My skin prickles. I doubt the president's speech will give the gritty details, but I may be able to glean an important piece of information out of it, something that will help me figure out what's next. "They're probably just eager to hear the latest news."

Elijah only nods, and then a hush falls over the group.

"Elijah, get over here," Tony demands. "It's starting."

Elijah nods for me to join him, and I gladly oblige. I want to catch every word the president has to say.

Raucous music blares from the radio, more fit for a game show than a presidential address. Then a raspy female voice says, "Cheryl Dare here, hijacking your airwaves along with my expert technical team."

An outcry of dismay circles around the fire.

"Are you kidding me?" Tony shouts. "How the hell did she manage...?"

Elijah notices my confused look and whispers, "She's a radio D.J., a shock jock who does outrageous stunts for the ratings."

Crap. I'll give myself away if I don't better hide my confusion over things I should probably know. Then again, how many people my age listen to the radio? Maybe I haven't given as much away as I fear.

"Shhh," hisses Imah. "I want to hear this."

Everyone immediately falls silent.

"Don't worry, my fellow Americans," says Cheryl Dare over the radio. "I'm not here to keep you from listening to the president. No, I'm here to let you all know I'm here for you. I'm outraged by these attacks. I mourn with you. If you need help or are looking for a loved one, call me and my team if you can. We'll do what we can to help you out. And I'll be popping in with important information as it becomes available. I was once your source of entertainment, and I hope to be that again one day soon, but for now consider me your source of information."

The group is silent, soaking in every word.

"My team and I are headed to Washington, D.C.," she continues. "We want answers, we want our voices heard. We'll be heading up a rally there soon, once enough people can get there to call it a rally. We're giving people at least a week to arrive if you want your voices heard. Join us if you can."

She gives a phone number people can call and also offers several locations from New York to D.C. where people can leave notes if phone isn't an option. Screeching feedback cuts her off, followed by static.

5

Everyone at the camp waits in silence for the shortwave to offer more. Finally, muffled voices break into the static, and a voice says, "Ladies and gentleman, President Reynolds."

There's a brief pause before the president speaks. "Thank you." He clears his throat rather loudly. "This has been a terrible, terrible time in our country. As president, I inherited a weak country militarily, and I'm sad to say that the worst of what I believed could happen has happened. I did as much as I could to strengthen America but have been blocked in many of my efforts. And because of this many thousands of American lives have been lost in these terrorist attacks. Billions of dollars of damage has been done to our infrastructure."

How many exactly is many thousands? The words echo in my head over and over again. My lungs search for air, but it's like I've been plunged into a cold lake and can't figure out which way is up. I push the panic away before it becomes too much and find a calm center.

Static from the radio pops in tune with the fire. The air is thick with the quiet of the people around me, their concentration all focused on the radio.

"I have been gathering information and making swift decisions," he continues in what sounds like a very rehearsed tone. "It is important now more than ever for all the citizens of our great nation to remain peaceful and civilized. This is very, very important. If you have a home that is safe and secure, stay there. The national travel ban remains effective until further notice. If you don't have anywhere to go, short-term shelters are being set up in public schools and buildings. The military, the National Guard, and FEMA are heading to areas to distribute food, water, and aid."

He goes on for a few minutes, detailing more specifics about how the citizens of the country are to proceed over the next days and weeks and how supplies will be delivered and distributed. This information I can handle without a panic attack. His speech has a hypnotic effect on me. His voice is more than familiar; I recognize it. It taps away at my brain, slowly dislodging something in there I've hidden away.

Then the president pauses and frantic voices rise in the background over static. It startles me out of the hypnotic state, chasing away whatever memory was trying to surface. My whole body tingles with anticipation.

A murmur rises from the off-gridders. Tony yells, "Shut up!"

"I'm sorry for the interruption," the president says. A subtle shift in tone, a strength to his voice stokes a fire in me. "We now know that our highly secure weapons system was hacked. It was—" he pauses as if for dramatic effect "—our own military weapons that were launched and detonated on our cities."

A collective gasp runs through the camp. One woman breaks down in sobs, and several others look like they're fighting back tears. Tony stands and hulks over us all. He sneers and cracks his knuckles, like he will single-handedly take on whoever did this.

And I feel nothing. I'm quite literally numb, my skull and fingers tingling with shock.

The president continues, "Several terrorists responsible for committing these terrible crimes have already been identified. I have just learned that one of the masterminds behind the attacks has been killed. The body of Jie Zhang, owner of the tech company Infinate, was found outside of New York City with evidence that the Chinese government is responsible for the attacks."

I inhale this information with a deep breath. The name Zhang rings in my head and I press my eyes shut against the mounting sorrow and rage filling the camp.

I open my eyes and look through a large glass window, gazing at a familiar city skyline. I'm still getting used to seeing the city from this angle. I'm much more familiar, and comfortable, with being down in the grittiness of the streets and subways that were my home before the Agency found me. Before they trained me...saved me.

My dress is little more than a tight-fitting negligee, nearly the same dark color as the long hair that hangs loose past my shoulders. I absentmindedly tap a hidden pocket in my dress, reassured by the thin flash drive tucked against my pelvic bone. A bead of condensation drips down the glass of white wine I hold but don't drink.

"Did you send the prep files for the hearing?" Zhang says in Mandarin into the phone, unaware that I understand everything. "I want to review them on my flight to D.C."

I force myself to turn away from the window and offer a half-dressed Zhang a timid smile. He sits on a disheveled king-sized bed, returns my smile before returning his attention to a laptop and his phone call. His black hair sticks up messily. His white shirt is buttoned but hangs loose at the waist because he's not wearing any pants. Thankfully silky red boxers covers enough of him not to be obscene. A designer suit jacket hangs neatly on the back of a chair, not a wrinkle on it. A sharp crease runs evenly down the pants carefully lain across the chair seat. Other than the disheveled bed, the room is immaculate.

Though I've taken this job to a more personal level than I ever have before, I try to remember that this is a job. And I'm doing what I have to do to get it done.

A pang of guilt runs through me as I think about what the information in the documents will do to him. He's not a bad man; he's got a family back in China and loves spending time with his nephew. It's not his fault he's meant to be a scapegoat. Which is what he'll be...when I get the job done.

I point to the bathroom and mime taking a shower, and Zhang nods absentmindedly. I steal a t-shirt from his bag, careful not to disturb the tidy packing job.

In the bathroom, I dump the wine in the sink, gripping the cool edge of the counter as I watch the pale-yellow liquid slip down the drain. I touch my lips to the rim of the glass and leave a deep red lipstick mark to make him think I drank it. The glass clinks as I set it down on the marble. I shed the tiny dress, which I will keep nearby until the opportunity to plant the documents presents itself. I'll get this job done tonight, one way or another.

Someone hisses "shhh" and I realize I'm gasping for breath. I'm no longer rooted in the memory but back fireside with the off-gridders. The president has continued talking, but the words don't make sense to my addled brain.

I picture the skyline I saw from Zhang's window. The point of the Empire State Building, the shine of the Chrysler Building. The girl in that memory—me, that was me—was not 13, she was a young woman. She was me from not that long ago. On a job to frame a business man named Zhang. There must be millions of Zhangs in the world, surely he's not the same one the president was talking about. The implications of them being the same are too big for me to contemplate.

There is no pushing down the panic this time. Imah is at my side with a bottle of water and a comforting hand on my back. She works her magic, and after only a few moments, I'm able to take a sip.

I catch the very end of the president's speech as he lists off the attacked cities. "Boston, New York, Philadelphia, Miami, Chicago, Dallas, Las Vegas, Seattle, San Francisco, Los Angeles."

Washington, D.C., I notice, is not on the list. It's a small detail that seems insignificant, but I note it all the same.

He finishes with "we must show our strength to the world and strike back at our attackers. The United States of America is alive and well."

I manage to squeak out a faint "thank you" to Imah for the water and slip away to a dark spot far away from the heat. The others are engaged in a lively debate about what this means for the country.

"We'll go to war against China," says one woman. Tears glisten on her face in the firelight. "It's what President Reynolds has wanted from the start. Now he has a reason."

Tony stands and points a finger at the flames. "Those bastards deserve what's coming to them. We should bomb them back to the Stone Age."

The group continues to argue, but I'm stuck on the memory. I walk farther from the camp and let the air cool my cheeks and hopefully my demeanor.

My instincts say the connection between what the president said and my memory are not a coincidence. I worked for an agency—no, the Agency with a capital "A." All I can remember about them is what I was thinking about in that memory, how they found me...saved me. How I was trying to frame a man named Zhang.

Panic mounts again as Elijah sidles up next to me, so close I can barely breathe. He takes my hand and squeezes.

"I can't believe it, our own weapons turned on us." His eyes shine with tears. They look black in the dim light. "We're headed to D.C. for the rally. Imah wants to keep helping people along the way, but she also wants a say in how the country gets put back together. We voted as a group, and mostly everyone agrees that you can come. Imah would like you to come."

I wonder if Tony was among the dissenters. He doesn't seem to take to outsiders, particularly me. But Imah wants me, and maybe Elijah, too. I sense he is hiding his desire behind Imah's wish.

"Do you think we'll go to war with China?" I ask.

"It's likely," he says. "That's why we all need to make our voices heard. Will you come to D.C.?"

I pause and consider before nodding. Though I'm probably not dependent on these off-gridders for survival, I have no one else. If these flashes of memory are true, I may be in big trouble. Unknowingly, Elijah is offering me somewhere to hide until I can figure out more about myself.

I shiver as he goes back to the fire, taking all the warmth with him as I wonder about who I really am.

6

The sea of refugees dissipates somewhat as we walk south, putting more distance between us and New York City. With each step away from there, I can breathe easier. The farther we go, the less evidence of the attacks.

The sky is gray with clouds, but the air and ground has cleared of ash. The leaves on the trees are green, and the wildflowers in the grassy spaces along the side of the highway are in bloom. I only remember a few days of my life, but I know what the seasons are supposed to look like, and what they feel and smell like too. Without any exhaust from cars or trucks, the smells of late spring run rampant.

A sweet, enticing scent reaches my nose. I stop right on the striped line of the highway and ask, "What is that smell?"

Elijah laughs, loud and hearty. His eyes glint and he takes my hand and guides me to a thicket of wildflowers. I'm stuck on the feel of his calluses against mine when he releases my hand to pick a small flower. It has yellow trumpet-shaped petals and greenery that vines up the trunk of a small tree.

"Honeysuckle," he says. I've heard of it, but it sounds magical coming from his mouth.

He shows me how to draw the tiny string in the middle of the flower through the petals and pauses right before pulling it all the way out. A bead of moisture forms, a teardrop waiting to fall.

Holding it between his fingers, he moves it towards my mouth and says, "Put your tongue out."

I step back, surprised and confused. "What?"

"Trust me." He smiles and moves it closer to my mouth.

I lean forward and stick out my tongue, careful not to make contact with his fingers. He pressed the flower to my tongue and a burst of sweetness hits my taste buds. It lingers for a moment before fading away. I straighten, a smile playing on my lips as I finally understand.

"Want another?" he asks.

I nod eagerly. He picks another flower and hands it to me, his fingers brushing my palm with a light tickle. I'm a little disappointed he doesn't place it in my mouth again. I can't help but stare as he tastes the honeysuckle, his tongue darting out to catch the sweet drop. Warmth spreads across my neck. I tamp down the sensation by using my fingernails to squeeze the skin on my inner wrist, effectively eliminating the blush.

We must sample a dozen before noticing our group is long out of view. I find that I'm laughing as we jog to catch up with the others. When Elijah pushes the sleeves of his shirt above his elbows and exposes his bruised wrists, my joy is cut off. I push to the front of the group, leaving him behind for the rest of the day's walk.

Once darkness has fallen and we make camp, I find myself next to him by the fire. His solid, quiet presence comforts my troubled soul and keeps my darkest thoughts at bay. I crave the relief as my few, disturbing memories burn brightest once the sun goes down.

I rub my temples in a useless attempt to suppress the mounting headache that started as soon as we stopped walking. Dinner of stale bread smothered in peanut butter churns in my stomach like hot lava. Elijah offers water from a canteen, and it soothes the throbbing in my head enough for my stomach to settle. My shoulders sag in relief.

"Better?" he asks.

"Infinitely better. Thanks." It doesn't feel like it's in my nature to exaggerate, but I find myself doing things that feel out of character in Elijah's presence. I pause and dare to ask, "How are your wrists?"

He rubs them, the bruising faded to yellow in most places. "Infinitely better." His mouth quirks in a subtle smile.

I can't help but smile back. "I'm sorry about..." I indicate his wrists, but feel there's more I should be sorry for that I just haven't remembered yet.

"It's okay. You were hurt, and scared."

And so many other terrible things he couldn't even imagine of me, like power hungry at having his life in my hands. I nod and turn away from his all too inviting gaze. We fall into silence, the conversations of the off-gridders swirling around us like smoke from the fire.

Despite my growing self-contempt at having so many unanswered questions in my head, I roll my tongue around my mouth as I decide how to pry for information without giving away how much of my memory I've lost. Instead, though, it's a personal question that pops out of my mouth. "Where are your parents?"

After a beat of silence, I add, "You don't have to answer that."

I've tried to remember more about my own mother,

but all I recall is a strong southern accent calling me a whore.

Elijah shrugs. We're sitting so close I feel the motion rather than see it. "Never knew my dad. Imah never did either, hers or mine. Our mom, she died of an overdose when I was twelve."

"I'm sorry," I whisper, kicking myself for bringing it up.

He shrugs again. "Imah was in med school and came home whenever she could to see me, but we're all like family here and I was taken care of."

"I can't imagine going to school long enough to become a doctor." I wonder how many years of school I attended before working for the Agency. Do I even have a high school diploma?

"I don't think she liked it, being a doctor," Elijah says quietly.

I'm surprised to hear that. Imah seemed like a natural when she was tending my wounds. Then again, we're all a mystery to each other, some of us even to ourselves.

"She's running for Congress this year."

"What?" My head jerks up, instincts kicking in that this is a vital detail. "House or Senate?"

"House."

"What state and district?"

He cocks his head to the side, like he can't quite figure out why I'm grilling him. How could he when I don't even know why exactly. "Twenty-first in New York."

"Oh, cool," I say slowly, failing to smooth over the awkwardness. It's so strange that Imah would go through all those years of school and training to become a doctor, only to give it up to go into politics, but I don't want to press the issue with Elijah. "What's it like living off-grid? Do you live in a house?" I'm suddenly desperate for a taste of what it's like to have a home to remember.

Elijah's shoulders relax with the change in subject. "It's a big, old farmhouse. We all pitch in and have jobs. All the mundane stuff, like laundry and cleaning dishes is split evenly, but then we all take on tasks that suit our skills. I'm good at fixing things." I stare at his face, his expression as warm as the flames. He bites his lower lip. When it slips out from between his teeth, it glistens in the firelight, as does his eyes. "It's quiet. And dark at night, so much darker than here. And beautiful." He looks up. "On a clear night, you can see the Milky Way."

I don't need to use my imagination to know the utter blackness of the void in my head, but that's not the kind of darkness he's talking about. I try to picture a landscape darker than this one. None of the streetlights are working, and buildings sit dark and foreboding off the highway. Campfires dot the land near us and there are some lights off in the distance where the power must be working, but it feels plenty dark. I close my eyes and imagine a night sky filled with stars, but I have no idea what the Milky Way looks like. Seems that's not one of the useless bits of knowledge I possess.

Elijah grabs my hand, startling me out of my reverie. To my surprise, I didn't hear him stand. He pulls me up and brandishes a flashlight. "Let me show you."

7

Hand entwined with Elijah's, I follow him through a stretch of damp grass. He doesn't let go as we navigate down a rocky slope and make our way across a long driveway to a corporate complex. He pulls me across an unlit parking lot.

Following a boy I barely know through an empty parking lot in the night might make me afraid, but one thing I know is that I can take care of myself. It begs the question of why I'm staying with Elijah and the off-gridders when I worry what might happen to them if my past catches up to me and I'm still with them. Then again, Elijah isn't exactly incapable of taking care of himself. Despite his boyish charm, growing up the way he did must have fostered resilience in him.

I swallow down my misgivings and continue to follow this boy to wherever he's taking me.

Elijah releases my hand, clears the dirt off a stretch of curb next to a parking spot, and gestures for me to sit. He scoots so close we're shoulder to shoulder, our outer thighs pressed up against each other. I press my palms against the concrete curb, grit digging into my skin, to remind me I don't deserve the gentle touch of such a boy.

It's a thought that is as pervasive as it is confusing. Why would I feel I don't deserve his touch? Is it because of my work with the Agency? Why would that make me unworthy? If only I could remember more...

With a click of the flashlight, the world goes black. My lids flutter as my eyes adjust.

"Look up," Elijah whispers, sweet breath tickling my cheek.

I turn my face to the sky and gasp. Millions of stars sparkle in the night sky. "When did the clouds clear?" I wonder out loud.

Elijah's fingers find mine in the dark. He rubs my knuckles with his rough thumb, and my death-grip on the curb loosens. I'm wound tighter than a boa constrictor around its prey.

"Almost as good as home," he says to the sky. "Do you know any constellations?"

"The Big Dipper." It's the only one I've heard of, though I probably couldn't point it out. The sparkles of light are an undecipherable maze to me.

"Too easy. Try this one." Taking my hand under his, he points our index fingers at the sky and traces a shape connecting the stars. "You know it?"

I shake my head.

"That's Ursa Major, a bear, his face up and his feet to the right. The hind part of his body and his tail—see them pointing down to the right—are the Big Dipper."

Now I see the ladle shape of the Big Dipper. But Ursa Major is new to me. Honestly, I'm having a hard time forming the stick figure into a bear.

Pointing at the two brightest stars in the ladle, his fingers—by extension my fingers—follow them to a new constellation. "And there's Leo, the lion. His face is also pointing up."

My mind forms an image and I giggle, the high-pitched sound foreign to my ears. I press my lips close to cut if off.

"What?" he asks, a little defensive as if I were laughing at him instead of at myself.

"Oh," I breathe. "It's just—it looks like a horse to me, not a lion."

He cocks his head and stares at the sky. "Hmmm. You're right. This next one is real easy to picture." Our fingers move as one across the sky. I lean closer to him to keep our hands together as his body turns.

He traces the stars, the serpentine shape evident to me before he tells me what it is. "A snake," I whisper.

"Hydra, the many-headed serpent, slain by Hercules." He pauses and adds, "I don't know any butterfly constellations."

I'm touched that he wants to find me in the sky. Too bad I feel more like the serpent who fights gods than a delicate butterfly.

"That's okay," I say. "I don't know any..." I refrain from finishing that thought with *thing* and settle for "either."

I slip my hand from his but stay pressed to his side. Maybe I can stay with Elijah and Imah and not remember my past. That wouldn't be so bad, would it?

A breeze stirs the air. The stifling humidity of yesterday has been replaced by cooler temperatures. I shiver. Our heads turn toward each other at exactly the same moment, our noses almost touching. We stare into each other's eyes, his like a world unto themselves. He tilts his head slightly as if inviting me to move closer, to brush my lips against his. I force myself to turn away with a funny little cough that gets stuck in my throat.

He rubs his arms absentmindedly, seemingly closing in on himself. "You really don't know any constellations besides the Big Dipper?"

"Not that I recall."

My breath is slightly ragged with wanting. To have his warm lips against my cold ones. To take that hint of affection from him and express my own towards him. To let my emotions flow from me like air from a flapping wing. The near kiss—the promise of something more blossoming behind it—unravels me.

I blame my stupid desire for the fact that I hear the crunch of gravel a second too late. A flutter behind us and then cold steel touches my throat. My instincts prickle a warning beneath my skin, and I let them take the lead.

I can't see much in the starlight, but I can tell the threat is a lone woman. I take a deep breath and let it out slowly and quietly, and then my other senses take over. A puff of hot air warms my neck as the woman exhales. The knife remains pressed to my throat. Her breathing is heavy and slightly erratic, which could be nerves, but I sense a heavier weight behind this.

I thank the constellations above that she chose to put the knife to my throat instead of Elijah's.

"Sorry to ruin your little date," comes the woman's raspy voice, "but I'm gonna need you to come with me."

I sense more than see Elijah's hand reach out. I narrow my eyes and grunt, hoping he gets the message to stay still. I can dispatch this woman without a problem, the confidence about this coming from deep within me. It scares and thrills me all at once. I let that confidence take over. I tell myself it's a survival instinct, and it's not that I like the idea of making this woman suffer.

"I don't think so," I say.

A growl escapes the woman's throat, rumbling in her chest and against my back. The hand pressing the knife to my flesh trembles. "My orders are dead or alive. I don't care which way you come, but the Agency will give me more if you're alive."

I nearly lose all my composure at the mention of the Agency, but instinct keeps me in check. I bide my time, waiting to see if she'll keep talking. She's playing it as coy as I am, though.

"I don't know what you're talking about." My voice is tight with the lie. "What agency? We're just a couple of kids."

I shrug, testing her with the motion.

She places her free hand on my upper arm and squeezes. "Don't move or I'll kill you."

"So kill me."

Elijah gasps. I want to shush him and tell him to stay the hell out of this. The knife presses deeper, draws blood, but it doesn't take my life. That's when I know she doesn't have the stomach to kill me.

8

At the sight of blood, Elijah shifts next to me, like he's about to do something stupid. I better end this before he gets hurt.

"I have nothing for you," I say to the woman. "Or for whatever agency your work for."

"Don't mess with me, girl." She squeezes my arm harder. "You come with me now or you die, your little friend too. Your choice."

Her final words are filled with such contempt, I wonder who I am to this woman. An inner battle wages inside me as a rush of rage fights with a spark of sadness. The rage builds in my chest, and my hands tremble as I try to hold them back from ripping into this woman.

I want to make her pay for threatening Elijah.

A buzzing fills my head and I see red. I bash the back of my head into her face, while simultaneously wedging my right hand in between my neck and her hand holding the knife. The woman grunts as the weapon flies out of her hand and lands with a clatter on the asphalt. She falls to her back and swears.

The fury of a thousand frustrations—the lack of memories, the guilt of surviving, the desperate need and fear of wanting to share my growing fondness for Elijah—releases itself in blow after blow upon the woman. Straddling her, I pound her face, chest, stomach. I barely restrain myself from giving her a pointed deathblow. Her screams turn to moans, which turn to silence. Yet my fists continue to rain down on her.

Hands wrap around my upper arms. I turn, poised to obliterate another attacker, when a stunned whisper halts my attack. "Stop. Please stop."

Evident in the dim starlight are the lines etched on Elijah's forehead, the open-mouthed expression of horror on his face. I sag to the ground as he releases me. On my side, I press my cheek to the ground. The cold of the asphalt seeps through my skin and tempers my hot head. My temples throb with pain.

I roll on my back, and a single tear slips down my face. The sky, Elijah's constellations in the stars, shift and blur. A rolling nausea seizes my stomach, and I turn my head just in time to avoid vomiting all over myself.

Elijah shushes me and helps me sit. He rubs circles along my back, like Imah did the day they saved me, and I shake and shake. I wish I could tell him that my reaction is because I'm revolted by my attack on the woman. But it would be a lie. It's my head injury that's made me vomit. There was nothing but sick pleasure running through my veins as I beat that woman to unconsciousness. I wanted her to suffer, maybe even to die.

Is she dead? I sit up and force myself to look at what I've done.

A dark puddle pools around her head. Blood seeps from her nose, washing down her face. The knife glitters harmlessly not far from us. She's wearing black, tight-fitting clothes. The similarity between them and my attire is not lost on me. She mentioned the Agency—a group I can no longer deny I'm involved with—sent her. An assassin? She was tasked to bring me in dead or alive, but she couldn't do it. A weakness I don't have.

The nausea makes it hard for me to move without wanting to throw up again, but I slowly scoot over to the assassin. I clean the knife on her shirt and take it for myself. I feel her neck for a pulse. Feeling the beat of it underneath my finger, I let out a deep sigh. She's a complication that would be better for me if dead, but I'm relieved I didn't beat her to death in front of Elijah. There would be no coming back from that, and for some reason, I want to be redeemable in his eyes.

Without warning, the woman bolts upright, blood dripping down her face. She grabs me in a chokehold, my throat constricting under her strong grip. Maybe I was wrong about her not being able to kill me, or maybe I pushed her to a new level of violence.

Stars burst through my vision as my last breath gets farther and farther away. Moments before I'm about to lose consciousness, a hand chops at her neck. Her fingers release me. I suck in gulps of air, my vision as starry as the night sky. Elijah pins the woman to the ground, straddling her much the same way I held him down.

Forcing myself to stand, to be steady and strong, I stride over, kneel next to her, and hold her own knife against her throat. "Go away and never come within a hundred feet of us ever again." When she stares at me with defiance in her sneer, I say, "Or I'll slit your throat and leave you for dead."

She smiles, blood staining her teeth. "I'll leave. But remember, you're the one with a mark on your head. The Agency won't stop until they have you."

Keeping the knife pressed against her skin, I nod to Elijah. He climbs off of her and takes several steps back. My vision swims, but I remain steady as I haul her to her feet and push her in the opposite direction of the highway. She laughs maniacally and runs into the trees beyond the parking lot.

Once she's gone, I bite back the bile rising in my throat and tremble so hard my head feels like it will rattle right off my neck. Elijah comes near and wraps an arm around me as my head lolls to the side and comes to rest on his shaking shoulder.

I manage to say, "It's okay. She's gone."

"Who was that?" he asks, his voice breaking. "What's the agency?" His silent tears wet the top of my head.

"I don't know. I don't remember her or any agency." Almost the truth. "She probably mistook me for someone else. You said things might get bad. Desperate people doing crazy things."

"Yeah" is all he says, but he squeezes me tighter to his trembling body.

I'm so dizzy, I don't know which way is up. I think I pass out for a minute. When I come to, I'm leaning heavily on Elijah. He's not shaking anymore and his arm is wrapped around my waist. With sure feet, he guides me back up the highway embankment. The darkness deepens as I nearly pass out again, but I hold onto consciousness.

He doesn't speak; I can only imagine what he's thinking. He keeps a hold of me, pressing together the pieces that are falling apart. I lean into his embrace. All the while, I know I don't deserve his comfort, but yet I'm unable to step away and support myself with my own two feet. The worst part is I've made him complicit in my crime.

I am weak.

I wish desperately on the stars he showed me tonight that my weakness doesn't make Elijah a victim of whatever mess I'm in.

9

Elijah doesn't mention the incident when we get back to camp. Everyone else is asleep, so we don't have to worry about explaining the semi-conscious state I'm in or the blood dripping down my neck. He guides me onto my borrowed sleeping bag and finds a bandage for my wound. Then he settles himself on the opposite side of the fire.

It's cold and lonely with him so far away. I stay awake long into the night, my few moments of sleep filled with nightmares that could be memories or simply terrors in my mind.

In the morning, Elijah tells Imah that I walked into a branch to explain the bandage on my neck. I keep to myself, clenched hands tucked up under my armpits as we walk. I can't stop thinking about how I lost control with that woman, attacked her in such a brutal manner. Sure, she was ready to kill me, but I took it too far. Worse, though, is how I felt about it, the power that radiated through my body as I beat her bloody.

And Elijah won't even look at me. Aside from glancing his way a few times, I avoid him as well. What he must think of me? I spend the morning walking with the group, listening to the others chatter while trying to ignore the events from last night running through my head on a loop.

A few hours into the morning, a rumbling in the distance carries on far too long to be thunder. The sound builds and builds until the asphalt shakes beneath us. That's when Imah gestures for all of us retreat to the grassy strip on the side of the highway. Elijah shoots me a worried look. My relief that he is no longer ignoring me is short-lived as a convoy of vehicles appears around the bend.

The line of tanks and armored vehicles—all manned by masked soldiers—seems like it will never end. They are so loud I'm forced to cover my ears, but that doesn't stop the sound from reverberating throughout my body. My stomach heaves with the vibration, and I'm having trouble keeping down my oatmeal from breakfast.

When a low-flying helicopter swoops in, a pressure wraps around my skull in a vice grip. The click-click-click of the rotors is barely perceptible over the roar of the convoy, but it thuds in rhythm with the pounding of my head.

A black helicopter flies in low—too low—over the training field where twelve of us trainees are practicing under the careful watch of Director Wolfson. He doesn't normally lower himself to attend target training, but rumor has it he has an eye on one of us for special-ops training. Rumor also has it that it's me he's interested in.

Despite the gusts of wind from the helicopter, I keep my rifle in position and shoot at the target 100 meters away. The bullet zips through the air and hits the center mark. Bull's-eye!

I, along with the other trainees, can't help but sneak glances upward as the helicopter spins in a tight spiral, upright but out of control.

Wolfson barks, "Did I say to stop practicing? What is your mantra?"

In unison we recite our training motto, "I am a soldier. I serve the Agency. It is my purpose."

I tuck my rifle to my shoulder and get back to target practice. Even with my focus back on the target and hours of training to stay focused in extreme circumstances—which a helicopter about to crash at any second definitely qualifies as—it's hard not to be distracted.

The helicopter swoops low toward the field. It smashes to the ground tail first, and the impact shakes the whole stadium. Metal pieces shoot into the air and a cloud of dirt plumes out from the accident site. Orange flames erupt out of the dust cloud.

Without orders, no one makes a move away from or toward the crash, though several trainees duck for cover. I stay put and shoot another bullet at the target. Not a bull's-eye but commendable given my surroundings.

"Rifles down!" Wolfson points at the wreckage. "Save the assets!"

All twelve of us immediately rush toward the helicopter in the hopes of saving whoever is in there. The dust hasn't fully settled and an inferno is raging, so I cover my nose and mouth with my sleeve and push into the debris. A wave a heat nearly forces me back, but I press on.

The windows are busted into a million pieces, but the frame is partially intact. There are two figures in the cockpit. The pilot in command struggles to unstrap himself from his seat. The other pilot is motionless. The guard of the helmet covers her features, but the many badges on her military jacket reveal it's Legend. Her call sign was well-earned for her heroics in war. She is a Legend.

One other trainee has made it past the smoke. I leave the conscious pilot to her and go for the more important asset of Legend. The smoky air is so thick it's hard to breathe or see, but I manage to finagle the belt open. The fire at the tail of the helicopter is growing, only a matter of time before it reaches the fuel tanks and blows us all sky high.

My movements turn clumsy from the lack of oxygen. I've got to get out of here. I pull Legend from her seat and drag her away from the wreckage. We're barely ten feet from the helicopter when an explosion rocks the earth and turns the world black.

A different helicopter hovers in the sky above the highway. The wind swirls dirt and leaves around, seemingly in slow motion, like the world is waiting for me to get my memory back, like it's waiting for me to make sense of who I am. I think it will be waiting for a long time. The convoy of vehicles comes to an end. The helicopter swoops away into the distance and the wind dies down. The debris settles into place, but my memory does not.

I sway unsteadily. A hand forces me down and pushes my head between my knees. The blurry image of a metal guardrail underneath my butt fills my vision, which slowly steadies out with my breathing. I lift my head. No helicopter, except for the one burned in my memory.

The same hand that forced me down helps me up, and I stumble and fall against a muscular chest. When I look up, all I see are Elijah's brown eyes set in concern.

He grips my arms to steady me. "You okay?"

"Yes," I say, but think no.

In that moment in my memory, I know I would have left Legend in that helicopter to burn if I hadn't been ordered to save her. *I am a soldier. I serve the Agency. It is my purpose.* I would have followed any order Wolfson gave. Any. The woman, the assassin, she was sent to kill me. She was following orders, too.

"Another memory?" Elijah asks.

"Yes." I blink back tears. An ache settles in my chest, but I refuse to cry. I thought regaining my memories would be a relief, would answer the question of who I am. But so far they've only brought anguish and more questions. I can't fit the pieces of me together. How do the 13-year-old liar, the young woman with Zhang, the trainee who follows orders at any cost, and the me who looks at constellations with Elijah make up the whole of me?

The violent things I've done, those things felt instinctual, my body telling me they were right while at the same time I recognized in a detached way that they were wrong. I don't feel like the same person my memories show me to be, even when acting in a way that fits with my memories. A piercing pain shoots through my temples and I sway again. This time Elijah's strong arms are there to keep me upright. Damn this head injury!

He settles back on the guardrail and sits next to me, leaving a good foot of space. Not like last night when we were pressed so close together. His expression of concern is replaced by a wary one.

He looks away, out into the distance. "Wanna talk about it?"

"No." I'm firm on that. I don't want to talk about my memory...or last night.

A long sigh escapes his lips, and I wonder what he's thinking. Did the convoy scare him? Or did it comfort him to know the military is here? Maybe talking to him would help me figure out what I'm feeling because I can't seem to push away the sense of dread that has filled me since seeing all those military vehicles rumbling down the road. Or maybe I'm dreading being hit by another memory. Or hurting someone else.

I shiver despite the warm air. Elijah pulls a gray

hoodie from his backpack and offers it to me. I thank him and pull it on, shoving my hands in the big front pocket. It smells like fresh spring rain.

"We should catch up with the others," he says, avoiding my gaze.

We head off down the long highway in silence, each step pounding in my head, a reminder of all the things I don't know and all the things I wish I didn't know.

10

We easily catch up to the group and soon approach a large rest stop on the side of the highway. There are more people gathered here than I've seen since the attacks, and it's set up like a makeshift hospital. Imah insists we stay to help in any way we can even though it's only mid-afternoon and it's a long way to D.C. She has a great capacity for helping people that won't be compromised.

The rest stop reeks of rotten, greasy food and unwashed bodies. Emergency lights in the corners and wall-length windows on three sides of the large room provide plenty of light to illuminate the injured resting on bright red Formica tabletops. The air is unpleasantly humid and claustrophobic. I peel off Elijah's sweatshirt and try to give it back to him, but he insists I keep it, so I tie it around my waist.

A quick sweep of the space tells me there are about twenty injured. Another thirty or so people loiter around— the noninjured, their stricken faces wearied. Two doctors in white coats tend to the wounded.

Imah sets down her medical bag on a free bench, snaps on a pair of plastic gloves, and issues orders to Elijah and Tony, the only other off-gridders who came inside. I've been sneaking looks at Tony all day and have been met with a vicious glare each time.

"See if you can find some disinfectant," Imah says to Elijah. He slips behind one of the fast food counters and ducks out of sight. "Who's in charge here?" she asks the room.

A tiny woman, 4' 11" and maybe 95 pounds, with tortoise shell glasses far too big for her face, skitters over. Her doctor's coat skims the floor, its sleeves hanging low, covering her hands. She stares at me a moment too long before turning her attention to Imah.

Everything about her is mouselike, including her squeaky voice. "I am." I expect her to raise a hand as if in a classroom, but she only holds out her hand for Imah to shake. "Dr. Bauman."

She points to a person on the nearest table. A sheet partially covers his body—I'm guessing he's a man based on his size. A bulbous belly blocks his head from view. I might have mistaken him for dead, if not for the uneven rise and fall of his belly underneath the linens. "We've organized everyone by severity of condition, starting here with the worst."

The mousy woman's gaze darts around the room, falling on a woman and pre-teen boy. She lowers her voice. "Head wound, heavy blood loss. Unresponsive since his wife and son carried him in on a wheelbarrow."

Imah opens her doctor bag. "Do you have anything to wrap his head?"

Dr. Bauman sighs. "We are out of anything sterile except for small pieces of gauze. There are the sheets, but I worry about infection."

I take a few steps closer and glimpse fresh blood seeping through the bandage on the injured man's head.

The blood puddles on the table, staining it a less cheerful shade of red. My stomach turns, not because of the blood, but because I know this man will die soon.

I think of the New York City skyline from Zhang's room and wonder, not for the first time, if he had anything to do with the attacks. And in turn, whether *I* had anything to do with the attacks.

I walk away from the dying man, not wanting to hear or see any more.

Rubbing my arms, which are covered in a layer of dirty sweat, I suddenly have the urge to cleanse myself. A large sign painted high on the back wall points me to the restrooms. I slip into the ladies' room and let my eyes adjust to the lowlight provided by a single candle. Apparently, the bathrooms don't warrant emergency lights. The candle, doubled in the mirror behind the sinks, gutters as the door swings shut behind me.

A young woman—thin but a muscular 5' 7", and older than me by a few years...if my guess about my age is accurate—comes out of the farthest stall. A fight between the two of us would be a match for the ages. I blink that strange thought away and watch her warily.

Her black, tight-fitting outfit is similar to mine, both made of sweat-wicking material. Where I have short-sleeves, she has a sleeveless top. My pants go to my ankles, and hers stop midcalf. There are no brands marking either of our clothes. Just like the assassin's clothes, too.

Definitely too similar to be a coincidence. My lips turn up in a funny little smile when I realize I don't believe in coincidences.

The smile isn't for her, but when she notices me standing just inside the door, she offers a friendly nod. I recognize the appraising way her eyes evaluate me. With one glance, she knows as much about me as I about her, and probably near as much about me as I know about myself. Maybe more.

Her short, dark hair is dusted with ash—seems the whole country is tainted by ash these days. I step to the sink, test the tap to find the water works, and wash my hands. It's the type of sink where you have to hold down the handle to keep the water running, requiring more attention than I'd like to give it. As I press the water on with one hand and rub my face with the other, I keep my peripheral vision on the young woman.

She sticks one arm under the stream as far up as she can maneuver it. The sink turns off and she rubs her arm all the way up to her shoulder. I watch her under the pretense of struggling with the sink to wash my own arms, acting more awkward than necessary.

My breath catches when she cleans the back of her shoulder, revealing a tattoo. It's a small snake coiled around her scapula, the green of it popping off her dark skin in the dim light. A tattoo I've seen before. But how the hell do I know that? She shoots a look of inquiry at me, and I fake a shiver and pretend it's the cold water that has shocked me.

The buzz of a tattoo needle reaches my ears and the smell of antiseptic invades my nose. The sting of the needle pierces my hip. My eyes water in bright, artificial light as I lie on my back on a hard table.

A girl lies on her stomach on a table next to me, the side of her head resting on her arms. On the other side of her are three more identical tables and three other people receiving tattoos. They are all on their stomachs; I'm the only one getting a tattoo on my hip.

"Doesn't hurt so bad, does it?" The girl winks, the skin

crinkling at the edges of her eyes. They're an unnerving chartreuse; I've never seen eyes that color before. Almost yellow. She's older than I first thought from her small stature, but probably not older than me.

I shrug, careful not to move the lower half of my body. "I've felt worse."

She glances at the woman administering my tattoo. The tattooist is wearing all white, from her simple button-down shirt to her spotless, plain sneakers. The same outfit as the woman hunched over the girl's shoulder. They are both engrossed in their work and don't appear to care that we're talking.

Still, the girl's next words come in a strained whisper, barely audible over the buzz of the needles. "Training's been brutal lately. Think we'll be ready for a mission soon?"

We shouldn't be discussing missions, but I'm always hungry for information. "What do you think?"

"A question for an answer," she quips. "So you don't know any more than I do. Well, all the recruits I know with tattoos have been on at least one mission. I'd say that means it's our time to shine."

A tingle of excitement rises up my spine and I struggle not to shiver. "Stay still," hisses my tattooist. I'll need better body control if I'll be going on a mission soon. I'll have to work on that in training.

She resumes needling my hip and the girl's mouth curls up in a grin. "Exciting times," she says, sharing in my exhilaration. Her lips pull down and her forehead wrinkles in seriousness. "What's with the hip tattoo? I've only seen the ones on the shoulder."

I look back up at the ceiling and let the glaring light wash my eyesight blind. "I follow orders, like everyone else." I resist the urge to smile, pleased with my facial control—

not many others get a tattoo like mine because I am special among the recruits. The only black-ops agent to come out of my class, and a black butterfly growing on my hip to prove it.

"Just a regular shoulder one for me," says the girl. She stretches her neck to get a glimpse of my tattoo, but she'll never be able to maneuver to see that side of me.

The girl's tattooist announces they're done. In a quick motion, she sits up, facing me, my budding tattoo in full view. "A butterfly. Hmm...haven't seen one of those before. An unusually delicate choice." She flashes her white teeth. I smile back but keep quiet about why I chose to get a butterfly tattoo.

Her tattooist, a frosty glare plastered on her face, steps into the space between tables, blocking my line of vision. "Turn around," she says to the girl.

The girl flips her legs around the end of the table, her back muscles tight and pronounced under her fitted tank top. I get a glimpse of her tattoo. A green snake curls around the protrusion of her scapula. As she moves to try and get a good look at it, her muscles ripple beneath the skin, making it look like the snake is dancing. The color is almost iridescent, and as it catches the light, it appears yellow before flashing back to green, just like the girl's eyes.

I gasp for air and see white-knuckled hands clutching the edges of a toilet, though last I knew I was at the sink. A voice with a tinny, faraway quality asks, "Are you okay?"

My only response is to retch into the toilet. I wipe my mouth and fumble around until I find the flusher. The clamor of the industrial toilet echoes in my head as I rest against the toilet seat, too spent to care about germs. Two memories so close together has wiped me out. A warm hand is pressed to my forehead. I scoot away from the hand as best as I can in the tiny bathroom stall.

"It's okay," the young woman says. She's kneeling too close to me, her blurry face dancing and weaving around like we're in a boxing match. "I was checking your temperature." Her face steadies in my recovering vision. "You don't have one. Head wound?" she asks.

I begin to nod, but the slight movement causes my stomach to roll. I swallow a few times and manage to utter, "Yeah."

She sits on the floor across from me. "Those are a bitch."

I manage a small nod that's more of a blink.

She holds out her hand. "I'm Breanne."

Without offering my name, I take it and grunt a greeting. Let her think I can't manage to talk right now. The less I share about myself, the less likely anyone will find out about Black Butterfly and whatever job I had before I lost my memory.

11

When I come out of the bathroom, I spot Breanne with a group of people huddled in a corner of the rest stop. They are all dressed in tight-fitting black clothes like her—like me—and are in their late teens or early twenties. Some sleep, while others sit with what I recognize to be a false casualness as they look around scanning the large room. For what? Threats and dangers? People like me?

I quickly find Elijah before Breanne notices me. I spend the rest of the morning helping Imah tend to the wounded. Seems I have some skill in first aid, not as developed as my fighting skills, but I prove to be an asset.

Dr. Bauman glances at me far too often, and I'm burning to know why. She hasn't given me any indication she knows me, yet my skin prickles under her gaze.

It's become a habit whenever we're around other people to examine each face closely. I keep expecting to see someone I know, to have a spark of recognition upon spying a familiar face. But there never is a spark; they are all strangers in my eyes.

My other worry is bumping into someone from my past that I don't recognize but they'll know me. So far no one—aside from the woman in the dark parking lot—has shown any sign of that. But like Dr. Bauman, occasionally someone will stare at me a beat too long. Do they know me? Are they from the Agency? Are they going to try and kill me? It's made me kind of paranoid.

It could be the person is studying my face in hopes of seeing someone they know, a loved one they thought they lost in the attacks. They're searching for a miracle. I don't think I believe in miracles, and I'm certainly not going to be one for them. Even with intact memories, we're all a little lost in this new world we've been handed.

The paranoia feels justified around Dr. Bauman with the way she is pointedly not looking at me whenever I get close to her. I do my best to stay near her to see if she lets anything slip, but she only makes polite conversation with Imah as they examine patients.

"Your kids?" she asks, gesturing to me and Elijah.

"Um, no," Imah says, a bit of bite in her reply at being mistaken for someone old enough to be our mother. "My brother and his friend." She directs her attention to the man on the table, who has a large cut on his leg. "Let's get this cleaned out. I don't have anything for the pain, but I'll make it as painless as I can."

He grits his teeth and nods. I hold a bag out for Imah to deposit the bits of debris she picks out of the wound. Then she cleans it with soapy paper towels, while I try to keep everything from making a drippy mess.

"How long have you all known each other?" Dr. Bauman asks from over my shoulder.

Imah jumps at the closeness and blows her breath out in exasperation, puffing her hair out of her face. "Well, I've known my brother all his life, and B's been a friend for a little while now."

"B, huh?" Dr. Bauman says with an edge to it. It

sounds wrong, more sarcastic than curious.

It sets me on edge even more, and I keep my head down and concentrate on bagging up the soiled paper towels. I breathe a touch easier as she moves to a patient a few tables over.

"This is going to need stitches." Imah pats my shoulder as I do one last swipe of the table. "Good job. Why don't you take a break?"

I can't keep a small smile off my face as I head to where Elijah is telling stories to a group of young kids. They are rapt with his tale of a dragon hiding in the cave, too timid to come out and discover all the magic of the forest around him. All of them look rather shabby with dirt and ash smearing their clothes and faces, but their eyes are alight with wonder at Elijah's words. His deep voice is perfect for the dragon's voice, and it cracks as he attempts a squeaky voice for a mouse that enters the cave and scares dragon. It's the most words I've ever heard him say at one time.

Shortly after I sit cross-legged in the back of the group, a little boy, no more than three, slides toward me and sits in my lap. My eyes go wide. The little body is heavier than I thought it would be, but I find his presence more comfortable than not. Elijah flashes me a smile when he notices my companion. He keeps the story going until Imah finishes her work and it's time to get back on the road. I pat the little boy on the head as his dad retrieves him.

Back on the road, Elijah and I walk next to each other in companionable silence, and I hope that means I haven't irrevocably damaged our friendship with my violent outburst the other night. Perhaps my work today with Imah and the cuddle with the little boy have redeemed me a bit in his eyes.

We're hot on the tail of Breanne and her group. After that memory of the tattoo, part of me wants to stay close to this person who maybe has a connection to my past and a part of me is reluctant to for the same reason. I keep tabs on them for the rest of the day. Like us, they are walking south on the highway. They are less subdued than I thought they would be, pushing and shoving, laughing loudly. It's like they're not in mourning with the rest of us.

As the overcast day turns dark, the off-gridders consider stopping for the night. Their committee approach to decisions can sometimes lead to a lengthy debate.

With an eye on Breanne as she continues on, I chime in for the first time. "I think we should press on a little farther." The off-gridders stare at me. "We haven't walked very far today," I add in as explanation, though it's not what's really motivating me.

Elijah nods in support, his wavy hair bouncing up and down. "I agree." The two quietest members of the group have spoken. That must count for something.

"All in favor of continuing?" Imah asks. Almost everyone raises their hands. Tony, of course, doesn't. "Then we keep walking. We'll be in D.C. in no time."

Elijah notices when Imah winks at me, and he let's out a deep laugh. It heartens me.

We end up passing Breanne's group as they stop on the side of the highway. The dark sky is swirling with black clouds and light is scarce, so about a quarter mile up the road, we also settle down. After helping with the fire and dinner, I grab a flashlight and tuck it into my waistband. I pull up the hood of Elijah's sweatshirt as I slip into the darkness, away from the warmth of the fire and the light banter of the off-gridders. Elijah notices but thankfully doesn't try to join me.

Off the highway, I track north. The ash muffles my footfalls. I keep the flashlight tucked away and rely solely on my night vision, which is particularly sharp. I'm a wraith stalking my target.

Slowly, I approach the group of dark-clad figures lounging around a fire, their faces lit up by the flames. I walk past their camp and circle back around. I settle on my stomach in damp grass, close enough to hear them but far enough away not to be spotted. I'm still as a statue as I observe.

Loud voices, the clink of glass on glass, and laughter erupt from the group. They're certainly not worried about keeping a low profile. I risk creeping a little closer. My moisture wicking clothes keep the wetness, if not the coldness, of the ground from reaching my skin. With a shudder, I realize cold and wet is far better than burning in flames. I swallow back the phantom stench of burning flesh and force myself to stay in the present. I can't afford to lose myself to a memory right now.

Their cheerful faces are easy to see from my new vantage point, and I note they are drinking bottled beer. Where the hell did they get beer? While so much of the country struggles, Breanne and her friends are drinking like it's a celebration. But what do they have to celebrate?

I'm not naive enough to think they're just some kids blowing off steam. I think of the flash drive tucked into a secret pocket, the man named Zhang being pinned as the mastermind behind the attacks, and an Agency that trains young women.

Mass chaos. China blamed. Mission accomplished. For what purpose I'm not sure, though I suspect it's somewhere in my addled brain. Would I be clinking glasses with them if my memory was intact?

The two people closest to me have their heads dipped toward each other in private counsel. This is a conversation I want to eavesdrop on. I army crawl, silent as a snake slithering through grass, until I'm mere feet behind them.

The pair are more subdued than the others, whispering in hushed tones, but my breathing is loud enough that I can't make out what they're saying. One turns her head toward her conspirator, her short hair and profile familiar. Breanne. The other is smaller, and I can't make out her features enough to see if she was also at the rest stop.

I slow and quiet my breathing, a technique my body instinctively does. Their hushed voices drift over. There's a good chance I might get confirmation of my worst fears about who I am, but I listen in spite of the danger of what I might learn.

"It wasn't just her clothes," Breanne says. "She had a mannerism about her, the way she appraised me but wasn't obvious about it."

"But you didn't see a tattoo?" the other replies.

"I checked her while she was puking. No tattoo."

I shudder over the fact that Breanne was able to check me for tattoos without me noticing.

"It could be a coincidence she was dressed like us," the smaller girl says.

"Luca," Breanne shakes her head, reproach in her tone, "you know there are no coincidences."

I mouth the name "Luca" to see if it's familiar on my tongue, but nothing registers.

Luca leans back on her hands, her strong arms rippling in the firelight. "There was one recruit I knew. She had a tattoo on her hip instead of her shoulder."

I suck in a sharp breath, struggling to keep my tingling body still. I want to jump up and tackle Luca, either to keep her quiet or demand more information from her. I'm not sure which. I haven't been able to see her face clearly, but I suspect she's the girl who got the tattoo at the same time as me.

The way she mentions me, almost too casually, I get the feeling we knew each other. Were we friends? I stifle a sad laugh, thinking, not for the first time, that I didn't have friends.

"On her hip," Breanne repeats. "So special-ops. What does she look like?"

Luca shrugs, like she couldn't care less about what I look like. It's an empty gesture because we, whatever we are, always evaluate other people. "Eighteen years old, five-six, one hundred thirty pounds. Fit, like we all are. She was a white girl with brown eyes and long hair so dark it was almost black."

That last part seems extra, an unnecessarily specific detail that betrays we were something to each other. But what exactly? And why is she referring to me in the past tense as if I'm dead?

Breanne shrugs again. "It could be her, or a million people who fit that description." She leans forward and holds her hands closer to the flames, reminding me of the cold seeping into my skin.

Luca turns to face Breanne, and I get a glimpse of her face in profile. She has a strong chin and a pointy nose like the girl from the tattoo memory. If only I could get a glimpse of those cat-like eyes to confirm it. "She was probably injured during the mission and is headed back to headquarters like the rest of us. If it's who I think it is."

I notice the shift in tense as if she's resurrected me by talking about me in the present tense.

"Maybe," Breanne says. "I can't shake the feeling there was something different about this girl, besides the tattoo."

Luca stretches her arms back, her shoulders popping with the movement. If I reached out, I could touch her. I stay absolutely motionless and concentrate on keeping my breathing quiet. "If she's the girl I'm thinking of, she was—is—different."

"Was?" Breanne finally catches the tense shift. She shoots a look behind her as if she knows I'm listening.

I tilt my face into the ground, just in case the firelight catches me. I take in the mixed scent of wet grass and soil.

When I dare to glance back up, Luca furtively glances

around at the others before tipping her head closer to Breanne. "I talked to her a couple of days before the attacks. I didn't expect her to survive."

"Should we be talking about this?" Breanne's voice has turned so quiet I almost can't hear it.

Luca dips her head closer and whispers, "Everyone here is in-the-know, right?"

"Yes. Was she?"

Luca nods once.

Affirmative. I had something to do with the attacks. I let the confirmation roll around in my head without really letting it sink in, all the while continuing to eavesdrop.

"She told you her mission?" Breanne says, the shock and disgust evident in her tone.

"No," Luca quickly answers. "Nothing like that. She wouldn't breach protocol. She had an intensity about her, a focus. She—" her voice breaks and she pauses "—did something I never expected her to do, not unless she was on a suicide mission."

"Well, if she was on a suicide mission and that was her in the bathroom, something went wrong."

"I hope so." I don't think Breanne hears Luca's mumble, but I do.

A smile quirks my cheeks. I press my face to the ground to smash it away. If Luca is right and I was on a suicide mission that had to do with the attacks, I not only failed my mission, but I'm also responsible for the terrible condition of the country. What the hell do I have to smile for?

13

Traveling with the off-gridders has taken on a feel of normalcy after only a few days. My role with them is becoming clear. I'm the girl who fills in the gaps, does any little task the others neglect. My observation skills suit me perfectly for this role, and the others have noticed. They have given me far fewer sideways looks and more nods of approval. All except for Tony.

So of course, it's Tony who catches me sneaking back into camp after spying on Luca and Breanne.

He grabs my arm and squeezes. "Where have you been?"

I pretend it doesn't hurt. "A walk." The lie comes easily, and he has no reason not to believe me.

He yanks me close so when he speaks, I can smell the sourness of his breath. "You might be able to fool that soft-hearted Imah, and you've got Elijah wrapped around your finger. Stupid boy, thinking with the wrong head. But I'm onto you. You're a bad apple, rotten to the core. I'm watching your every move. Don't fuck with my family."

I reach for his hand, wanting to break each finger as one-by-one, I pry them off my arm. Then we settle on opposite sides of the fire where, thankfully, I can't see Tony.

I force myself to focus on Elijah, to stare at his sleeping form, as a constant reminder not to beat Tony to a bloody pulp. What hurts the most is that he's probably right about me being rotten, and it'll probably be Elijah and Imah who pay for my selfishness in staying with them. But there is nowhere else for me to go. And there's nowhere else I'd rather be.

It takes all night for my rage to settle to a slow burn in my chest. Morning dawns in much the same way as yesterday where we pack up and make our way south towards D.C. Each step away from New York is a little lighter than the last. Maybe the physical distance from the spot where I was found is buoying me. More likely, it's the way Elijah snatches glances at me when he thinks I'm not paying attention.

I'm *always* paying attention, especially to him.

Or maybe it's how every time I cleaned a wound yesterday, Imah patted my hand and offered a compliment. That and the headaches have lessened to the occasional dull ache behind my eyes.

Our group continues to tail Luca and Breanne until we stop at another rest area. I breathe a sigh of relief. Without them around, it's easier to push aside what Luca said about me being involved in the attacks. It was a mission, and I was trained to follow orders. I may have played a role in the attacks, but not all of the blame can fall squarely on me. That's what I tell myself to ease the guilt.

With most of my memories still locked away, I start to believe that maybe I don't need to remember the past. My life can reside in the present and the future I want for myself. Maybe.

I try not to think too hard as Imah removes her doctor kit to care for the injured—fewer here than at yesterday's rest stop. As I clean another wound, Elijah sits nearby, an eager group of children in a half circle in front of him. Their dirty faces are rapt with wonder with his dragon and mouse story.

I dare to dream of a future that has nothing to do with agencies, secrets, or lies.

I'm high on the hope of a new beginning when we finish our work and hit the road. A flutter on the asphalt catches my eye. A butterfly is incapacitated on the ground, one wing twitching in a feeble, pathetic motion. It's covered in soot except for one spot of velvety black peeking out.

For a second, I imagine I am the butterfly, fragile in these conditions, flittering around with no memory, lost in a dark world. It's a stupid thought. I am nothing like this beautiful creature.

My foot jerks out and stomps down hard on the poor butterfly. I move my boot away and stare in horror at what I've done. Ash smears the delicate wing, or maybe it's the tears in my eyes that make it look so blurry.

"That must have been hard," Imah says, and I yank my gaze from the carcass to her face, wrinkled up in sympathy. "Destroying your namesake."

Crushing the butterfly...hard? It was too easy.

Concern lines the edges of Imah's eyes, like she feels sorry for me, or maybe she's sorry for the butterfly. She touches my arm gently, treading lightly. I wonder if Elijah warned her about what can happen when someone touches me without consent.

"It was the merciful thing to do," she says. "It was suffering. Now it will fly again to the afterlife."

It wasn't mercy that moved me to kill the butterfly. In that moment, when the wings and tiny body crunched underneath my boot, my chest pounded with power, the ability to take life with a single stomp.

I was delusional to think I could move beyond my past and focus on the future. I am no butterfly; I am a predator.

I rub my temples.

"Still getting headaches?" Imah asks, mistaking my attempt to scrub away the defect in my brain for pain.

"Not as many as I was, and not as bad," I say, my voice breathy.

My chest constricts and I can't get enough air to my lungs. Imah guides me to the curb and we sit together. She rubs my back in steady circles and instructs me to take deep, steady breaths. My arms shake as I hold the curb, willing the world to stop quaking. But it continues to shake and blur, and this time I recognize that I'm about to fall into another memory.

14

A high-pitched hiss sings through the air. The bomb makes a direct hit on the Empire State Building. More bombs rain down and explode. It's like a fireworks show during the day. It's only minutes before the iconic building begins to collapse, and then there's too much debris for me to see the sky anymore. The confusion and terror are worse than anything I could have imagined.

An explosion rocks the earth and sends me sprawling on my ass. Shards of wood and broken glass rain down like shrapnel on a battlefield. My arms whip up to cover my face. My jacket is fortified with light armor and protects me from the worst of the blows. I jump to my feet and join the exodus of people trying to get out of the city.

Another boom rumbles nearby as a subway station blows up. I keep my feet under me this time, my eyes scanning through the chaos, searching for one particular man. I lost him as I stood in awe staring at the Empire State Building falling. A mistake.

A ringing in my ears deadens the sound of more explosions and the screams of the people me. I press on, navigating as quickly as I can through the mounting wreckage. I pass the bodies of innocent bystanders, but I ignore them, the calling of my mission stronger than any other need.

The air grows smokier with each breath. What I wouldn't do for a gulp of clean air. An eerie quiet settles over the city as the explosions cease. Ash swirls around in a tornado of heat.

Then the building in front of me creaks and groans. It shudders in place before it collapses, sending a plume of dust and flames right for me. I turn and flee the other direction. My armored jacket weighs me down, so I throw it off in an attempt to move faster. In a moment of panic, I lose all sense of direction.

Imah's steady hand guides me back to the present. My body shakes with terror. I let it out with one long exhale and find stillness.

"Better?" she asks.

I nod, not ready to test my voice yet. On the road, the others have moved ahead of us and are getting smaller by the minute.

Imah notices where my gaze falls. "Don't worry about them. We'll catch up easily enough."

Mumbling incoherently, I reach for my hip flask— given to me by Elijah—and take a swig. Imah's steady hands continue circling, sending me comfort, peace.

"You're fighting the memories."

It's not a question, so I don't offer an answer. My memories are all horrors. Why would I want them?

Her hand breaks contact with my back, leaving coldness behind, and she turns to face me. "How much have you lost?"

I stare at the ground, unwilling to admit the truth.

"It's more than the day of the attacks, isn't it?" It's not so much a probing as a polite request for confirmation.

I nod, still refusing to look up.

"If you want to learn who you were, you have to embrace those memories, no matter how hard." There's no judgment in her tone, but there's plenty of it in my own head.

"What if I don't want to?" I whisper.

"I'm not one to judge. Your past is your business to remember...or not." Sincerity shows in her soft expression, in the tiny lines framing her eyes.

I wonder if Elijah has mentioned anything about the assassin that attacked us. Surely not if Imah's continuing to treat me with such kindness.

"But it's hard to figure out who you want to be without knowing who you were," she says.

My fingers brush the concrete curb in a rhythmic manner, back and forth, back and forth. It would be easy to open up to Imah, tell her how frightened I am of delving deeper into my past. To confide in her the horrible memories.

I exhale long and slow, sending out the urge. It's too risky for both of us. Not until I know more about myself. I have to know what I've done, so I can know if it's safe to tell her. I have to remember what I've done, so I know if it's too horrible to tell her. I'm afraid it is.

She lets me have my silence and rifles through her bag. When I look up, she opens her fist to reveal an electronic device as small as her pinkie fingernail. A dark brown stain covers most of the shiny metal. I make out a few minuscule numbers marking it like a serial number, though there are more I can't read as they're obscured by dried blood.

"What is it?" I ask.

"You were holding it in your hand when we found

you."

"Oh!" My lips stay open in exclamation.

She slips a hand into the folds of her skirt—bright yellow today—and pulls out a pendant on a delicate silver chain. "And this."

The pendant is a butterfly with metal wings and a black oval-shaped jewel as its body. Even with the sun behind a mountain of clouds, the jewel glints in the lowlight. I stare into its dark depths, and like the eye of a predator, it stares back. I shiver and wrap my arms around my middle.

Imah pulls my hand from its protective fold, turns it over, and gently places the device and necklace in it. "I have no idea what this tiny thing is, but maybe these personal items will help you remember what is important to you." She pauses. "There's one more thing."

She stares me in the eye, and I feel her appraising me. I must come up worthy because she digs through her pack once more and pulls out a flash drive. "I haven't seen what's on this. Obviously." She chuckles. "How would I have without a computer?"

Then she holds it out to me and slowly lets go as I take it.

"Thank you," I say in a cracked whisper, though I'm not sure I want any of these things. There's no way for me to know what they mean, and I've reached a point where I wish I could erase every new memory of my past.

I stand absentmindedly, clutching my possessions in a tight grip. After a moment, I offer Imah my free hand to help her up. She takes it and doesn't let go immediately after standing.

"When you're ready, I'm always here to talk to." She puts her hands on either side of my arms and gives a small squeeze. "No matter what happened to you in the past, no matter what kind of person you thought you were, the future is wide open, especially for someone as young as you. We can't change the past, but we can always make a brighter future for ourselves."

As Imah strides away to catch up with the rest of the group, a dangerous feeling hangs in the air, outweighing the prickle of mystery over the items. She has imbued in me a sense of the impossible, she has allowed me to hope.

15

We stop for the night at a small diner not far off the highway. Only three people require minor medical attention, one of whom injured herself cutting up a pineapple. I'm guessing the number will increase again as we approach Philadelphia.

"B, be a dear and look for some disinfectant," Imah says. "These tables are disgusting."

I don't find any behind the long counter, so I slip through a steel door into the kitchen area. As a reflex, I flip the light switch, which, of course, produces nothing. The tiny window in the door to the dining area is the only source of light.

A flash of metal glints in the dark. At first, I think it's only light reflecting off the flat top grill in the back. When the light begins to move in a slow, taunting circle, I know I'm in trouble.

My muscles tense and I crouch. My vision adjusts to the lowlight and the shape of a woman comes into focus, the deadly point of a big butcher's knife prominent in her hand.

She shakes a plastic bottle in her other hand and it makes a sloshing noise. "Looking for this?"

It's the disinfectant. Her white teeth shine brightly as

she shoots me a taunting smile. A grumble in my throat threatens to become a growl. I can't see the color of her eyes, but I know it's Luca. More than an inkling is growing in me that we have a complicated history.

She laughs, a deep rumble in her throat. "Well, you gonna come and get it?"

I whip out both the pocketknife Elijah gave me and the knife I stole from the assassin, one in each hand. I feel dangerous enough when I'm not armed, but with two weapons, power surges through my arms. I think carefully as I weigh what my next move will be. My knives look like sewing needles next to Luca's giant blade.

She takes a step to her right, and I immediately step to my right as well. She takes another sidestep and we circle each other. I move with surefooted strides on the tile floor. I have her on size and arm reach, no problem, but her steps are quick and light. Her advantage is her quickness.

We reach a narrow point in the kitchen, mere feet separating us. I can almost reach across and touch her with the tip of the assassin's knife, and even with her shorter arms, her longer knife would reach me if she thrust out.

She stops sidestepping and I match her. The light from the kitchen door catches enough of her face for me to see her eyes, which are less yellow and more green than I remember. Her face is scrunched up in a cocky grin.

In a swift motion, she tosses the bottle of cleaner in the air. I know this trick and stay motionless, letting it crash to the ground. The plastic splits and spatters disinfectant on my boots and ankles. The solution gurgles as it goes down the drain in the middle of the floor. I glance down and the tiles glisten with moisture.

A mistake. Luca lunges at me.

I twist away from the advancing knife and kick her in

the stomach, sending her into a counter full of pots and pans. They rattle loudly, and one falls to the ground with an earsplitting crash, the noise echoing in my sensitive head.

I slip a little on the cleaning solution and drop the pocketknife, but I regain my balance before Luca does.

She steadies herself and laughs. "Well-played. What else have you got for me?"

I'll show her what I've got. I plant my left foot in a dry spot on the floor and flick my right foot up in a blindingly fast movement toward her wrist. I'm quick, too. The butcher knife flies from her hand, connects with the wall to my left, and lands with a clatter on a flat-top grill.

Wide eyes show her momentary shock, but she quickly regains her composure and plasters that cocky smile on her face. She holds out her fists like a boxer. I feint a stab at her hands, but she holds her position.

"C'mon, you can do better than that, Raine," she says.

Rain, snow, sleet, fog, hail. I scream in my head for my brain to shut up with the stupid lists. Then I pitch forward, my ears ringing. Raine, with an E, not the precipitation.

My name.

Black spots pepper my vision. A sigh escapes my mouth as my body deflates and I lose control. I'm passing out, vulnerable to Luca and whatever she wants to do to me. This is the end. I feel a slight sense of relief at the thought.

A sea of identical gravestones shaped like crosses shine in the moonlight. I sit in a patch of grass separated from the graves by a small, circular driveway. The few trees dispersed throughout the smooth patch of grass inside the circle offer me a moment of peace before tomorrow when I leave for New York City.

I lean against a scratchy tree trunk, rest my eyes, and meditate, picturing a successful outcome to my mission, no matter what that means for me personally.

There is no distinct sound, no shuffling feet or cracking branches, to reveal that someone approaches, but I sense them all the same. I open my eyes to see Luca slip out from among the gravestones. She crosses the driveway, and I let her sit next to me.

"The sun will be up soon," she observes.

I rub my hands in the grass, already slick with dew. "Yes."

"That's when I leave."

"Me too." It comes out as a weak whisper.

She rests her hand on mine, effectively stopping my nervous rubbing of the grass. "I've never seen you nervous."

"I'm never nervous." At least I never have been for any of my other missions.

She cups my hand in both of hers. "It's a big one." She reads the question on my face. "I know because mine is too. Everyone's on edge. I think we all have big missions." A flicker of fear shines in her yellow eyes—no hint of green in them tonight—but then it's replaced with resolve. "It's what we're trained to do."

I nod. I will obey my orders, like everyone else. But tonight—morning really—before the sun rises, I want to do something purely for myself.

Leaning in, I grab the back of Luca's head and pull her close. Trembling lips meet her steady ones. There is no hesitation in the way she returns my kiss. An emotion between passion and desperation passes between us.

I've kissed many people. For money. For secrets. Once a kiss was forced upon me. But I've never kissed anyone on my own terms.

My heart beats up against her chest, all my training lost on Luca's lips. I break away before we get too carried away. Then I flee, leaving behind Luca and my small place of solitude among the graves. It will be the last time I see her.

16

A harsh brightness assaults my senses. I recall a saying about a tunnel and light and following it, but none of it really makes any sense. Am I dead?

A shadow breaks up the light. Arms hold me tight around the middle and a chest rises and falls against my back. Somehow, I ended up sitting on the wet floor, carefully cradled by a woman. Not dead.

"What happened?" The voice, unassuming but deep, belongs to the shadow above me. "We heard crashes."

"We were messing around, play-fighting." Luca's husky voice sounds loud so close to my ear.

"She's injured." The shadow sounds accusing now.

"I know," Luca says. "It was stupid of me. Something we used to do for fun."

The thump of a door closing filters out the light. Elijah stands above me, his russet hair framed by the light of the kitchen door's circular window, like he's wearing a golden halo.

Luca's light breath tickles the tiny hairs on the back of my neck. Why didn't she skewer me or break my neck? Did she just say something about play-fighting? Sure didn't feel like play to me. Nothing at all like the night in the

82

cemetery either, a kiss full of passion and endings.

I shudder the memory away. It's hard to reconcile the woman I kissed with the one who attacked me in the kitchen.

She releases her vice grip from around me and moves her hands to my sides. "You okay, Raine?" she whispers.

I jump at the intimate gesture and pull away from Luca with as much grace as I can muster. "Yes, I'm fine."

"Raine?" Elijah asks.

"It's my real name. I should have told you," I say, hoping he doesn't mention my memory issues. "I'm sorry."

"You've had other things on your mind," Elijah says. "Need my help?"

I try for a soft, apologetic tone. "No, thank you. Sorry about the noise. I'm okay, really."

He leaves it at that, taking my words for truth, and heads to the door with a half-glance back. I press my lips shut and hold my limbs still. Let Elijah leave, keep him away from this mess and whatever demons of my past Luca holds.

"Wait!" Luca yells. I grab her arm, not wanting her to make a move toward Elijah, but she only grabs an intact bottle of cleaner from a low shelf behind her. Luca stands, making sure I'm steady enough to sit on my own, and hands the bottle to Elijah. "You need this, right?"

Elijah nods and leaves without another word. Using the shelf to steady myself, I stand.

"Shit, Raine." Luca rubs her forehead. "I didn't realize how injured you are. You should have told me." She paces the small space, boots squeaking on the wet floor. "Of course, you wouldn't tell me. You never back down from a challenge. And you always keep everything so close to your chest."

I'm glad at not having to participate in this one-sided conversation.

She stops in front of me and stares at me with those chartreuse eyes. There's deep, unnerving feeling projected at me. "Injured is better than what I thought was going to happen to you. Are you sure you're okay?"

I nod. The blackout wasn't because of my injury; it was from the shock of hearing her say my name. I have a name, a real name.

Luca reaches for my hand but thankfully pulls away at the last second. I'm treading dangerous waters staying in here with her, but she's talking about me, about what happened. Now that I know I'm not in bodily danger, I feel a pull towards her, a warmth thawing my insides. Maybe that's what friendship is, though it seems we may have been more than friends. I imagine that Luca, with her snake tattoo and cat eyes, cares for me, and the warmth spreads.

I risk a smile, knowing it's my turn to add something to the conversation. "I got out."

"Well, I'm happy you did, even if that means you failed your mission." She grins and lightly punches me in the shoulder. "Not that you'd ever tell me anything about it." My shoulders relax when I realize I don't have to explain how I got out of the wreckage of the city, because I couldn't even if I wanted to. "What the hell are you doing with these hippies?"

"They're not hippies." I'm surprised I'm so defensive about them. "They call themselves off-gridders, people who live off the land."

"Whatever. Off-gridders then. What are you doing with them?" She shakes her hands, waving off the question. "Never mind. I know you won't tell me. Tell me this. Are you meeting at Agency headquarters? Initial reports said the Pentagon was hit, but they retracted that. Of course, it wasn't a target."

Luca is spewing vital information, and I've hardly said a word. I offer her a reward for her loose lips. "I'm headed to D.C." Then I throw her a curveball. "How long have you been following me?"

The yellow of her eyes sparkle. "Of course, you knew I was following you. And here I thought I was being stealthy. It's hard to out-spy a top spy." She winks and her mouth quirks up in a way that makes me wonder how well she knows me. "Just since last night. I saw you sneak away from my camp and followed you. I tried not to eavesdrop too much. I only wanted to see you, talk to you in person."

I stare at her for a moment too long. "I should get back out there. They're probably worried."

"I should go, too. I'll go out the back, the way I came."

She lingers a minute before turning and heading to a door at the back of the kitchen. I can't believe I didn't notice the exit there. Between that lapse and the unhinged reaction to learning my name, I wonder how much further I can slip before I really screw up, although I think I already screwed up big time on the day of the attacks.

When she opens the door, the gray light outside creates a petite Luca silhouette. "I'll probably see you again. We're heading the same place, right?"

She turns, not waiting for an answer, and the door closes behind her with a dull thud. My brain reels under the new information: Agency headquarters, the Pentagon not a target, my name.

I mouth it, "Raine." It's kind of hippy, more fitting for someone like Imah, and I can't help it as my lips pull up into a smile. I know my name.

17

We stay the night at the diner. I deflect most of Elijah's questions about Luca, claiming I don't remember her very well. The truth...for once. And I'm sure as hell not sharing the two memories I have of Luca.

"So, can I call you Raine?" Elijah asks. I relish in him saying my real name, but the joy doesn't last long.

"Do you mind sticking with B for now?"

He tilts his head like he wants to ask why, but all he says is "sure."

A darkness comes over his features, and I wonder if he's thinking about the assassin I beat up. He claims to be tired and settles down near Imah, and I don't blame him. He can't deny the danger of being close to me. I'm exhausted anyway and fall asleep without a problem, but I wake with many thoughts in my head.

We hit the highway, always moving south toward D.C. And I'm closer to having to make a choice between staying with Elijah and Imah and going out on my own. I could follow Luca to headquarters. Perhaps going somewhere I've been is the key to unlocking my past. There's a third option of going off on my own and forgetting about my past, but somehow, I don't think running from my past will make it go away.

Maybe it's time to be open to the process of actively trying to retrieve my memories, like Imah suggested. That night, in a quiet spot not far from the fire, I mentally lay out my scarce recollections like cards on a poker table. Too bad it's probably a losing hand.

Being pinned down by a beam, flames licking their way toward me. Struggling to free myself, and a growing hopelessness that I'd never get out, until strong hands save me.

The hotel room with Zhang. The same Zhang the president mentioned? Were the documents I provided the evidence that tied him to the attacks? From everything I've learned from Luca and Breanne, if Zhang was involved, he was probably manipulated by me and the Agency. It seems the Agency's headquarters is in the Pentagon, so are they part of the U.S. government?

The yellow-green eyes taking in my tattoo as Luca also got one. Mine a black butterfly on my hip, a smug sense of satisfaction that it marked me as a special-ops spy, the only one in my class of trainees. Hers a green snake on her shoulder blade, just like Breanne's. Both of us poised to start missions, the excitement over it palpable.

I close my eyes and remember Imah's warm hand making slow, methodical circles on my back as I recalled New York City crumbling under the attacks. Heat and suffocating smoke, panic rising, all the while searching for a man. Countless people dying around me. Somehow, I got out when so many others didn't. No clear recollection on how that happened, though it does bring to mind those strong hands reaching for me.

My face burns as I try not to think of my most recent memory of kissing Luca.

And nothing of my life before training with the Agency except for a snapshot of me at 13. I slam my fist into the grass, my skin burning with anger and frustration and my insides frozen with fear and longing. Who am I?

My hand finds the front pocket of the sweatshirt I've permanently borrowed from Elijah. It's only a little bit too big, a perfect fit for a sweatshirt. My fingertips lightly brush something cold. I pull the electronic device and the butterfly necklace from the pocket, leaving the flash drive inside. I haven't looked at any of them since Imah handed them over.

Elijah settles in next to me, giving me the excuse I need to turn off the leaky faucet of thoughts flooding my mind. He offers me a small candy tucked into a shiny purple wrapper. "Looks like you could use a treat. Found a couple in my backpack. They're probably old. Sorry." He shrugs apologetically.

He twists his own wrapper to reveal a small chunk of dark chocolate and pops it into his mouth. I do the same with mine. It melts delectably on my tongue and I close my eyes to savor the bittersweet taste. A slow rumble of pleasure starts in my throat and sinks into my belly. How could I have forgotten the simple pleasure of a piece of chocolate melting in my mouth?

Through my fluttering lashes, I spy Elijah's satisfied smile, warmer than any fire. My mouth curls in the corners before I remind myself I'm no good for him. I don't need to remember my whole past to know that inside the ice chamber in my chest is a black center, rotten to the core. Just like Tony said.

But Elijah never fails to draw me in with his kindness and inherent thoughtfulness. His simple innocence, the thing that makes me want to sprint away from him before I hurt him, is also the thing that makes it hard not to fall for him. There are no games with Elijah. Not like with Luca; it's all games with her.

Then there's Imah. Her goodness seems to bring out the goodness of everyone, even me. I see her helping people and I want to help as well. She and Elijah make me want to be a better person, make me believe I can be a better person.

Elijah reaches for my hand, but instead of grabbing it, he caresses it with his thumb. His gentle strokes shoot tingles up my arm.

"You have this effect on me," he whispers.

The butterfly effect. A single flutter of a wing can have a catastrophic impact on the future. Is that what I do as the Black Butterfly?

Elijah goes on, "I'm so aware of everything you do. The way you clench your fists when you're having a memory. Or how most of the time when you smile, it doesn't reach your eyes, but every so often, they crinkle at the edges...that's how I know it's a real one. Like I'm unconsciously following your every move."

I didn't even know that I was doing all those things, and that he was noticing. What have I done to this poor, misguided boy? And how can I make him stop evoking all these complicated feelings in me. Yet, I'm pleased he's learned my secret body language...as much as I know I shouldn't be. I suppress a groan.

He clamps his mouth shut as he stares at my lips, which are locked in a grimace.

"Oh shit," he says, surprising me with the swearword. He rubs his hand through his hair. "I just realized how creepy that sounds. Sorry."

He turns and stares toward the fire where the other

off-gridders rest or are engaged in quiet conversation. Against my better judgment, I cup his chin in my hand and steer his gaze back to me.

"It was sweet." Then with a giggle—I can't believe I'm giggling—I say, "Sweet in a stalkerish way."

My bad joke has the intended effect, Elijah smiles and his eyes light up in genuine joy. I know his real smiles like he knows mine. I release his chin and run a finger down his arm, lingering over the rough skin of his hand. Touching him is magical, prickles of emotion travel up my arm.

Dangerous.

The sickly yellow, almost-healed bruises on his wrists catch the firelight. An image of me pinning him down is replaced by him staring in horror at the assassin after I beat her to a bloody pulp. I swallow and pull away, putting some space between our bodies. My brain goes back to the first time I saw Elijah. That moment bombards my senses.

Where did Elijah say they found me?

18

A click sounds in my brain and turns to a ringing. "You said you found me just outside the Holland Tunnel, right?"

His eyes widen at the abrupt change in subject, but he nods and remains silent, waiting patiently for me to explain.

"But you live upstate, off the grid." I'm not exactly sure where I'm going with this, but my instincts are telling me that this is important and to keep talking it out. "It wasn't long after the attacks that you found me, right? And transportation was halted immediately. How did you get down there so quickly?"

"We were staying in New Jersey, just outside the city."

The ringing intensifies, but I talk over it. "What were you doing in New Jersey?"

"Imah had been asked to attend an environmental summit in the city," Elijah says without hesitation. "We were staying with friends instead of the hotel where the summit was. Imah doesn't care for hotels. Too much waste."

"And the other off-gridders came too?"

"Yeah, to support Imah." He cocks his head like he's trying to figure me out, but I'm doing my own figuring in

91

my head. "They were at a campsite, while Imah and I were with our friends. That's why we have so many supplies. We were planning on staying for a few weeks."

"An environmental summit in the city," I say, mostly to myself. The noise in my head cuts off, and I'm left listening to Elijah's soft breathing and the hiss of the fire. "So you were supposed to be in the city on the day of the attacks."

"Yes." He stares into my eyes, and I see questions building in his.

I touch his hand again, very briefly. "I'm glad you stayed with friends and not at the hotel. I'm glad you weren't there when it happened. And that you found me."

It's true, though that doesn't erase my fear for Elijah and Imah and what it means for them to be near me. I offer him a smile, knowing he'll see it doesn't reach my eyes.

Later, I'm restless in my borrowed sleeping bag, so I walk away from camp and Elijah, who is sleeping near me. I stare up into the night sky and find Hydra, the serpent. No butterflies in the constellations. The stars twinkle at me, sweet and innocent from afar, but deadly balls of burning gas up close.

Footsteps slip through the dewy grass. I'm pretty sure it's only Elijah—anyone trying to sneak up on me would make far less noise—so I lie back, hands behind my head, and wait for him. His face appears above me, his brow wrinkled in concern.

"You shouldn't wander off alone so late," he admonishes me.

One side of my mouth quirks up in amusement. If only he knew how well I can take care of myself. On second thought, he knows a little something about how I take care of myself.

I cringe on the inside but wave him off with a casualness I don't really feel. "It's fine." Then for some reason, I add, "I'm fine."

He gets down on his side, facing me, head propped up on his hand. "Cold out here."

"I hadn't noticed." Another lie as the cold seeps through my clothes straight into my back, making its way into my chest. Or maybe it's the ice in my heart that makes me shiver. "What do you want?" I ask more harshly than I intend to.

"Thinking about how I was supposed to be in the city on the day of the attacks. How by chance, I wasn't. Life is short. Too short to pass up on doing what we need to do." His stare is intense, the whites of his eyes bright in the moonlight. "There's something I've been wanting to do," he mumbles so all the words jumble together.

His gaze flicks up to the stars before turning back to me, burning me with its passion.

Quick as a snake sinking into its prey, Elijah leans over and presses his lips to mine. I react by instinct, opening my mouth to let his tongue brush mine. The warmth of his breath spreads into me, down my throat into my chest.

Warning bells ring in my head. Danger! Danger! Danger! I don't care. I want this, I need this.

Even if I could remember my past, it doesn't matter. In this moment, neither of us has a past and the future doesn't exist. All that matters are his full, soft lips on mine. The heat of our mouths mingling together. He pulls away before I do.

His face is closed, pensive for a moment, and then it breaks into a grin. "Thought you might punch me if I did that. Glad I took the chance."

I can't smile back. The ache in my chest is too strong, like I've plunged myself into freezing cold water. I'm waiting for the frostbite to set in. No longer in the moment, I know I can't have this forever. I'm too broken for him, too dangerous.

"You shouldn't have, Elijah," I say. "You've seen the kind of shit I'm messed up in."

He grabs my hands and squeezes. "Don't care. Whatever happened in the past is done. I see you here and now, and I like you."

I turn away so he doesn't see the tears hovering in my eyes. "I may not remember everything, but my past is there, and it's not going to leave me alone. Please. It's not safe. I'm not safe."

I abruptly stand and practically run back to camp, hastily wiping my tears. Everyone is awake and huddled around the radio, listening intently to a man with a southern accent that reminds me of my mother.

Elijah arrives shortly after and settles himself closer to me than I can handle right now. My discomfort is quickly forgotten when I recognize the voice of Cheryl Dare coming over the shortwave.

"That was Herman Tully calling in from an undisclosed location. That was a loaded interview, so I'll give you a quick wrap-up. Mr. Tully is claiming that the attacks were perpetuated by the United States government. He says he has a credible source inside the CIA who confirms his claim. When asked why the government would attack its own cities, murder its own citizens, and blame it on China, Mr. Tully said he could only speculate, but he believes that the government wants to go to war with China. He claims the U.S. is threatened by China's booming economy, their growing military strength, and their cyber supremacy. Mr. Tully says the president has wanted to go to war with them from since before he came into office..."

Static cuts in, and her words break up into incoherent syllables before succumbing completely to white noise.

The camp erupts into outrage. Heated discussions begin, most of the off-gridders deciding the man is crazy, but a few—Tony among them—admitting his theory has merit. Then it spirals into a debate about war. Imah takes on the role of moderator, and Elijah remains silent but listens intently. I can't handle listening to their theories over what is really going on, any more than I can handle my own memories and conflicted feelings over what to do next.

I don't have to fake a headache as an excuse to go to bed. I drag my sleeping bag as far away from the others as I can without being rude.

Soon after everyone quiets down, Elijah settles close to me. I feel the heat of his body as I try to fall asleep. His presence isn't enough to keep me from tossing and turning with nightmares for the rest of the night.

19

The ash has thickened again as we make it to the outskirts of Philadelphia. Our entire entourage detours off the highway to stop at a hospital as Imah wants to see if she can be of help.

We enter two at a time through a revolving door, which seems an absurd type of door to have at a hospital. The lights flicker off and then buzz back on. The hospital must be running on generators. Last we heard from the nightly radio reports is that power has yet to be restored to many areas.

A woman who looks old enough to be retired sits behind a sterile-looking wraparound desk. Her thick, old-fashioned glasses can't quite hide the bags under her eyes. Errant pieces of frizz escaping her tight, gray-haired bun indicate she's been there awhile.

She looks us up and down and purses her lips at our ragtag bunch. "The hospital is indefinitely closed to visitors at this time. Emergency care is open, but only for those in dire need."

A short, overweight man in a rumpled security uniform clomps over with a heavy tread. He waves his arms at his side, trying to usher us out, as if he could actually intimidate any of us. He's a sad excuse for security. Imah stands her ground.

"We're not here for a visit or for care. I'm a doctor and would like to offer my services for a few hours." She grabs me and Elijah and pulls us to either side of her. "These two come with me. The rest can stay in the lobby."

The security guard takes in Imah's flowing orange skirt and folds his arms across his chest. "I'll need to see some credentials."

"Mr.—" Imah squints down at the man's I.D. badge "—Sanchez, please let me introduce my brother, Elijah, and his friend." She conveniently leaves out my name. "I am Amelia Crawford, M.D., licensed to practice in the state of New York."

A low buzz stings my ears. At first, I think it's the lights, which flicker sporadically, but then I realize the droning noise is in my head. *Amelia Crawford.* That's Imah's real name! Amelia Crawford, M.D., who is running for Congress. Why do those facts feel so important to me?

Imah squeezes my hand. I shake my head and the buzzing ceases.

She clears her throat and puffs out her chest, seemingly growing taller in the process. "I am not in the habit of carrying around my medical license. I haven't driven a car in thirty years and don't carry my driver's license with me. I would be more than happy to wait while you look up my credentials, but I suspect your computer systems are not operating and it would be a waste of everyone's time. It is my understanding that people are in need of medical attention and I can give that to them. Can you in good consciousness turn me away?"

Mr. Sanchez blinks in rapid succession and glances at the woman behind the desk, who nods. "I wasn't trying to be rude or dismissive, Dr. Crawford. Of course, the hospital could use your help. Let me escort you to the emergency wing."

I nudge Elijah as we ascend a wide, stark staircase lit only by emergency lights, Imah and Mr. Sanchez a few steps ahead of us.

"I didn't know Imah's name is Amelia Crawford," I whisper.

His gaze stays trained on the steps. "Does it matter?"

"No. It's just your last name is Aarons, and I thought…"

What did I think? That they had the same last name? That Imah was her legal first name? *Amelia Crawford.* What is so important about that name?

"We have different fathers," Elijah mumbles to the ground. "Different last names."

"I'm sorry. I didn't mean anything by it." I lightly elbow him and attempt a joke. "I don't even remember my last name."

Elijah's head jerks up, and that's when I realize my mistake. He doesn't know the extent of my memory loss, and I've given him a piece of information I'd rather not share. He opens his mouth as if to ask me about what I just revealed, but a door banging open in front of us interrupts him.

We've reached a grayish-green hallway bustling with activity and light. Stretchers laden with injured people line one entire side. A low moan emanates from a person at the far end. It almost sounds like the word "help," but it rumbles on far too long to be articulate.

Mr. Sanchez pauses by the door, like he can't decide whether or not it's safe to leave us unattended. "Just down the hallway you'll find Dr. Long, head of emergency. He can help you."

Imah reaches out and shakes his hand. "Thank you."

She manages to be gracious and grateful when all I want to do it punch the prick of a security guard in the face. She weaves her arms through mine and Elijah's, keeping some much-needed distance between the two of us. I feel Elijah's probing gaze on me, but I ignore him.

Imah leads us down the hall past the stretchers, right into the heart of the emergency wing. The lights flicker, a reminder of all that is wrong in the world, but before my thoughts wander too far down that path, a tall, thin man in a white doctor's coat intercepts our path.

Imah flashes him a warm smile, releases me, and shakes his hand. "Dr. Long?"

"Yes." He holds out a hand stained with a dark brown streak that looks like dried blood. He glances down at it and yanks it away. "Forgive me. We're out of gloves and I just came out of surgery."

"Dr. Amelia Crawford," Imah says in introduction, and my ears start ringing. I shake my head in hopes of dislodging the noise, but it continues. She gestures to me and Elijah. "Do you have a spare room where these two can shower and rest? And then you can have my services for a few hours."

Dr. Long flicks his greasy black hair out of his eyes. "We can use all the help we can get."

"Are your CT scanners or MRI machines working?" Imah asks. She grabs my arm again and pats my hand. "B here has a bit of a head injury, and I'd love to have her looked at after I help out."

A cry of pain comes from a room down the hall. Dr. Long turns distractedly and yells, "Felicia!" He turns back to us. "I'm afraid power is too unreliable for our machines to be up and running."

I breathe out a sigh of relief that no one is getting inside my head today.

"No worries," says Imah with an apologetic smile at me. "How can I help?"

A woman in colorful but disheveled nursing scrubs hurries toward us. "Yes, Dr. Long." Her posture and face are droopy with exhaustion. "What do you need?"

"An empty room with a shower for these two," he points to Elijah and me, "and then brief Dr. Crawford on our patients and procedures. She's going to be helping us out this afternoon."

He doesn't pester Imah for credentials. At least Dr. Long can recognize a helping hand when he sees one.

Felicia hurriedly escorts us through the busy emergency area and into a dark corridor. She takes us to an empty room near the end of the hallway. "Hot water is limited. There should be towels and soap in the bathroom."

A high-pitched scream echoes its way to us. Felicia's hands fly up. "I have to go. Dr. Crawford, come with me."

She runs from the room with Imah in tow. The dim afternoon light filters in through a frosted-glass window, but I flick the light switch anyway. The overhead light brightens slowly with the familiar hum of a fluorescent fixture. It helps to drown out the unending ringing in my ears. The room is small with a curtain divider in between two beds. Elijah disappears into the bathroom and emerges with towels, handing one over to me.

"Soap's on the sink." The words are quiet, halting. "Ladies first."

Awkwardness has settled over us. It seems he's lost the nerve to ask me about my slip-up in revealing I don't remember my last name.

I touch his shoulder and offer him the realest smile I can muster. "Thanks. I'll save some hot water for you, if you're lucky."

"You better." The sparkle returns to his brown eyes and his mouth twitches at the edges in a ghost of a smile.

As I undress in the bathroom, I try not to think of how much I'd like to reveal everything to Elijah. Confide in him about my faulty brain, give him the gory details of the few memories I do have, and confess my worst fears about my past.

I touch my lips as water cascades over my face and recall Elijah's mouth upon mine. How I'd love to breathe in his warm breath again. I stifle a moan in my throat.

I shake my head of the thought and turn the water to cold. There isn't enough soap in the world to cleanse myself enough to be worthy of him.

20

The stream of cold water shocks my senses, easing the soreness in my muscles and the raw areas of my feet. No matter how good of shape I was in before, walking in dirty socks and heavy boots over the last few days has taken a toll on my feet. I use the hard bar of unscented soap and scrub under my nails. I lather it up in my hands and rub it into my hair, massaging my scalp. It feels divine.

For a moment I allow myself to believe I'm a normal girl, at home in my own shower, maybe getting ready for a date. That's what normal girls do, right? I close my eyes and listen to the steady spray of water. It's foolish to think such things, so I reluctantly stop daydreaming and resume scrubbing.

The suds slide down my stomach to my hips. The wound over my tattoo stings and I suck in a breath. In the dim light, I make out the inked black butterfly, one of its wings slightly disfigured. The pain is not so bad. I've felt much worse.

My left shoulder smarts as someone grabs my arm from behind.

"Don't you leave this house without my say so." In her anger, my mother's accent deepens.

The ancient air conditioner hums loudly from the sole window in the living room of the trailer, blocking out most of the hot Florida sun. Dust motes float all around us, suffocating me with the reminder that I've been trapped here for all of my 16 years of life. Now only the flimsy, dirt-brown door stands between me and freedom. Well, that and my mother, who tightens her grip on me.

When she jostles me, my bag strap digs into my sore shoulder. "I'm leaving, Mom, and you can't stop me."

As I try to pull away and reach for the door handle, she rips back my arm. My shoulder dislocates with a sickening pop. She doesn't let go. Black dots mar my tear-stained vision. I push forward against the pain, but she persists in holding me from the door.

I slap her across the face with my free hand. One swift yank frees my injured arm, which hangs limply at my side. My hand, still tingling from the slap, finds the coldness of the knob. I fling open the door and escape down the metal steps into the suffocating humidity.

My mom screams from the doorway, "Don't come crawling back when you've had to sell your body in order to eat! I won't take you back, you little whore!"

The insult would sting more if I could remember a time when I thought she cared about me.

A muted banging brings me back. My vision blurs. Cold water pours over my head and even colder ceramic numbs my bottom as I sit on the floor of the shower.

Shit. How long have I been in here?

"Raine!" shouts Elijah from outside the bathroom door, and I love the sound of my real name on his lips. He bangs again. "I'm coming in."

"No! Don't!" I yell before he comes busting in on me. "I'm okay."

My hand shakes as I reach up to turn off the tap. A shiver takes over and I stay on the frigid, wet floor until it passes. Another knock sounds. Can't he let it go and give me some privacy?

"I'll be out in a minute," I snap.

Muffled movements taper off to silence, and I hope that means he's not coming in. I wrap the rough hospital towel around my shoulders, still unable to kick the shiver that's from more than the cold water.

I had a mother once, not that long ago. And she hurt me, and I hurt her. Maybe she wasn't very nice, but she was a mother all the same. And I had a home once, too. A dilapidated dump, but a home. What else did I leave behind that day? And where did I end up going? How long before I ended up in New York City? A wave of shivers sweep through my body.

I dry my hair as best as I can with the already damp towel and put my dirty black outfit back on. I suppose clean clothes are a luxury now, and probably one I don't deserve anyway.

Elijah is perched on the edge of one of the stripped beds when I leave the bathroom. His gaze is fixated on the dull tiled floor. I sit near him but not too close.

"Sorry," he mumbles.

Damn. He thinks I'm mad at him when he was only looking out for me.

"It's okay." I hit him on the shoulder with the intention of being playful, but it's more awkward than anything else. It seems to work, though, because he finally looks at me. I get the full brunt of his concerned eyes, and my heartbeat kicks up a notch. Whoa!

"I slipped and fell. It's kind of embarrassing to admit." I stare down at the floor and bite my lower lip to seal the deal on my lie.

Elijah touches my chin—a calculated risk on his part, given my track record of beating up people who touch me—and gently tips it so I'm staring into his eyes again. "I don't believe you."

My eyes widen ever so slightly. How did he see through my lie?

He grabs a hold of my hand. "You can tell me," he whispers. "Whatever's going on. Even if it's that you can't remember."

When I avert my gaze, he lets go and clasps his hands in his lap. His shoulders slump, but when I glance at him, his gaze remains on me. There is an earnestness to his expression but not in a pushy way.

And that urge to confess rises again. The memory about my mom, how she hurt me and I slapped her and then left. What I said about her boyfriend when I was 13. How I know Luca and what I think I am. What I did with Zhang and how I planted documents, ones that have something to do with the attacks. And more. I want to tell him everything, even the things I haven't allowed myself to think about.

But I keep it all locked in tight. I hang my head in shame and tell a partial truth. "It was just a memory coming back. An unpleasant one about my family."

He brushes the back of my hand ever so slightly with his thumb. "Do you want to talk about it?"

I shake my head, not trusting my voice to lie again about myself, so I pick another lie. "I think I used all the hot water." I apologize with a small smile.

He rewards me with a small grin that washes some of the concern off his face. "That's okay. I'm used to cold showers." I raise my eyebrows. "Oh, no. Not because of that." His blush goes all the way to his neck. "Part of living off-grid."

As he disappears into the bathroom, I rest on the crinkly mattress and stare at the ceiling. The fluorescent lights flicker with a buzz. Hot shame fills me as I think about the horrible person I was, I am. I don't even have the guts to admit it out loud.

Elijah and Imah have a right to know they have been harboring and caring for someone like me. I should have the courage to tell them. But I am scared and tired. They have given me a place in this fucked up world. They've given me a sense of hope at times. And it's spilling over into my emotions. I have a chance to build a new life with these off-gridders. Forget the past. Start over and be a good person.

But I don't really. My past will catch up to me eventually, and I don't want Elijah and Imah to be collateral damage. A tear rolls down my cheek and lands on the bed with a soft plop.

The shower squeaks off and I roll over to face the wall, pretending to sleep as Elijah comes back into the room. I feel his presence at he leans over me, and I breathe steady and deep. His fresh soapy scent smells like rain. His footsteps creep away, the light switches off, and the door shuts with a quiet click. I am left alone to think about who I am and what my future holds.

21

Acold sweat paralyzes me as I wake from a sleep I never intended to have. Trembles take over, starting in my legs and radiating up my whole body until my teeth are chattering. I suck in deep breaths until the shaking subsides, but the iciness chills me from the inside. The droning buzz I haven't been able to stifle most of the day goes silent when my body finally stills.

The last image from my dream—nope, more than a dream, a memory—lingers. Me trapped. No escape. Mission: failed. The details are fuzzy, fighting to stay hidden, but the panic and despair are sharp, biting emotions that are—were—all too real.

I sit and blink in the dim hospital room. A quick glance out the window tells me I've been out long enough for darkness to have overtaken the landscape, which before the attacks probably blazed with light at night. The clock on the wall reads 10:33. I watch the minutes tick by as I contemplate my next move.

I know what I need to do.

I stretch and do warm-up exercises, the rhythm of them coming easily. Enacting my plan requires me to sneak out of the hospital. I better get moving.

A thorough search of the room and bathroom offers up a few useful items: gauze, antibiotic ointment, a pair of scissors, adhesive bandages, and medical tape. The scissors come in a handy leather pouch, which I tuck into the interior pocket of my pants where I stowed the pocketknife. I toss the other items into a small garbage bag and use the drawstrings as a strap. I fill my hip flask from the sink.

A peek out the small window in the door reveals an empty hallway lit only by emergency lights. I slip out of the room with silent footsteps and hold the handle so the door shuts without a sound.

To my left—the direction Elijah and I came from when escorted to the room—the hallway eventually turns to the more brightly lit emergency section of the hospital. To the right, a bright red Exit sign leads to a staircase. This is my route.

As I reach the landing, I hold the door open behind me and take one last glance back. Elijah's shy smile and deep-set eyes flash in my mind. I freeze the image for a moment before turning my back on the only people who have ever cared for me, as undeserved as it was.

I don't bother silencing the shutting door and take the stairs two at a time. My pace is steady but deliberate. Even if Elijah and Imah decide to search for me, they won't find me. I may as well be a ghost, my short presence with them dead and buried under the heap of shit that is my past and probably my future, too.

I fetch the tiny electronic device and the necklace Imah gave me from another one of my pockets. Using my fingernail, I scrape off the dried blood and stare at the 7-digit number imprinted on it, committing it to memory. My hand drops open, and the device falls to the ash-covered asphalt without a sound. It crunches under my boot with a satisfying grind. Then I put the necklace around my neck and set off as the wound on my tattoo twinges beneath my clothes.

Under the cover of night, its shadows embracing me like an old accomplice, I reach the highway and begin my search for Luca and the group of agents. It's where I belong. I will go with them to headquarters. I can't be sure of the consequences of returning, but I'm damn sure I'm tired of hiding from my past.

The highway is dark and lonely and my thoughts are equally as black. I keep a brisk pace, just short of a jog, best for keeping the churning thoughts from spiraling too deep. Miles pass underfoot and hours tick away in my head. Stars shine above me, but I avoid their allure, too painful a reminder of the night with Elijah and the constellations.

Finally, the dancing light of a fire offers the promise of finding my quarry. I sneak up on the camp to find it's only a group of civilians. Every last person is asleep. I continue down the highway on silent steps and inspect several other similar camps. I move on from each one, a phantom none of them will ever know was there.

The eastern sky lightens from navy blue to sapphire to a fiery orange. I've come to hate the color orange. I focus on the ground. Better to stare at the cracked gray asphalt than to ponder my past. I quicken my pace, a renewed sense of urgency surging through my veins.

A sharp whistle, meant to mimic a bird call but clearly made by a human, echoes off the road. I snap my head up to find Luca staring at me from the edge of her camp. A bustle of activity commences behind her as the group readies themselves for another day of travel.

A wry grin spreads across her face. "I thought we'd lost you."

My heart's not in it, but a small smirk plays at my lips. "I'm never lost, only purposefully missing."

The hearty laugh that escapes Luca's mouth sounds genuine. "You and your pretty words. To what do we owe the pleasure of your presence?"

"Heading back to headquarters. Figured I'd tag along with you." And hopefully find out some key information I'm seeking.

I narrow my eyes playfully. Her cat-like gaze fixes on me as though she wants to embrace. I wrap my arms across my chest.

"Are you nervous about going back?" Her question holds so much more than words.

The witty banter, which a moment ago felt natural, fails on my tongue. I smile, a full one, like I have a secret—which, of course, I have many of those. It buys me time to find my voice.

"I'm never nervous." I hold out my hand to demonstrate, and I'm pleased to find it remains steady.

The garbage bag at my shoulder rustles as Luca pokes at it. "Let's get you a real bag. Only a few more days until we get to D.C."

I swallow through the lump in my throat. "Yup." Only a few more days until I face my past and find out if I have a future.

22

Traveling with Luca and the other spies is not all that different from traveling with Elijah and the off-gridders. A little more boisterous, and definitely full of sophomoric humor and laughter, but it's laced with the same sense of purpose and direction. We march on toward Washington D.C., a mission of some sort on each of our minds.

Luca stays close to me the whole day, though most of the others greet me with wary glances. After giving me a brief hello, Breanne keeps her distance. I'm being treated like an outsider, even though I'm pretty sure I'm one of them. Then again, maybe my status as special-ops marks me as not quite fitting in here either.

In the afternoon, the sun peeks out of the clouds. The smoggy mess of sky turns bright and happy. With the sun on my face, my body feels warm but my insides remain coated in ice. I can't let it thaw or that ache in my chest might become too much for me to stay focused. Missing my new friends isn't a weakness I can afford.

B no longer exists. I am Raine, the Black Butterfly, cold-hearted spy.

With fists clenched, I face forward, ignoring my thoughts and Luca's sideways glance of inquiry, and march on. We pass a Welcome to Delaware sign. One more state to go and then D.C. My stomach twists with anticipation, and adrenaline makes it easy to push forward through the pain of the blisters on my tired feet.

By noon, the sun pounds down on the asphalt, creating a soup of heat. I've long tossed Elijah's hoodie into my bag. A much welcome chill returns after the sun sets. The sky remains clear, but I avoid looking at the stars as they twinkle to life. After helping to set up camp for the night, I stare into the fire, welcoming the blindness that comes from the bright flames.

Luca shares her meal with me when she realizes I don't have any provisions.

"The food sucks anyway. What I wouldn't give for a chocolate-covered doughnut. Didn't the Agency give you provisions?" She's fishing because she knows I heard her tell Breanne that she didn't expect me to come out of my last mission alive. Why would the Agency give a dead girl provisions?

"No" is all I say.

But she can't leave it alone. "Why not?"

I shoot her a withering look, and she throws her hands up. "Right, right. Like you'd tell me. I should just stop asking, huh?"

"That would be nice." I can't help the smile that spreads across my face. Luca's constant search for information is annoying, but for some reason, she entertains me. "But you won't."

Her tongue darts out, teasing me. "You know me all too well, Raine."

The intimacy of the way my name falls from her lips burns me. I turn away, hoping to hide the blush creeping up my face as I think about our kiss in the cemetery.

Embarrassment over how little control I have over my body temperature right now only fuels the heat. I am the worst special-ops agent. I can't even stop myself from withering under Luca's attention like a love-sick school girl.

I clear my throat and regain my composure, but the self-satisfied grin on her face makes it clear she sees right through me. She spares me more mortification when she excuses herself and disappears into the dark night surrounding our camp.

Head down, I creep away from the campfire to find a quiet place to cool off. I catch Luca's hushed voice on the breeze.

"No, she's here right now." She pauses as if listening. "Yes."

Bubbles of suspicions rise in my stomach at her tone. The copse of trees bordering the highway make for good cover. I slink behind a thick tree, careful to tread lightly on the mess of leaves on the ground. I peek around the trunk, and the half-moon provides enough light for me to spy on Luca.

She's on a cell phone. If anyone would have access to a working cell phone in a time when most people don't have power, it would be one of us. Unbidden, I suddenly remember she's good with technology, better than good, an expert. It's her specialty.

It occurs to me that in the president's speech, he said the military weapons systems were hacked and our own bombs destroyed our cities. It's likely that Luca—at least in part—was responsible for hacking the weapons system and detonating the bombs.

While my brain is rapidly putting the pieces together, my ears are trained on Luca's conversation.

"Do you think she would just tell me that?" she hisses

into the phone. A long pause follows before she says, "She's on our side."

An indistinct voice comes from the phone and Luca slaps her free hand on her thigh. "Well, she always has been. Why would it change now?"

Her end of the conversation is vague, but how could this be about anyone but me?

"Acting weird?" Luca asks after a moment. "Not that I've noticed, but I haven't talked to her much." She falls silent and paces a tight line along the guardrail. "I can try, but I can't promise you results."

Yelling, too garbled to understand, issues from the phone as Luca holds it away from her ear. After it quiets, she brings the phone close to her face again.

"Yes, ma'am," she says all official sounding. "I'll consider it a mission."

She taps the phone and places it in her pocket. With a low sigh, she sits on the guardrail and stretches out her legs. Then her posture slumps in on itself. She lets out a disgruntled groan as she redoes her ponytail.

I lean against the tree trunk and slide to the ground in one silent movement. Any desire to continue spying seeps out of me. So now I'm a mission for Luca.

The Agency must know I failed my last mission. The one with Zhang and the attacks—I'm sure of that—but those crucial details of how it all went down that day still elude me. Without the particulars or any real information about this new mission for Luca, I can't be sure what's coming. If it were a simple matter of the Agency wanting to find me, their problem would be solved now that they know where I am. They need something from me. But what?

I'll have to stay extra alert around Luca and the others. Not that I trust them, but this is just more proof not to. I rub my eyes as fatigue sets in. I haven't slept in over 24 hours, and it doesn't look like I'll be getting much in the next few days. Luca's muffled footsteps head back in the direction of camp. I look to the stars and find the constellation Hydra, praying to the serpent that I will find my answers in D.C.

23

All the next horridly hot day, I wonder how far Elijah, Imah, and the off-gridders have traveled. With each step forward on the steaming asphalt—as I leave behind Delaware and enter Maryland—I picture their faces twisted in sadness over missing me. As much as they shouldn't be sad about my departure, I want them to be. It shreds my insides to realize how much I miss them.

When darkness finally falls, we make camp. I sit away from the others, like I often did with the off-gridders, but no one comes to keep me company like Elijah always did. I silently pout, hating myself for caring that no one here cares about me...until Luca saunters over.

"Wanna take a walk?" she asks.

Not with you, I think, but I shrug and say, "Sure."

Once we're out of earshot of the others, I smooth my hands over my pants and make the mental shift from brooding sap to savvy spy. Luca can't know I plan on pumping her for information, so I better play it flirty.

She steps over the guardrail and sits facing away from the highway. I slide over next to her and nudge her with my shoulder. "So what are you going to do to me now that you've lured me out alone in the dark?"

"Ravish you until you beg for mercy." She attempts a joke, but her tone falls flat.

Her guilty conscious working overtime, serves her right for taking that mission.

I pretend not to notice her lack of enthusiasm. "Oh, like you could ever force me to do anything I don't want to."

Luca's face is dead serious when she says, "You know the Agency could force you to do whatever they want. They have. They've forced us all."

"What have they forced you to do?"

We sit in silence for several long minutes counted off by the chirp of crickets. It feels so quiet in this post-attack world with no hum of traffic and buzz of electricity.

"A lot of things," she finally says. I wait patiently and am rewarded. "The attacks, so many dead. It was me. The bombs in New York City were me. I sent them there while I sat at a computer in a tiny room miles away." She hangs her head. "You know I shouldn't be telling you this."

The honesty unnerves me, and I shift uncomfortably on the hard metal. I match her honesty. "They want you to turn me in."

"But why would they need me to turn you in?" Luca's eyes are questioning slits in the dark—more cat-like than usual. "Did you go dark without their permission?"

Seems I went dark without anyone's permission, even my own. But I can't tell her about the extent of my memory loss, and I don't know how much the Agency knows. Perhaps a dash of the truth will suffice. "Did they tell you I'm suffering from memory loss?"

"Memory loss?" She stares at me in confusion, but then her eyes widen as it dawns on her. "Your head injury, the one your friend mentioned when we fought in that greasy old diner."

I nod, but keep my mouth shut, not trusting myself to speak for fear of revealing too much.

"Damn. How much did you lose?" she asks, as if my memories are napkins that were scattered by a strong wind and can simply be gathered back up.

I look her straight in the eyes. "Enough."

Her eye roll is unmistakable. "Why do I even bother?" Abruptly, she kneels and grasps my hands, all irritation replaced by sincerity. "Raine, you have to let me turn you in. I don't know what you've done, but they're desperate. Do you even remember what you've done?"

The desperation is palpable. It's there in her raspy voice, in the slight shake of her hands, in the dilated pupils nearly blocking out the yellow of her eyes. I shake my head no, taken in by her vulnerability. Is it calculated, a ruse to get me to give her what she wants?

Luca pulls her hands away and sits in the grass. "They'll find you eventually with or without your tracking chip."

I think of the electronic device I smashed in the hospital parking lot, the one Imah found me clutching in a bloody hand. The Agency must know I destroyed it. Does that mean they knew where I was the whole time before that?

Luca grabs my hands again. "You don't even have to let me do it. Turn yourself in. I don't care...just give me some credit. Tell them I told you to do it."

"You want me to turn myself in to save you?" I ask slowly.

"My track record with missions isn't exactly squeaky clean," she says, her eyes pleading. "Do you remember when Legend's helicopter crashed?" I nod. "That was my fault. I misprogrammed something in the auto-pilot and almost killed the best helicopter pilot who ever lived, one of the Agency's most important assets."

"Doesn't your success in the attacks wipe that out and prove your competence to the Agency?"

"From what they told me, you're screwed already." It's a deflection, but I let it slide. "They've asked me to take you in, alive. You know what that means, right?"

I can guess. Torture, or worse.

"Do the honorable thing. Turn yourself in and say I convinced you to do it."

Anger boils in my gut. I snatch my hands away, shove them into the front pocket of Elijah's sweatshirt, and stand.

"Honor?" I say. "What the hell do any of us know about honor? We're spies, assassins, criminals. Just because we do it on the orders of the Agency, doesn't make it right." I'm shouting now. "We're no better than the dirt you're sitting on!"

"I know...I know, Raine." She stands and faces me, grabs my upper arms and holds tight. "But we can't say these things. Think them all you want, but we can't say them. We're not supposed to have opinions. We're soldiers. You've crossed a line, and they're not gonna let you come back. You're a sinking ship. Don't pull me down with you." She falls at my feet. "Please. If you ever thought of us as friends, do this for me."

Backing away from Luca, from the desperation that makes my insides quiver, I turn and run. Her pleas sound too sincere, but my instincts tell me not to trust her, and my instincts are always right.

You can't trust any of us.

24

I'm stalking through the brush and trees on the side of the highway, loud and fuming. I take my knife and hack at a branch under the pretense of gathering firewood. The nerve of Luca to ask me to give myself up to save her.

Me or her. Who does she think I'm going to choose? I rocket the knife into the soft earth, grab a branch with my bare hands, and pull. Crack—it snaps and goes down at my feet. My palms sting where the bark pierced them.

Even if everything she said is true, who wouldn't choose to save their own skin? She's playing on our friendship, but I'm no sucker. Who's to say we were ever really friends?

I pause a moment in my tirade and wonder if maybe I should turn myself in. I'm doomed anyway, so I might as well, right? That's what Elijah or Imah would do. No, that's what Luca wants me to think. She's a snake, with the tattoo to prove it. She can slink her way out of this without making me a martyr. Turning myself in at Luca's request would make me look weak. I need to come in on my own terms in order to keep any leverage I have.

Why does she have to try and make me feel guilty? And how come it's working?

My amnesia has made me soft, and I can't be soft.

A tree trunk becomes the subject of my wrath as I kick and punch it, my breath coming in short, gasping spurts. My heart races, and I've lost my cool control.

A branch snaps to my right, and I snap my head up. Three black-clad figures, who blend seamlessly into the shadows of the night, surround me. They encircle me, poised to fight.

A fourth stands off to the side, oddly nonchalant in his posture. His sheer size—6'5", 250 pounds—is impressive. All their faces are under ski masks, only their eyes and lips visible.

I stand, keeping an eye on the one outside the circle. Rage over Luca resurfaces, replacing my sorrow. It ripples through my chest, into my arms and legs, all the way to my fingertips and toes.

I size up the fighters—possibly assassins. No, if they were assassins, I would've never heard them coming. Someone wants to see me fight, maybe to size up my skills. I think it's safe to assume these are the people Luca sold me out to, members of the Agency. And now they're here to claim their prize.

Too bad my knife is firmly implanted in the ground outside the circle of fighters. On second thought, I'm glad I don't have a weapon. I flex my hands; they will do just fine against these foes.

The ice is back in my chest. My breathing is steady. My head clear. The misplaced rage fuels my fire to fight.

A wolfish snarl curls my lip, and I shout, "Come on!"

The fighter directly in front of me darts at me first. She's curvy but fit—5'3", 130 pounds.

Quick and aggressive, she charges in. The blade in her left hand flashes as it catches the little moonlight reaching past the trees. She may be fast, but she's not smart, too offensive in her fighting style. I disarm her with a kick to her wrist. The weapon shoots out of her hand and lands in the fallen leaves with a crunch.

Her tongue darts out between her teeth and back into her mouth. Then she hisses long and low. We circle, staring down each other. She moves with more caution now, waiting to make her move. When we circle around so my back is to the man outside the circle, the curvy woman glances at him.

Her mistake. And my chance to strike.

Fast as a hawk diving at a mouse, I plunge to the ground and tackle her at the ankles. She goes down easily, but curls into a ball, taking me with her as we somersault through the brush. Halting our momentum with the tips of my boots, I pin her to the ground and press my elbow to her throat.

I feel absolutely nothing as she gags and flails and finally stops moving. Her eyes roll back in her head as she passes out. The steady rise and fall of her chest beneath me tells me she's not dead, just unconscious.

Elijah's face flashes in my mind, and I stop short of crushing the woman's windpipe. Instead, I kick her in the ribs and leave her body on the ground.

The other fighters have followed us and resume their formation around me. Two are close by, and the big one, clearly the leader, remains outside the fray.

A lean man to my right turns his head to the leader, who nods once. The lean fighter approaches me, stopping a few paces away. He's unarmed, which makes me think he must be a very skilled fighter.

He smiles and the holes in his ski mask are big enough to reveal deep lines around his eyes, betraying his age. Still, he's not to be underestimated. An older fighter means an experienced one, and he looks plenty youthful in his lithe movements.

He twists his neck with a crack, crouches low at the knees, and points a finger as if to say, "Your move, girlie."

I take a step to my right, he follows suit, and so begins the circling before the battle. Not breaking eye contact, we're both careful to step over my first victim as we move. With only one other fighter left, there's not much barricading us, but I'm not running from this fight.

Adrenaline pumps through my veins, just enough to give me heightened senses but not enough to hinder my breathing or heart rate.

After a few more circles, I decide the thin man isn't going to make the first move, so I carefully plot mine. Leading with my left foot, I take two shuffle steps toward him, feint a left hook, and swing my right fist at his jaw. His head jerks backward, avoiding the blow, and he advances on me.

Before I can make a second attempt, he wraps his arms around me in a straitjacket of a hug, pinning my arms to my side. His embrace is firm, a python with a tight squeeze on his prey.

I slide down out of his arms before they get too tight. Then, I roll away backwards, before quickly popping up to my feet. This time, he wastes no time before attacking. He runs straight for me, probably hoping to catch me off guard before regaining my balance. But I'm too quick.

I duck under his fists. I kick out and my boot makes contact with his knee.

A sharp snap and his agonized cry tell me he's down for the count.

The third fighter, also a man, is average in just about

every way: 5'9", 160 pounds, muscular but not overly bulky. He's so nondescript in his black outfit, he could pass for a wisp of shadow in the dark. My mind is on overdrive taking in all the little details that could give me an edge in this unfair fight. I've already fought two battles, and I'm injured.

Despite his unassuming appearance, I know better than to think this fight will be an easy one. Surely, they saved the best for last when I'm at my most fatigued.

Sweating profusely, my heart pounding in my chest, I'm a bit disheartened when he charges me. I suck in a breath and prepare for the onslaught.

Punch. Jab. Kick. His blows come quicker than seems humanly possible, his limbs blurred lines as they come at me. Sweat forms in places I didn't know could sweat as I dodge each attack, backpedaling as he advances.

My heel grazes something poking out of the ground, and I unceremoniously fall flat on my ass. The fighter swoops on top of me, straddles my waist, and pins my hands above my head.

His smile peeks through the thin slit of his ski mask. But he hasn't bested me, not yet. I kick up, and he dodges my foot, so I miss the sensitive place between his legs. Expecting this, I throw him off, springing up like a jack-in-the-box. He back-rolls straight up to a standing position and crouches low.

We begin the old circling routine again, knees bent and ready, arms out waiting to strike. My chest heaves, and my legs wobble ever so slightly. We've fought our way into a more heavily wooded area. Between the darkness and the sweat trickling down my face, I can barely see my opponent.

I swipe my eyes with my sleeve, and that's all it takes for him to make his move. He's on me in a split second, hands encircling my neck. His thick fingers tighten around my windpipe so tight I can't even cough. He lifts me off the ground by my neck and squeezes even harder.

If the second fighter was a python, this guy is the larger, stronger anaconda. And I'm about to be suffocated and swallowed whole.

"Enough!" shouts the leader.

The fighter hesitates for half a breath before he releases me. I collapse in a heap of shaking limbs. Sharp, rasping gasps issue from my raw throat. I fold in on myself, face pressed to my knees.

For a moment, when he first released me, my heart beat in joy to know I was alive. The elation has quickly faded, and now I wish he had ended it. My life would be so much simpler if it were over.

25

When I'm recovered enough from the near strangling to look up from my folded position on the ground, it takes a minute for my eyes to adjust to the darkness. Through tear-stained vision, I see the leader towering over me and the last fighter, the only one to defeat me, standing slightly behind him.

It's hard to tell, but the way the leader leans over me, feels like it's meant to be comforting, nonthreatening.

"It's time," he says in a deep voice I recognize somewhere deep in my brain.

"Time for what?" I ask in a hoarse whisper.

"To come home." He holds out a hand. It's a casual gesture of help, but it feels more like a contract. It's not "take my hand and I'll take you home"—whatever home is. It's "take my hand and agree that I own you."

Kneeling now, submissive below this man whose face is covered with a mask, I clutch my hands to my chest. Yet, I consider his offer. Freedom is a steep price to pay, but it may be worth it to find answers. Despite my dread, I long to know about my failed mission.

He leans down, so his breath tickles my ear. "What is left for you here, Raine?"

I wince at the sound of my name, so familiar on his lips. I know the answer. Nothing. There is nothing left for me here. I almost believed I had friends in Elijah and Imah —and Luca. But I can't commit my friendship back to Elijah and Imah. And Luca, well, she's proven to be no friend.

The ice hardens once again in my chest. I reach out…

A voice cries, "No!"

Then a hand swats mine away from the leader. Luca's chartreuse eyes catch mine through the dark. They're drowning in sorrow as if she's actually remorseful over what she has done.

She pounces on the man and yells, "Run!"

Dumbstruck, I stand there watching their scuffle. Lucky for me, the last fighter also seems too surprised to move.

Luca shoves the leader against a tree and looks at me, her cat eyes pleading. "Go, Raine, please. It's your last chance."

As I turn and flee, I think I hear her shout, "I'm sorry."

Despite the fatigue in my legs, they carry me quickly through the wooded area. I head deeper into the trees rather than back to the highway. It's too risky to be out in the open.

Once I lose the cover of trees, I head south on a small highway, still moving towards D.C. and hopefully to the truth of my past. The road is mostly dark and deserted, my footsteps echoing off the asphalt. I pause only to take off Elijah's sweatshirt and tie it around my waist.

I run for hours, sweat running between my breasts and lungs burning as they pump at maximum capacity. My mind also works at full capacity the whole time, deciding my next course of action.

The rising sun glints off the sign for a big discount store. I jog down the exit ramp, across the barren street, and into the empty parking lot. People must be lying low, focused on surviving and heeding the president's advice to stay home, or for those who don't have homes, staying in shelters.

The glass doors to the store are dirty but intact, and a firm tug on them tells me they are locked. A small miracle in this mess of a world that no one has looted the place. I laugh at the idea of people taking care of each other. How nice a concept, and how foreign a concept to me.

Others may be caring for each other, but I have to take care of myself right now.

A small pang runs through me when I take a rock and smash it through the glass door. The shattering echoes across the parking lot but quickly dies down, and quiet is restored to the dawn. I find a sturdy stick to clear away enough glass for me to fit through.

The inside of the store is darker than I expected, not even the emergency lights are working. I left behind the meager bag of supplies I had from the hospital. My knife—Elijah's knife—is somewhere in the leaves by the fighters, so I'm back to square one.

I know I'm alone, yet I tiptoe quietly through the aisles.

I find a flashlight and batteries and tear into the packages. The single beam does little to lessen the oppressive darkness, but at least I can see the floor in front of me.

Taking a deep breath, I take stock of what I need and narrow the list in my head to what I absolutely need, which isn't much.

The first thing I must do is treat the blisters on my feet, which have broken open in a mess. I grab bandages, antibiotic ointment, and several pairs of socks. My feet sigh in relief as the ointment starts to numb the blisters. The new socks make me feel like I'm walking on clouds. A travel-sized deodorant gets added to the pile. I'll put that on my feet before I set out again to keep them dry and prevent new blisters.

Next, I focus on weapons. The selection here is impressive. There are no handguns but a dozen different rifles to choose from. I bypass the rifles—too conspicuous—and study the knives, which are locked in a case. This time I smile in satisfaction as the glass shatters, opening up the world of possibilities inside.

I select a small pocketknife reminiscent of the one Elijah gave me, a large utility knife with spring-assisted opening, and a multi-tool with all kinds of fun functions. My favorite is the badass needle-nose pliers, which serve the dual purpose of intimidation if I should have to threaten someone.

My mental checklist is dwindling as I find a new pair of boots, some fresh clothes, and a sturdy backpack. I swipe a really nice watch that has a compass and tells the time in several different time zones. It's a bit heavy on my wrist, and probably too rich for my new persona, but it's way too useful to resist.

I break in my multi-tool clipping the tags off of everything. Behind the counter, I find the tool to snap off the ink security tags on the clothes and backpack. My hands are steady as they work, and my mind is relaxed for the first time since waking up after the attacks. It's amazing what a sense of purpose can do.

I slip the utility knife into my boot, handle-up so I can

easily access it, and store the pocketknife in one of the front pockets of my new hunting vest. I would love to fill each of my pockets with knives—and a handgun if they had them—but I need to be light so I can travel quickly. I reluctantly turn my back on the hunting gear and head to the food section, filling my bag with water and ready-made food.

An atlas—didn't know they still printed those—with a map of Maryland allows me to chart my route. Just south of here is another fairly large highway that meets back up with I-95 in Baltimore, which I'll then take to D.C. with whatever other citizens are headed there.

There's just one thing left for me to do: change my hair. It's weird to feel attached to a look I neither put much effort into nor particularly like. But it's what I know, and that's hard to move away from given how little I know. In the hair-care aisle, I find a dye that promises to turn my dark hair to bleach-blond in 30 minutes.

The bathroom is damp and rank. I unscrew the cover of the flashlight and set it on the sink so it works like a candle. I use the scissors on my multi-tool to chop my thick hair to just below my ears. The result is uneven, but I'm okay with that. Brown water chokes out of the tap so I opt for bottled water to start the transformation of my hair to bottle-blond.

My brain is churning with all the possibilities in front of me while the required dyeing time passes, my scalp prickling ever so slightly. I contemplate the different scenarios I may come across and my reactions to each one. I compartmentalize, organize, and analyze as I've been trained to do.

Failed mission or not, I'm ready for the next phase of my life by the time I douse my hair in bottled water and dry it. Even in the dim light, I can tell the new color is a bit conspicuous, but I figure I'll hide in plain sight rather than try to blend in with all the upstanding citizens.

The only thing I keep is Elijah's sweatshirt. I shove it into the bottom of my backpack, not wanting to think about it but not wanting to let it go either. The necklace Imah gave me is hidden away in its pocket.

I'm heavy with supplies but oddly light of heart as I slip back through the hole in the glass doors. I squint as my eyes adjust to the brightness of the fully risen sun. When my vision returns to normal, my heart skips a beat at the figure waiting for me, hands folded across her chest and cat eyes crinkled at the edges in a smile.

Luca.

26

I fiddle with my backpack straps, adjusting the weight, pretending not to be surprised by Luca. My heart rate calms with a few quick breaths, but it's hard to pretend I'm not shaken by her presence. She was supposed to stay with the other spies. Sure, she helped me out with the fighters and their leader, but I pinned that down to a guilty conscious for turning me in, not because she actually cares what happens to me.

But here she is, like a bad habit I can't kick. But I can use this to my advantage.

"Nice hair," she says, the flirt back in her voice. So different from the frantic shouts I last heard from her.

A slow breath raspberries out my lips, no need to feign exasperation. "What do you want?"

"To spend time with my favorite spy." She closes the gap between us and links our arms together. "Seriously, blond is good on you. But does that mean I have to call you Blond Butterfly?"

I pull my arm away. "Seriously, Luca. What the hell do you want?"

"Relax, Raine. You're safe with me."

Her face turns serious, but I doubt I'll ever truly trust

her. How can I trust anyone when I don't trust myself?

Luca whistles and waves her hand in front of my face to get my attention. "Look." She turns and pulls the neck of her shirt down to reveal her shoulder where the tattoo is. The coiled snake is slashed through the middle, a straight red scab marring it. "I took mine out, too. They can't find us now, not through our tracking devices."

I recall the crunch of my own tracking device under my boot outside the hospital in Philadelphia. Interesting development that Luca has removed hers. I put that information in my back pocket to pull out when I need it.

"Exactly," I say. "Not through our tracking devices. But like you said, they'll find me—both of us—with or without the devices. I've failed a mission, and now you have too. They won't let this go."

"We'll go underground." She taps a toe and lightly punches a fist into her hand over and over again, a bundle of energy. "I know people who will help us, but they all have ties to the Agency. What about those hippies you met on the road? Will they help?"

"No. I'm done with them." I twist my face in disgust to mask my fondness for my former companions, but it doesn't fool Luca.

"You really care about them, huh?"

"It doesn't matter. I'm going back to the Agency." After a beat, I add, "On my own."

"You can't." There's that concerned look again, the one where her eyes are slits. "They'll annihilate you."

"Maybe so, but that's what I'm doing."

"That's what you're doing, going back there." She takes an aggressive step towards me, but I stand my ground. "That's suicidal! You'll be tortured. They'll kill you." Her glare is angry, eyes shining yellow in the sunlight.

"I need to do this. And no one, least of all you, is going to stop me."

"And you won't let me turn you in, will you?" She's standing too close, trying to block my path, but we're in a big parking lot and her small body can't keep me here. "Don't bother answering, not that you would. I thought letting you go meant that you were getting out, not going back in. Now I'm screwed because I helped you and you won't disappear with me. This is a mistake. It's all a big fucking mistake."

I take a step forward, push her out of my way, and stalk away. A glance back proves she's not following me, just staring dumbly with her mouth half open.

"Raine!" Luca yells after me. "The Agency is really pissed about what you did, whatever it is you did. Be careful, okay?"

The smile I give her is genuine, confident. I think we really were friends before all this. But she lets me go easily, maybe a little too easily.

I move forward on my own. Whatever Luca is up to is her business, just like my business is my own. It seems like she's trying to do the right thing, make amends for what she's done. Assumptions, yes, but I file it away all the same.

The day turns hot and muggy, and miserable. Sweat soaks my back, my shirt sliding against my skin with the rise and fall of the backpack. How did I ever live in Florida? I picture my mother's cruel face as she pulled my arm and my shoulder popped out of place.

Don't go there, I think.

I force my brain to ignore my past and focus on the future.

All day long, I keep a steady pace and eat or drink while I walk. It's not until the sun begins to set, and I'm drenched like I just got out of the shower, that I stop and take a break.

My feet throb in my new boots, so I tend to them first. As I pull off my socks, they stick to my blisters, which are an oozy mess. I clean them with water, glop on fresh ointment, and re-bandage them, hoping they won't get infected. Then I slather deodorant on any open skin. I have a lot more walking to do in the next few days.

Grinding on all night, I reach I-95 as the sun rises. My new, ostentatious watch reads 5:43 a.m. People are already out in groups—both small and large with the occasional single traveler—heading south, always south, toward D.C.

I slip into my new persona of a young woman, friendly but not too friendly, curious but not weirdly so, and as nonthreatening as possible. My hunting vest goes slightly against this new look, but it was too practical not to poach. It hides all my weapons but still allows me easy access to them. I smile as I pass a family of two middle-aged adults and two teen kids when I read the sign for Fort McHenry Tunnel in Baltimore. My heart rate hitches with my erratic breathing.

A tunnel. How could I have overlooked there being a tunnel?

Though I don't remember the details of my last journey through a tunnel, panic rises in me at the thought of going through one. Elijah and Imah found me just outside the Holland Tunnel. The panic of before going in the tunnel is fresh in my mind. Chasing Zhang. Failing my mission. Saliva fills my mouth, and it's hard to swallow.

I pause at the unmanned toll booth. Travelers stream by. One bumps into me and raises a hand in apology. He holds a flashlight. It'll be dark. I should get my flashlight out. I use one of the booth seats as a place to hold my backpack. My hand shakes as I paw through my stolen possessions and finally feel the cold metal of the flashlight.

Step by step, I force myself to move closer to the tunnel. All around me people are talking, some even laughing. The mood isn't jovial, but it's definitely the lightest it has been since the attacks. D.C. is within reach, less than two days away by my calculations. Everyone can taste it, and it propels them forward, except for me. All I can taste is the sourness as my breakfast threatens to come back up.

I stand outside the entrance to the tunnel, frozen in place, a butterfly caught in a web of fear.

A woman walks by carrying a baby. I focus on the baby's chubby face. He—she?—opens their mouth in a slobbery grin. I flick on my flashlight and follow that baby face into the tunnel. It's my anchor until we travel deep enough and lose the outside light, the baby's face swallowed up by darkness. Now the beam of the flashlight on the pavement in front of me is the only fixed point to focus on.

Voices and the shuffle of feet reverberate off the walls, the words and steps a chatter whose meaning is lost in the disorientating nature of too many echoes. Laughter bounces down the tunnel. More sounds echo all around me. I turn around and try to follow them, but they fade away into silence. I swing back around, my light following me, feeble in what is becoming a suffocating darkness.

I'm in a pocket of solitude. Where have all the people gone? I swing around again and lose track of what way I'm supposed to be going. My breath comes in short, raspy gasps. My head spins.

I fall to my knees, my flashlight clanks to the ground as I lose my grip on it, and on reality.

27

Flames lick at the mouth of the tunnel. Smoke is sucked in, creating a current that blows my hair forward and into my face. Screams, so many screams, cry out nearby and are lost in the chaos of a falling city.

Firm arms cradle me, and I'm carried into the tunnel. The fire provides plenty of light for me to see Zhang's ash-stained face. He's breathing hard under the weight of me.

"Can you walk?" he shouts.

I nod, and my head throbs with pain. He gently drops me to my feet, grabs my hand, and pulls me deeper into the tunnel before my addled mind can process much of anything but the turmoil around us.

Zhang is several inches smaller than me, but he tugs me along like he's the strongest man in the world. We leave behind the flames and the light they provided. There is so much smoke. I can't see it anymore, but I can feel it swirling around me, in me. My lungs scream for fresh air. And Zhang continues to pull me deeper into the darkness, a compass pointed in the direction of safety. If we make it out, he's going to wish he left me behind to die. Nothing good awaits him at the end of the tunnel.

"Hey, Blondie, are you okay?"

I'm on my hands and knees when the voice breaks through the memory. I'm having a hard time getting my bearings. A light is shining right at me, and I shield my eyes to see who's speaking, but it's too bright for me to make anything out.

A hand hoists me up by the elbow, and the beam of light floods the wall instead of my face. A tall, thickset, scruffy-faced man is peering at me, curiosity and concern in his squinting eyes.

"It's the claustrophobia," he says. "I've seen it bring the bravest of men to their knees."

"Blondie?" I ask, still slightly confused.

He points at my head, and only then do I remember I dyed my hair.

"I'm guessing that's not natural." He steadies me and then holds out a hand. "I'm Al."

I shake his hand, feel hard calluses beneath my softer skin. "B."

He grabs my flashlight off the ground and gives it to me. I hold on to it like I'll never let it go.

"Bee. Like the bug?"

"Yeah." Just not the one he's thinking of. "Thanks. I, uh, don't know what happened there."

Al shrugs. "Like I said, claustrophobia."

He gestures down the tunnel. I take the cue and start walking, the constriction in my chest lightening now that I'm not alone. Al has no trouble filling the quiet.

"I'm a coal miner, so I'm used to places like this. But it takes some getting used to. The first time I went down in the mines, woo-ee, could hardly breathe. Nearly cried my first ride down the shaft. It don't bother me anymore. I'm a shift-boss now." There's unveiled pride in his voice. "You headed to D.C.?"

"Yes." I keep my eyes and flashlight aimed at the ground in front of me.

"Me too. Not much of a talker, are ya? That's okay. No sense in engaging in a bunch of chitchat if you ask me. I only talk when I need to."

I chance a look at him and see he's smiling, making a joke at his own expense.

He slaps me on the back and chuckles. "I find in dark times like these, a cheery disposition goes a long way to help others forget about their troubles. Helps me forget my troubles, too."

A shadow passes across his face, and I figure he's lost someone in the attacks. My stomach twists in guilt, but I push it down. No sense thinking like that now.

Al hums a tune I don't recognize, the smile back on his face. After a few notes, he picks up his one-sided conversation. I learn all about his 15-year-old daughter, how when she was little, she would eat her waffles frozen and liked her hair in two braids, which, he informs me, he would do himself every morning. He doesn't mention a wife, so I wonder if she isn't in the picture or if she was killed in the attacks and is the reason for the shadow of sadness that passed across his face.

Before long, a hint of outside light brightens the walls. We hoof it up the last incline to find the bright, welcoming mouth of the tunnel. I suck in a few deep breaths of warm, humid air. It's oddly refreshing compared to the stale tunnel air.

I turn to see Al staring at me, his smile now a permanent fixture.

"We made it." His teeth are crooked and stained with spots that match the brown of his beard. He pulls out a packet of cigarettes and offers one to me.

When I decline, he asks, "You mind if I smoke?"

I tell him I don't, though when he lights up and the smoke puffs around us, I find my chest tightens a little. I've had too many bad memories of smoke, and not enough good memories of, well, anything really.

Al's chatter carries us all the way to midday when we take a break at an indoor rest stop. It begins to rain while we're having lunch, each munching from our own provisions. Fat raindrops slap the big glass windows, washing away the last remnants of ash.

"That'll help clean things up," Al says with a mouth full of granola bar. "It's kind of like living down in the mines with all this soot covering everything." He finishes his bar, takes a swig of water from a canteen, and pats his stomach. "A few more meals like this and another day of walking, and I may just lose this Santa belly of mine."

He laughs so loud several people turn to stare at us. I laugh along with him. Let them stare. Al stands and holds out his hand to me like a prince offering to escort the princess to a ball. "I'm happy to have the company the rest of the way, if you are."

I tell myself traveling with Al will be good cover. That his outgoing personality fits right in with my idea of hiding in plain sight. I tell myself it's not because I'm lonely and I like Al's company.

As I take his hand, he loops my arm through his and we head outside into the rain. He pulls a baseball hat out of his bag and wiggles it onto my head.

I'm good at telling lies.

28

Al and I travel together all day, his chatter leaving no room in my head for thoughts about my screwed up life. I just listen to his. He tells how he got Tammie, his high school sweetheart, pregnant and started working the mines to pay for their "shitty old apartment." He goes on and on about that apartment, how they had practically no furniture and shopped meal to meal, eating lots of instant noodles.

Listening to Al, I barely notice how hot it is, the sweat coating the skin underneath my hunting vest. I'm happy for the rain splashing gently down. I do a nice job of pretending I'm just a young woman listening to an old friend tell a story.

Then Al's voice rises to a higher pitch. "Cheyenne was only three months old when her mother left in the middle of the night and never came back. Well, 'cept for that one time, but she was all meth'd up, and I wouldn't let her see Chey. She used to send Chey a card every year for her birthday, sometimes weeks late, but one always came. We moved in with my mom after that. Thank God for her. Helped me raise Cheyenne right."

I breathe out in relief; his pain has nothing to do with

the attacks.

He winks, like he's worried he's making me sad with his life story. "Tammie always wanted to travel the world, but there wasn't much opportunity for that growing up in Podunk, Pennsylvania—that's not a real place, you know."

"I know," I assure him.

It stops raining, but Al tells me I can keep the hat. We've put in a lot of miles today. D.C. looms ever closer as the sun sets, and Al turns chatty again.

"Tammie made it as far as Philly."

My insides freeze when he mentions Philadelphia—one of the cities taken out in the attacks. I stare at him open-mouthed, guilt creeping up my belly and into my chest. This is how reality comes crashing back, and all of a sudden, the story I was escaping into gets too real. It's counterproductive to keep coming back to putting the blame on me, but it's hard not to with what I know.

I'm not going to ask what happened, but he's going to tell me anyway.

"We don't know for sure, but we think she was lost in the terrorist attacks." His Adam's apple bobs up and down, like he's holding back tears. A deadness clouds his eyes, but then he blinks and it's gone, the sparkle back. "It's not like I loved her anymore, not for a long time. We never even got married. And she lived hard and probably would've died young, but to go like that. And she is—was—Cheyenne's mother..."

I swallow through the lump in my throat, unable to speak. What would I say? *Sorry, I think it's my fault your kid's mom is dead.*

Al wipes the tears from his cheeks. "I know a lot of people are going through the same thing. We're all mourning someone. I keep telling myself it's put things in perspective for me. I don't want Cheyenne to end up like her mom, or like me. She deserves a better life, that's all any parent wants for his child, a better life. My mom—God rest her soul—did her best raising me, but she was mostly alone after my father died—coal mining accident. She did great with Chey, too, before she died. But it's hard not to get trapped in small town life."

I'm barely listening anymore. Bile rises in my throat and my breathing has become shallow. So much destruction, and so many lives lost. And now one of them is all too real. It doesn't matter that she didn't have a great life; it was a life. How many of those who died were good people?

Al is still talking, lost in his own sadness, oblivious to my mounting panic. "That's why I'm going to D.C. I want to see if there are better opportunities somewhere, not for me, but for Cheyenne. I'll be damned if she ends up with a miner."

He realizes I've stopped keeping pace and am ten feet behind. My chest is heaving, but hardly any air is reaching my lungs.

"Hey, Blondie!" he calls. He hurries back, sits me down on the guardrail. "You okay?" I can't answer but don't have to. "Of course you're not. None of us are. I'll tell you this, though. It will be okay, eventually. Even if it ain't until the day we meet our Maker."

He pats me on the back a little too hard, but the kind gesture reminds me of Imah. In the height of all this tragedy, there are still good people in the world. People who are willing to help a monster like me. I know I'm masquerading as one of those good people—doing a good job of fooling them—but I think they would be kind to me even if they had an idea of my past, and I suspect Imah might have had an inkling of what I am. Despite that, she chose to take care of me and show me kindness. She believes I have a second chance, that I really can remake myself. Even if I don't believe those things.

Tears squeak out of my eyes, and I try to pass them off as a side effect of hyperventilating.

"Easy there, kiddo," Al says.

"I'm okay." I gasp, gaining a tenuous hold on my emotions.

He pulls a water bottle out of my backpack and offers it to me. I nod my thanks as he takes a swig from his canteen.

"You know, you remind me of my daughter. She's quiet like you, takes after her old man." I manage to smile at that. "She's always dyeing her hair, too. She uses that powdery drink stuff because it's cheap. Chey knows we don't have much money." There's that flash of sadness on his face again, but like before, it quickly disappears. He hauls me up, sets me on my feet, and gives me another pat on the back. "Waddya say we find somewhere to rest before it gets too dark?"

The clouds have cleared out, making way for the stars, which I still can't bear to look at. I focus on Al as he wanders, not caring where we stop for the night. I'll leave him tonight anyway. Can't risk entering D.C. with him in tow.

In the moonlight, we spot a fast food joint just off the highway. It's a hotbed of activity. Good for hiding in plain sight. It's been set up as a makeshift triage center, like the ones Imah made us stop at. My heart twists, and I swallow down the memory.

Al peers into the window. "We should find somewhere else. We'll be in the way here."

I place a hand on his arm. "No. Let's stop. Maybe we can help."

"Yeah," Al says with a big grin on his face. "Good idea."

One step into the place and I freeze. The tiny, mousy doctor I met while on the road with Imah is scampering about the restaurant, helping the wounded. I remember her name, Dr. Bauman. I remember *her*.

She's from the Agency.

29

I take a step backward and bump into Al's soft body. I swing around to face him and try to control my heart rate, which has ratcheted up. I push him out the door.

"You're right," I say. "We'll be in the way. Let's go."

"No," he says in a far too loud voice. "I think we can help." He waves into the open doorway and yells, "Do you need help?"

When I turn, Dr. Bauman is staring right at me, a knowing, simpering smile tugging at her lips. In a panic to leave, my palms begin to sweat.

"B!" Dr. Bauman scampers toward us. "How nice to see you again. Why don't you and your friend come in, and we can all have a nice chat?"

My throat feels thick, and it's hard to swallow. Before a full-blown panic attack can kick in, I fight my way past Al into the cooling night and run. My legs pump fast, in time with the backpack bouncing against my back. I run with no thought of direction of where I'm going. I run to escape.

I come to a dark alleyway that reeks of weeks-old garbage and skirt behind a dumpster. My hands and legs are shaking so badly, I can't stay upright, though I didn't run very far. I collapse on the soiled ground, a sticky substance covering my pants.

Clomping footsteps head into the alley, too loud to be the doctor's. They stop near the dumpster.

"Blondie!" Al's voice echoes off the buildings. I listen to him cough and heave, all the while straining to hear if anyone followed him. "B! Where are you?" He's wheezing now, the only sound besides my ragged breathing.

I step out from behind the dumpster and walk cautiously forward until Al spots me. He's hunched over but manages to smile. He's breathing so loudly. My senses are piqued for any evidence that someone followed him.

I hiss "shh," grab his hand, and pull him against one of the buildings that make up the alleyway. Hand still entwined in Al's, I peer around the corner and examine both ends of the street. Slowly, I count to five hundred, keeping a diligent watch the whole time. No one appears.

Al's wheezing subsides. The air seeps out of me with a long puff, and I slide to the ground. He slides down with me, his calloused hand clutching mine.

"That doc knew you," he whispers. "I don't like the look of her. That's the kinda lady that smiles when poking a needle into yer arm. Who is she?"

I shake my head, my eyes wide.

"You're in trouble." He's not asking.

My chest is tight with panic. "Yes. I have to leave you. Get to D.C. as fast as I can."

"No." He squeezes my hand. "I'm staying with you."

Fat tears wet my cheek. "I can't let you come with me." My tone isn't as forceful as it should be.

"You don't have a choice. I'll follow you wherever you go. And you'll never outrun me." He lets out a chuckle that turns to a cough.

I choke out a laugh. "It's dangerous, being with me."

There is so much kindness in his eyes, I can barely stand to look at him. "It can't be that bad."

"It is." I stare him down, trying to make him understand how truthful I'm being. *Please say you'll leave*, I think, but I can't get the words out.

"Every hero needs a sidekick. I'll be yours."

Too bad I'm not hero. Still, I gulp down any further protests. If only he hadn't followed me, I wouldn't have to make this decision.

I pace the short width of the alley, my mind on overdrive. He'll slow me down. Staying with me puts him in danger. But the Agency has seen his face, so maybe he's in danger already. It's easier to keep him safe if he's with me.

"Blondie?" Al breaks into my thoughts.

I face him as he stands, take in his kind face. As much as I want to convince myself it's safer for him if he stays with me, even I can't concoct such a lie.

"I'm staying with you no matter what. Don't make me chase after you." He holds out his hand to shake in agreement.

In my most cowardly move yet, I take his hand and shake, possibly sealing an awful fate for him.

All it took was to see one person from the Agency, and I turned chicken shit. So much for being a badass spy. I'm going to let Al come with me for a little while longer. Because I'm selfish, and scared, and weaker than I ever imagined. My capacity to take advantage of the goodness in people continues to amaze me.

"We need to be quick and quiet," I say, not quite able to keep eye contact with him.

Al gives a low chuckle. "Two of my strengths."

I grab him by the shoulders and shake him. "Seriously, Al. This isn't a joke. You need to do what I say when I say it. Can you do that?" I'm still scolding myself for not leaving him behind. It'd be better for both of us. I should leave him behind…

"Sorry, Blondie. I'm all in." The narrow set of his eyes and hardened jaw tell me he's being serious for once. "Let's get to D.C. and see if we can't find a better future for you and my Cheyenne."

I wonder how long before Al comes to regret his decision to stick by my side.

30

My nerves are at an all-time high as Al and I sneak down empty roads in the night. We should reach D.C. some time tomorrow, so our best bet is to stay off any major highways the rest of the way. That's what my head tells me, but my fluttering heart tells me nowhere is safe. I'm too close to the wolf's den, and I'm bringing an innocent with me.

We walk with arms linked, masquerading as father-daughter. Al can't help but chatter most of the way, but at least he manages to keep his voice low. I don't bother telling him to shut his mouth. I doubt he'd listen anyway. It all sounds like one long hiss in my ear because I'm too high-strung to pay attention.

My gaze darts back and forth, constantly scanning the area. The streets are dark enough that all I pick up are the big things, the silhouettes of trees and buildings against the slightly less dark surroundings. My hearing searches past Al's whispers and our footfalls, straining for any alarming sounds. All my instincts work at maximum capacity.

What am I doing? I should have ditched Al ages ago. I should have never stayed with him in the first place. He has no idea what he's gotten himself into.

Something darts across our path. I hear it more than

see it. I shove Al behind me and take a fighting stance, reaching for the knife in my boot.

Behind me, Al chuckles. "You're tighter than a—well, I won't say what in such company. It's only a squirrel, Blondie. Got a lot of those in Podunk, Pennsylvania."

I turn on him and flash the knife in his face. "Did I tell you it was okay to make a joke?"

The darkness can't hide the downturn of his lips, the wrinkle of hurt around his eyes.

"Sorry," he says, dipping his head.

Too far, I think. My many skills don't seem to include being nice to the people who deserve it. I'm all points and hard edges, especially when I'm on high alert like this. I stow the knife back in its hiding place in my boot.

In my best effort at an apology, I mumble, "Don't worry about it. Let's keep moving."

"Okay, kiddo." Al taps the brim of my hat and relinks arms with me.

We've taken all of three steps when a choppy whirring pricks my ears. The lights of a low flying helicopter approach us. Where the hell did that come from? There's no time for panic. My instincts guide me.

"Move! Now!" I pull him along with me toward the nearest cover, a parking garage a few blocks down.

We have as much chance of reaching the garage before the helicopter reaches us as a mouse has of getting out of a viper's den alive, but I'm good at beating slim odds. A wrecking crane and some other abandoned construction vehicles serve as temporary cover and get us to the garage.

Seconds before we reach safety, the helicopter's spotlight lasers in on us. Sirens blare—from what direction, I can't tell. A maelstrom of lights and noise whirls around us.

We duck under the boom gate and enter the garage. It's empty and in disrepair, littered with chunks of concrete with rebar sticking out of them. There's an old excavator sitting there rusting. Skirting over the debris, we run straight through to the opposite end, only to find more vehicles approaching. They're all blacked-out SUVs, surely not the regular police.

A string of swearwords fly from my mouth. The flashing lights illuminate Al's shocked expression, and even he has nothing to joke about.

This isn't supposed to happen. I'm supposed to sneak into the Agency, take them by surprise. But they found me first. And now I've mixed Al up in all of this.

A warning siren blasts three times.

A voice comes over a megaphone, "We have you surrounded! Come out with your hands up!"

I'm casing the place for a way out. I see an elevator and stairs, but what the hell good would it do us to head up. Our only exits are covered, but I've got to find a way to get Al out.

On the far side of the garage, I spy a break in the concrete where there's a gate, probably for maintenance workers. I lead him deeper into the garage towards the gate. It's locked but nothing I can't handle. I bust the rusty padlock with one clean kick.

The sirens aren't as loud here, and I can talk without shouting. "I'm gonna go out there, turn myself in. You stay here for two minutes and then bolt. They want me, not you. Use the trees, buildings, whatever you can to stay out of sight. I don't think they'll find you, but if they do, tell them..." I cast my mind around and realize he doesn't have anything to hide. "Just tell them the truth. You met me on the road, you have no idea who or what I am."

His eyes are wide and his mouth is half open.

I shake his shoulders. "Understand?"

He blinks once, twice, then his eyelids flutter like he's just waking up. "No." His voice comes out hoarse but determined. "I won't let them take you."

He wraps me in a hug rivaling a boa constrictor's squeeze. I squirm and try not to find comfort in his warm, protective embrace.

"You don't understand. I'm more than in trouble. I *am* trouble. These people who are after me, they won't hesitate to kill you."

I can't risk telling him more in case they catch him. He needs to have plausible deniability.

The warning sirens blast again. "Come out now! This is your final warning!"

They must think I'm trying to lure them into a trap if they haven't come in yet.

"Let them take me," Al pleads, his breath hot in my ear. "I have nothing to lose."

"You don't know what you're saying. Your daughter, Al, you have her to lose."

"No, no, no." He falls to the ground in a blubbering heap. "I don't."

My heart skips a beat. A cold ache freezes my insides. "What do you mean?"

He only cries louder.

I slap him in the face and scream, "What do you mean?"

"Cheyenne, my beautiful baby girl, almost all grown up." He stops, tears glistening in his bushy beard, as he looks up at me. No, no, no. Don't say it. "She was in Philly with her mom when the terrorists attacked."

I open my mouth to scream, but nothing comes out

but a low moan. My stomach lurches and I lose my dinner all over my shoes. Then I'm on my knees, sobbing, apologizing, telling him I'm sorry over and over again.

He holds me, strokes my hair, tells me it's okay. Al, who lost his daughter and her mom, who lost everything, is comforting me.

"Blondie," he cries. "It's not your fault. It's not your fault."

"It is," I croak out. "That's what you don't understand. I'm a government spy. I'm a part of this. I helped make the attacks happen."

He cups my head in his hands and looks deep into my eyes. "How old are you, Blondie?"

I'm caught off guard to think too hard about the question and answer immediately, "Eighteen."

"Just a babe, not much older than my Chey," he says more to himself than to me. "And so much like her. Stubborn, independent." He shakes his head and embraces me in another hug. "Whatever you did isn't your fault. You're mixed up in something bad, that's for sure. But a terrorist attack isn't one teenager's fault."

He pulls away and looks at me with such caring, such love, that I want to believe him. I almost do. But I can't deny the truth of what I am.

Al squeezes my arm hard and yanks me to my feet. His handling of me is surprisingly rough, and I think maybe he's changed his mind about me.

He grabs a scrap piece of rebar off the ground. I brace for the impact, welcoming the payback I so badly deserve. The blow never comes. Instead, he shoves me through the open gate, slams it shut, and wedges the piece of rebar through the slats, effectively locking me out.

I grab the gate and frantically shake, but it doesn't so

much as budge. Through the gate, I paw at the rebar and try to pull it out. It's stuck in so tightly, I might as well be trying to move the entire parking garage.

I press my body as far as I can through the openings between the metal slats of the gate, but I'm too big to fit through. "What have you done?"

"I'm saving you." A slightly maniacal grin takes over his face. "Like I couldn't save Cheyenne."

"No!" I kick, punch, throw my entire body against the gate. Nothing. I'm stuck outside looking in. I shove my face against the gate, metal biting my flesh. "Al, please. Don't do this. I don't deserve this."

"You're wrong about that. You don't deserve whatever shitty lot you got handed in the first place." He presses his lips to my forehead and kisses me in a fatherly way. "God bless you, Blondie."

Without a look back, he's off and running toward the exit. Boots echo off the garage walls, telling me I'm out of time. The agents finally decided to enter despite the risk of a trap. Either I stay here and get caught or I get moving and make damn sure Al's sacrifice isn't for nothing.

31

I turn my back on that damn gate and duck under the bushes lining the side of the parking garage. While the Agency is preoccupied with Al—sweet, innocent Al—I move away by instinct and training. I keep low and quiet, sidling along buildings when I can. Once I'm a few blocks away, I run. But my mind is not on the escape.

What is wrong with Al, sacrificing himself for me? What is wrong with me for letting him?

Even as I'm forming these questions, I know the answers. Can't I even admit to myself that I'm relieved by what Al did? His life isn't as important as mine because I have important work to do.

Besides, my concern for others doesn't trump my desire to save my own skin, self-preservation above all else. As much as I try to deny it, I know that as much as I feel real affection for Al, I also let him sacrifice himself. Surely, I could have overpowered him if I really wanted to.

I shake my head. None of these thoughts matter now. The bottom line is that allowing Al to stay with me was a mistake. I should have ditched him the second we left the tunnel. It was a moment of weakness, one that can't happen again. The stakes are too high, not just for me, but for anyone who gets close to me.

In my head, I chant two words in rhythm with my pumping legs: moving forward, moving forward, moving forward. Maybe if I think it enough, I'll have the strength to follow through with going back to the Agency. No more deviations.

By the time I've found my new path on Route 1, the road is very quiet. I resolve to travel through the night, as I'll likely reach my first destination before sunrise without Al here to slow me down.

Don't think about him, I tell myself.

I've had little sleep these last few days, but my body is ready to be pushed to its limits, so long as I don't stop. Then I might never get going again.

It's only when I've slowed to a walk, Al's cap still tugged down low on my head, that I notice my cheeks are damp. I wipe my eyes with the back of my hand, but it does nothing to stem the flow of tears.

Five minutes of self-indulgence in my emotions, that's all I give myself. Then I dig in and continue with a brisk walk. I've come across a few other lone travelers and running might draw unnecessary attention.

I pass a woman muttering to herself, shuffling more than walking. A little while later, a young man walks with the slow, steady pace of someone who is tired but determined. Not too long after, an old man staggers and swerves his way down the road, raising a brown paper bag to his lips every few steps.

I walk by them and others, my determination growing with each step. I'm in a pretty seedy part of town when I make a stop to visit Legend, who owes me a favor for saving her life, even if I only did it on someone else's orders.

She's not pleased when I barge in on her and some

guy in bed, especially when I tell her why I'm there, but she agrees to do what I ask. Though I never mention the Agency, she probably thinks I'm working under their orders, which means those are her orders, too.

Back on the road, the slim moon and stars light the change from run-down urban area to the more upscale part of D.C. As the road continues south, more trees line the sidewalks and a quaint, grassy island divides the northbound lanes from the southbound ones. The island ceases, and the buildings take on an even more regal feel. I'm heading right into the heart of D.C.

My feet know the way.

I take in what sights I can make out in the dim light, the museums and Capitol building silhouetted against a sky that is slowly lightening in preparation for daybreak. The National Mall teems with people, mostly sleeping in huddled masses. A few who are awake talk quietly amongst themselves. The stench of unwashed bodies permeates the air, and everyone is haphazardly scattered across the expanse of lawn, some with tents but mostly out in the open.

No one pays any attention to a lone girl silently slipping through the crowd.

At the edge of the reflecting pool, I stand and watch the sunrise in duplicate, first turning the sky and water light blue, then a pale pink, and finally flashing a brilliant orange before fading back to blue. It all happens quickly, though it feels like I stand there a very long time.

Reflecting pool is an apt name for this still, silent body of water. But too much self-reflection is bad for anyone, especially someone like me.

My feet find their momentum again as more people wake and go about their day. There's a rhythm already established, though none of the masses could have been here for very long. Most of the people have tired eyes, their hair and clothes in need of a wash, but a hopeful mood permeates the atmosphere. Fires are lit to cook breakfast. Water bottles are passed around. Music pops up in little pockets: the strum of a guitar here, the vibrato of a violin there.

I picture Elijah and Imah here with the off-gridders. Maybe they've already arrived. On second thought, probably not, given Imah's tendency to stop and help people along the way. I imagine them fitting in so perfectly, in a way I'd never fit in, even with my plain clothes and silly hair.

There's only one place for me.

I make one more stop to drop a note in one of the locations shock jock Cheryl Dare mentioned when she broke in over the radio before the president's speech. If she's willing to help me, I'm ready to accept it.

Then it's time to head to the Agency's headquarters. I know my way now, and it's not far. Just a bridge—thankfully not a tunnel—and a ride on a secret elevator, and I'll be back where I belong.

32

Silent as my namesake the butterfly, I creep past the 9/11 Memorial near the Pentagon. I arrive at a small service complex for Arlington National Cemetery. The wall that surrounds it is rough under my fingers as I slide my hands across the fake stone. The sensation confirms I'm here for real, not in a dream or a memory.

I head down a driveway that snakes the perimeter. Parking spaces are lined up next to buildings huddled together like a small fortress. I follow my feet almost to the end and stop at the smallest building in the group. A single door is all that adorns one side, the same generic beige color as the building. But where the building is stucco, the door is painted metal. There is no lock or handle on the door, not even hinges.

I lightly touch my hand to the cool metal and close my eyes. Listen to the quiet sound of my own measured breathing. Feel the steady pulse in my wrist beating in time with the one in my neck. Ignore the thrumming of my heart. What good is a heart if it can't love?

I stay there for twenty seconds, twenty minutes, a lifetime.

A low buzz drones on and on in my head, building up

to a terrible headache. I remove my hat—Al's hat really—and rub my temples. I inhale and exhale long and hard and try not to think of Al or Imah or Elijah. I need to discard them from my thoughts in order to do what I need to do.

Finally, I place my foot just to the right of the door. I tap the spot with a particular sequence of Morse code. The door slides opens in near silence to a mirrored elevator car. A rush of cold air greets me from inside.

I don't hesitate as I step in. The time for wavering is over; I must be resolute in my actions and thoughts.

The door shuts, sealing me in. Infinite reflections of my own face stare back at me. My expression is stony, showing none of the fear I'm barely holding back. The fake blond hair looks absurd and juvenile in the fluorescent lights of the elevator car. I place Al's hat back on my head and pull it down low.

While much of the country suffers with prolonged power outages, this building is, of course, in perfect working order. It's not subject to the power grid. Imah would like that, but I very much doubt she would like anything else that goes on in here.

With the press of a button, the elevator car zooms down. My empty stomach turns over. When was the last time I had a meal? Or slept?

Not important.

My ears pop as I travel down, deep into the ground. The car pauses in its descent. A feeling of weightlessness lifts my body for a fraction of a second before the car lurches down again. I lose my footing and my face smooshes into the mirrors, knocking my hat askew. My greasy skin leaves a smudge mark, obscuring my features so I no longer have to stare at the many reflections. I fix Al's hat and wait for the elevator to arrive.

When the door slides open, my hands are slick with sweat but steady. A long marble corridor stretches out in front of me. The floor and walls are shades of black and gray, but they reflect the light so it doesn't feel as dark as it should. Most importantly, it's empty.

Etched in a copper plate on the floor are three sentences, each on its own line.

I am a soldier.

I serve the Agency.

It is my purpose.

I step over those words and down the long Gray Mile, footfalls echoing off the walls. That's the first thing new recruits see after they've put to rest their old lives, just before they begin training. There's no turning back once you've reached this point.

Sure, agents use this corridor throughout training and once they've become full agents, but there's no walk like that first one.

At least for me there wasn't...not until today. I have the same butterflies in my stomach as I did that first time. The same sheen of sweat on my brow. But not the same intentions. Back when I first took this walk, an older agent leading the way, I was innocent.

There was an excited air to my steps. I was leaving behind my old, miserable life with an abusive mother, a string of deadbeat stepfathers, and the life of crime that followed leaving home.

There was hope for a better future. I was going to be trained to be one of the most-skilled government agents in the country. I was going to make a difference. No more getting pushed around. I would be the one doing the pushing. I was beyond naive.

Now, walking down this corridor alone, I am no longer

a green recruit. I am the Black Butterfly. I have returned to my cocoon where I first transformed into a special-ops agent. One with ice in her veins. One who followed orders no matter what. One who set up an innocent man and helped destroy the country.

I'm here for one last mission. And after that, I don't think this butterfly will fly again.

33

The Agency's entire compound is high-tech, so there's no need for a receptionist who sits at a desk greeting people and answering phones. Who would be calling? All our missions are classified above top secret. There is simply an eye scanner at the end of the Gray Mile. This is the part that makes my knees weak.

Once I use this scanner, the Agency will know I'm here. I already ran through all the likely scenarios in my head and came up with a plan for each one. I tell myself not to think about what's at stake and to focus on what I came here to do.

It's go-time.

Removing my hat again, I squint and lean toward the panel. With a deep breath, I open my eyes wide. A beam of infrared light scans my retina. The panel beeps, and an elevator door slides open with a faint whoosh. Like the elevator at street level, this one is all mirrors, broken up only by panel on the right side with a keypad. I punch in a number.

This time when the elevators zooms down, my stomach stays in place, a hard rock of nervous energy forming in it. The lower I go, the more persistent the droning in my head becomes. A deep ache pierces my forehead. It's not like the headaches from my head wound. These pains are a reminder of my training. I'm a soldier, here to serve the Agency, and only the Agency. Personal agenda has no place here.

I shake my head to loosen the thought, buck against my training. I'm not the soldier I once was. I'm not here to blindly follow orders. And without any direct orders from the Agency, I'm making my own.

The irony that the Agency is deep within the bowels of the earth—hell territory—is not lost on me. Finally, the elevator stops its descent, and there is a pregnant pause before the doors part. And who should I find at the gates to hell when they pop open?

None other than Luca. With a gun pointed directly at me.

She looks like shit. Black bruises bloom under both eyes, and there's a slump to her posture.

I flash a smile like I'm expecting to see her, all the while my brain never stops working, zipping through scenarios before landing on the one with the best chance at success. Luca is a pivotal player, one I thought I would have to track down, but she walked right into my game without any effort on my part.

Her tight expression reveals nothing of her thoughts or feelings. Agents are trained to suppress emotions, and certainly not show them if we happen to have any. The fact that she is here at headquarters means she got caught or turned herself in.

If I had to guess, I'd say she turned herself in, which means the Agency knows about our conversation outside the store where I disguised myself. They probably sent Luca here to try and rattle me, catch me off-guard.

"I'm turning myself in." I position my hands palm up and hold them out like an offering.

"Noted." She keeps the weapon trained on my chest. "I'm to take you to a holding cell until you can be further processed. I need to search you for weapons."

"Can't I just give them to you?"

She sighs, and her whole body sags deeper into itself. She must have really taken a beating.

"You know you can't. Hand over your bag and then stand with your hands on the wall." She gestures toward the wall with the gun.

I further appraise her appearance, looking for more hints as to the state of her body and mind. There is a large bruise peeking out from the neck of her shirt, dark purple in the middle and yellowing on the edge. It looks like it goes all the way to her shoulder.

With slow, nonthreatening movements, I shrug off my backpack and give it to her. Instead of searching it, she throws it over her shoulder and gestures for me to turn around. I do so and place my hands on the wall. She holsters the gun and pats me down, removing all the weapons from my vest and the one near my waist. She stows them in my backpack. I swear she feels the knife tucked away in my boot but leaves it there.

Luca doesn't cuff me, simply takes my elbow and guides me down several hallways. We pass other agents, none of whom I recognize, nor do they pay any attention to us.

When we reach another elevator, she shoves me in and we zoom up a dozen floors to the holding cells. Breanne, of all people, is the guard on duty. She nods at Luca and glares at me as we pass.

"Give me a few minutes with her, will ya?" Luca

winks at Breanne.

She nods her head knowingly and leers at me. "Take all the time you need. I'd like to see this one put in her place."

I seriously hope Luca isn't considering trying anything with me. I'll knock her on her ass, consequences be damned. I think she has more sense than that, though.

At a door about halfway down the hall, Luca stops at the keypad and punches in a code. She pushes me through, follows me in, and shuts the door behind us. The walls are padded, and the cell is empty except for a metal toilet and sink. There is one too-bright fluorescent light on the ceiling, protected by a transparent, plastic box.

Luca lets go of my elbow but takes hold of my hand. I snap it back out of her reach. I check my anger, measure my breathing to keep calm. I'll need Luca before all of this is over, so I have to get her on my good side.

She shoves the backpack into my arms. "Take it. You're gonna need it."

I falter, barely snatching it up before she releases it. "What are you playing at, Luca?"

With a slight tilt to her head, she squints at me appraising me anew. "Why are you turning yourself in?"

My gaze takes in each crevice in the tiny box of a room. There aren't normally any cameras or listening devices in these rooms; the Agency doesn't want what goes down in the cells recorded. Still, I'm being extra careful.

"It's not bugged," Luca confirms. "No one can hear us."

I turn the question on her. "Why did you turn yourself in?"

"How did you know I turned myself in?"

"Lucky guess." Which is mostly the truth.

She rubs her temples, like she's got a bad headache, or maybe it's a droning in her head like I have. "I'm going to tell you because I need you to understand you can trust me. Do you trust me?"

"Yes," I whisper.

I do think I can trust her. It's me that shouldn't be trusted.

34

Luca's throat bops up and down as she swallows. She takes several steps towards me, moves the backpack to the floor next to us, and rubs my arms in an affectionate way. Then she opens her mouth and lets out a slow sigh, the warmth of it washing over my face. It calms me, almost as if she's drugged me with her breath.

"What they did…Raine, what we did…the attacks, the destruction," her words come haltingly, like there's a physical impediment to her saying them. She clears her throat. "It was wrong. So many people died. And what the hell for?"

Her gaze falls to the floor. She grips my forearms tight and sways like she might faint. She recovers and gives me that appraising look again.

"We get orders. We've been trained to follow without question. We're told it doesn't matter who the orders come from, that they're the government's will. I always thought they came from someone important—not the idiot president —but someone else important who cared about the country, cared about the people."

Her eyes plead with me to explain. "How…tell me how these attacks were good for us? So we can frame the

Chinese and go to war? Seems a stiff price to pay to justify an unjustifiable war. I signed up to do good. I knew that maybe meant taking out the bad guys, and I was okay with that. Killing the bad guys to keep the good guys safe. That's violence I can stomach. But we took out the good guys this time, the ones I thought we were here to protect."

The circulation in my hand is being cut off by her viper grip on my forearm. My headache has reached near unbearable proportions. Luca's eyes are slits, her mouth clenched in pain. Her head falls on my shoulder, and she lets out a quiet moan.

"You feel it too," she whispers, no hint of question in the remark.

In this place where it all started for both of us, where our minds were molded and warped, it's almost impossible to kick the training. But I have to fight past the pain and do what I came here to do. She's saying all the things I need her to say. Now I need to act on them.

I grab her shoulders and shake her. Her eyes snap into focus. "Luca, we don't have to follow their orders. We don't have to be soldiers anymore."

"I know, I know. It's all been a fucking lie, Raine. Did you know I'm the one who hacked the system and launched the bombs in New York City?"

"Yes, you told me that."

My hands shake at the mention of New York, but I push the feeling down and steady myself. Her emotions are as strong as my own, and I practically taste them they're so potent. I also can't help but feel a little impressed with her hacking skills.

"And it's fucking eating me alive," Luca says quietly. "I'm here to fight against the Agency. No matter how hard it will be. No matter what it means for me. For us."

Those chartreuse eyes of her shine with unshed tears, and I'm undone. My insides twist with agony over our shared crimes and the guilt that started before I even remembered I had done something terrible, a guilt I've had since I woke up on the Jersey side of the Holland Tunnel. There's more to come, too, guilt over crimes I have yet to commit.

She takes a step away from me and shakes out her arms and legs, like she's warming up for a marathon. "I'm done with being a soldier for the Agency. From now on, I'm doing what I want. Do you know where I went after I last spoke with you?"

Worry twists my insides. I gulp down my dread, but the word comes out hoarse when I ask, "Where?"

"I tracked down your friends."

I muster all my training to shut down my emotions… and fail. My stomach roils with nausea, and heat prickles at the corner of my eyes.

"Why?" My voice wavers over the question. The panic and fear outweigh the anger and keep me from beating her worse than the Agency already did.

"For information. I wasn't getting anything from you or from the Agency, nothing useful anyway. So I tracked them down. Wasn't hard, you know. Their band of hippies stopped and helped so many people. It left a pretty hot trail."

"And then?" I barely whisper.

"And then nothing." She narrows her eyes, taking in the concern I'm trying so hard to conceal. "I knew you really cared about them. Who would've thought…?" The last part she says more to herself than to me. "Don't worry. They're fine."

She tugs on my hair, I think in an attempt to distract

me. "I liked it better black."

She's staring like she's never seen me before, and the tiny room suddenly feels claustrophobic. I'm barely breathing as Luca leans in toward me. A beeping noise kick-starts my heart and breaks the moment.

"Shit!" She looks at her watch. She presses a button on it, and the beeping stops. "I don't have much time. The point is I'm not the Agency's soldier anymore. And I don't think you are either. I'm here to help you. What do you need me to do?"

My eyes fall on Luca's bruises. I'm tempted to ask how she got back in good with the Agency. I want to know how she's still alive after failing the mission to turn me in and taking out her tracking chip. Those are questions more of curiosity than necessity, and we don't have time for that. I cut to the chase.

"Evidence," I say dumbly. My words come in a rush as I pull a written list out of my hunting vest and shove it at her. My head throbs worse than ever.

Ignore the pain, I tell myself, and the compulsion to obey. The mission is more important.

"We need proof. I don't know if it exists anymore. I can't imagine they'd want a paper trail on this. The best bet to finding it is—"

Luca cuts me off, "The mainframe computer. Shit. I don't have access."

"Me neither. Do your best. Trick someone into accessing it for you if you have to. I need that evidence." I wait to drop my next request. "And I need to know about Zhang."

"Zhang! What do you know about him?"

My face burns hot, my damn circulatory system betraying me. Thankfully, Luca doesn't know about my mission to frame Zhang and what I did to get close to him. "Plenty, but that's not important. He's not dead is he?"

Luca shakes her head.

"He's here, right?" I ask. "You can get me to him, can't you?"

She flashes a genuine smile. "I already have, of course. He's being held in this hall."

The pieces of the puzzle are starting to line up. "Can you get him out?"

"Not likely. We have strict instructions about Zhang, and I'm not cleared to move him."

My focus is back, despite the raging headache, which I do my best to ignore. The scenarios are churning, my trained and honed brain on overdrive. "Can you hack both of us out?"

Luca chews on a nail as she thinks. "I can get you both out of the cells by overriding the security mechanisms on the door, but I can't do that from here."

"Do it. How long will it take?"

"No more than ten minutes." She heads to the door but then turns back. "What about Breanne? I won't be able to escort you out."

"I'll take care of her," I say, though it won't be easy. "Give me five minutes alone with Breanne before you cut Zhang loose. Got it?"

"Yeah. I can do that. What else?"

"There is one more thing." I play it like I'm reluctant for her to do it, like I can't even suggest it.

"What is it, Raine? I'll do anything."

I've never seen her cat eyes so sincere. She really has changed. And here all this time I've been thinking people can't change. Though, that's not important anymore.

"I have an envelope in my locker with...personal

things in it. Can you get it for me? I'll give you the code."

A grin lights up her eyes. "Like I'd need the code to get into your locker. That I can break into easily enough. But how will I get it to you?"

"I need you to contact Legend first." I give her the details on how to cash in on my favor with the infamous helicopter pilot. "Once you get the evidence and my stuff, meet me..." I pause, trying to think of the perfect place. "Meet me in the place we kissed."

Luca coughs into her hand, a blush creeping along her neck up to her face. "I'm glad you remember it."

I'm playing to her weakness, and right now it's that she has a guilty conscious...and she actually cares about me.

"Me too," I say honestly, while at the same time pushing down the mounting guilt gnawing at my insides.

35

Luca pounds on the inside of the door and is let out. I peer through the small window to the hallway. It's only a moment before the back of Luca's head is replaced by Breanne's face. She points two fingers at her eyes and then at me to show me she's watching me. As if I would expect anything less of her. Her face moves away from the glass and out of sight, but she'll probably stay close to the door. Not that she has any reason to believe I'll be getting out soon.

My instincts were right about Breanne when I saw her in the bathroom at the rest stop. I remember now that she's one of the most skilled hand-to-hand fighters in the Agency. But I'm the Black Butterfly, and I'll have the element of surprise on my side.

Luca left the backpack with me, so all the weapons I filched from the store are back in my possession. I take stock of them, strategically placing as many as I can on my person and opting to keep the utility knife out and in my hand. I take a swig of water and put the bottle back in the bag with the rest of the supplies. I prop the backpack up against the wall right next to the door.

Now all that is left is for Luca to remotely open my

door.

While I wait, I run through fight scenarios and stretch my legs, exercising my mind and body. It keeps me alert and ready. A glance at my watch shows me it's been about eight minutes since Luca left. Any minute now, she should be busting me out. I stand at the door, crouched and ready to ambush Breanne.

My breathing is calm and steady, my heart rate normal. But my fingers itch for a fight. The lock on the door clicks so quietly, I almost miss it. There is no handle on the inside, but a light push on the door opens it.

I slip on my backpack and peer out to find Breanne a little ways down on the opposite side of the hallway from my cell. She's examining her nails and doesn't see me. I inhale nice and slow and then let out a long exhale. Oxygen pumps through my veins...and adrenaline.

I charge out the door, ready for a fight for the ages.

Breanne spots me immediately and reaches to her side for her holster. I pitch the utility knife toward her. It flies end over end and lodges itself in her right shoulder. The injured arm hangs slack at her side.

She reaches across her body with her good arm, yanks out the knife, and tosses it to the floor. Then she goes for the holster again, but I'm on her before she can release the pistol from it.

We crash together so hard my teeth rattle. Even injured, Breanne is stronger and quicker than I am. She pushes at me with one hand and forces me against one of the cell doors. The handle jams into my back. A squeak escapes me as pain shoots up my spine.

I jab a finger directly into her wound. She flinches and grunts. The moment of weakness is enough for me to gain the leverage I need to push her across the hall and smash her into the wall.

I go for the gun at her hip, but she lands a punch square on my jaw. I reel back, not from the pain—the adrenaline is pumping too hard for me to feel much pain—but from the impact.

We stare, sizing each other up, seeing who is worse for the wear.

Blood drips down her fingertips and lands in soft drops on the floor. The sound punctuates our heavy breathing, hers more strained than mine. The knife glints in the light, resting beneath Breanne in a puddle of blood on the tile. She shakes out her good hand, the one that just punched me.

If she gets her hands on the gun, it'll be the end of me.

As if in slow motion, her good arm moves across her body as she tries one more time for the pistol. I spring backwards, throwing my hands out behind me to support my fall. As my palms hit the ground, I swipe my leg at her ankles, making sure she'll land on her injured side.

She tips sideways but is quick enough to pull the gun from the holster and aim it straight at me. She hits the ground with a thud and fires, which throws her aim off just enough that the bullet whizzes past my shoulder.

I lunge toward her, grabbing the knife off the floor, before she can get off a second shot. I stab it into her thigh and strike with my freehand at the gun. The weapon flies into the air, crashes into the tile, and slides down the hallway.

I scramble for it and receive no challenge from Breanne. I seize it, stand, and hold it pointing down at her.

She stares up at me with wide eyes, pupils dilated. Her chest heaves as she sucks in ragged breaths. I confiscate her ear piece. I didn't see her activate it to call for back-up, but I may have missed it in the fighting.

All is quiet on the device when I stuff it into my ear.

"What do you want?" Her voice comes out hoarse.

"I need to talk to one of the prisoners." My voice is steady, and my breathing has already begun to even out.

"How did you get out?" She's stalling. The ear piece is still silent, so I think I have time.

I look up and down the hallway at all the doors. There's more than I have time to search. And none of them are open. I check my watch. It's been five and a half minutes. Why the hell hasn't Luca opened Zhang's door yet?

Breanne's blinks are becoming longer, her posture more slumped. I shake her.

"Zhang, the Chinese prisoner! Where is he?"

She barks out a laugh, her teeth shining with blood. She spits red onto the floor. That's all I need to see in order to know she'll never tell me.

It's not her fault really; it's the Agency's. She's just following orders like a good spy. Just like I used to be.

A banging echoes down the hallway.

Time's up, I think.

But no agents come storming down the hallway. No one in sight but me and Breanne, who is passed out cold. Not dead or mortally wounded, not as long as someone finds her within the next hour.

The banging sounds again. This time I see an open door and rush over to it. Zhang's pale, slightly manic face stares at me from the threshold. His eyes widen, and his mouth forms an O when he recognizes me.

He backs into the cell, frantically shaking his head. It seems he wants nothing to do with me. Can't say I blame him. If everyone didn't think he was dead, he would be number one on the most-wanted list. His country probably isn't too happy with him either, given he's the reason the world thinks they attacked the U.S.

A ruckus in the hallway captures my attention. Cell doors are banging open all along the corridor, and the prisoners are escaping. They look dazed and fearful at first, but when they realize no one is there to tell them where to go, they head right for the door at the end of the hall to the stairwell.

For a moment, I panic, but then I realize this could work to my advantage. More chaos means more time before I'm caught.

I duck into the cell, grab Zhang by the elbow, and hold the gun to his stomach.

"You're coming with me."

I steer him toward the stairwell. I push past the other prisoners, some who glare at me until they see the gun. Then they let us pass unharassed.

Zhang looks over his shoulder, fear in his eyes…and hatred, too. He doesn't have to like me for what I need him to do, though he does need to trust me enough to heed what I have to say. We reach the end of the hallway and are about to disappear behind a door.

"Blondie!"

The familiar voice stops me in my tracks, and my heart leaps into my mouth.

36

Keeping the gun on Zhang, I swing around to the source of the voice. Al waves from the middle of the hallway. His face is bruised and he's hunched over, but he's alive, and smiling.

"Holy shit!" A sob escapes with the swear. Hot tears scorch my cheeks. Al is a wrinkle in my mission, but a welcome one, an important one. I thought I'd never see him alive again. "Come on, Al. I'm gonna get you out of here."

He's already lumbering towards me. Al wraps his arms around me in a bear hug. I want to squeeze him back, but with my hands occupied, I nuzzle my face into his chest. My eyes search his, and I barely see his pain hidden beneath all his joy.

"I'm so happy to see you, Blondie. You made it." Then his eyes crinkle in concern, and his head darts around as if he's taking in his surroundings for the first time. "No. You're not supposed to be here. You were supposed to escape. Go anywhere but where they wanted to take you."

There's no time to explain why I seemingly wasted his sacrifice by coming to headquarters on my own. I want him to understand that my mission is more important than my life, and when he turned himself in, he allowed me to come here to do what I need to do. I don't have time to explain, but maybe one day soon, he'll understand.

"We need to move," I say. "Follow me."

All the other prisoners are gone for now, though I doubt they'll make it out of the Agency. Breanne lies unconscious on the floor. More agents will be here any second. I can only hope that the other escaped prisoners prove enough of a distraction that they won't key in on Zhang and Al immediately.

I guide them onto the stairway. For his part, Zhang seems resigned to come along. He's not fighting me at least. I keep a firm grip on him. Maybe he realizes he'll never escape this place on his own and he's hoping I'll help him. He would be right to think that, though I'm not doing it because I'm some kind of altruistic savior. I'm simply on a mission.

We head up flight after flight of stairs. We're almost where we need to be when news of the escaped prisoners gets out. The ear piece buzzes with instructions for all available agents to report to the wing with the holding cells. They'll be closely monitoring the surveillance cameras, and most of the stairways have them. They'll know I'm with Zhang.

Al begins wheezing and falls behind. I stop at a maintenance floor and make Zhang open the door. Luckily, it's empty. I squeal for Al to hurry up, and we enter the relative safety of the non-monitored area.

Then I radio in under another agent's name that I have Zhang, an unknown prisoner, and a rogue agent in my custody. Giving them a false location, I tell them that I'm injured and not mobile, the rogue agent is unconscious, and Zhang is detained. That'll hopefully keep them chasing their tails while trying to find us.

I give Al a water bottle and let him sit. I shove Zhang to the ground and keep the gun pointed at him. The maintenance floor is dull and dim compared to the shiny marble parts of the Agency. It suits the shady nature of mine and Zhang's relationship.

Zhang keeps his gaze downcast. "I should have known you were trouble." His accent has a slight lisp, and I notice a chip in his front tooth.

"It was my job to make sure you didn't." I practically hear the seconds ticking away, but I have to do this right.

"You were very good at your job, Miss Winters."

"Raine," I correct him. I catch Al's look of confusion, but don't bother explaining. Where would I even start? "My name is Raine," I repeat to Zhang. "It was a shitty job to have. I'm sorry you got mixed up in all of this."

"Sorry?" Despite the gun at his chest, he's up and in my face, doing a damn good job of pretending to be taller than he is. "You framed me for the terrorist attacks. I've been tortured by your government. My country thinks I'm dead, and my government is calling me a traitor. Do you know what they'd do to me if they found me alive?"

"China wasn't responsible for the attacks." I pause a beat, wait to drop my bomb. "The U.S. government attacked its own cities."

Boom! Zhang gasps, tries to take a step back but can't because of the wall.

Al stares up at me. I turn away, unable to witness the tears that course down his cheeks and get caught up in his beard. Surely, he's thinking of his daughter.

I focus on Zhang. "The attacks were orchestrated by the U.S. government. It was my job to plant evidence on you, implicating the Chinese government. It was a conspiracy, a big fucking conspiracy."

Zhang grabs me by the shoulders, his face twisted in disbelief. He slams me against the wall once, twice, three times. I let him, my teeth rattling with each impact. Then Al is there—on his feet much faster than I imagined he could move—and pulling Zhang off me.

"Leave her alone. She's just a girl, like my Cheyenne. Let her talk."

In Al's meaty grip, Zhang has shrunk back down to size. He nods, and they look to me for an explanation.

I slide down the wall to a sitting position, the reminder of Al's daughter a heavy weight. The ringing in my head that started when I first entered headquarters has increased to a wail. I turn down the ear piece, unable to bear all the chatter. Nausea washes over me.

I close my eyes against it, take a deep breath. Focus on slowing the beating of my heart. Breathing in and out, in and out. The nausea passes.

Al sits next to me and pats my leg. I check my watch and see I need to burn a few more minutes before the next phase. I boost the volume on the ear piece, and it seems the other agents haven't figured out where we are.

"I can't take back what I've done." I'm staring at the wall as I speak, talking to Al and Zhang but unable to look at either of them. "This wrong is too big for me to right. The only thing I can do is tell the truth."

Zhang bends down, gets right in my face. "What is the truth?"

I open my mouth, ready for the first time in a long time to talk about my past.

37

“The truth?” I sigh, the fatigue of my life squeezing the breath out of me. Al and Zhang’s attention is on me like the laser pointer of a sniper rifle. “The truth is I was once a mean, scared girl who ran away from home. It wasn’t long before I got involved with the wrong people, ended up getting arrested for running an illegal gambling ring.”

Zhang snorts in derision.

“I was good, too good,” I snap. “I rose so high through the ranks that when shit went down, I became the scapegoat.”

Then I plunge into what happened next, quickly telling them about the first meeting with my court-appointed lawyer. His suit and briefcase were expensive looking, and his name was followed by a bunch of abbreviations. None of it added up to him being a public defender—I had good instincts then, even before my training. I didn’t question it, though. He was on my side, and I was scared of going to jail.

We plead out the case. I got community service, and he persuaded the courts to send me to what they thought was a facility for at-risk teens.

That’s how I ended up with the Agency. After a brief

orientation where they claimed to train troubled youth and place them in work programs, I was given the option to stay and learn what they called a "trade" or leave.

I laugh, the bitter tone loud in the small room. "Not much of a choice. Stay where there was a bed for me and hot meals, maybe make something of my life, or leave and end up back on the streets. I stayed. I took their tests, ate their food, took their classes."

Silent tears wash down Al's ruddy face, for his daughter or me, I don't know. Maybe for us both. Zhang's expression is hard and stoic, but his attention is rapt.

I continue in a dead tone, "The training was rigorous but fulfilling. We were told we were the elite, chosen to serve the government. Our strengths and weaknesses were assessed, and we were placed in special groups. I was top in the class in many areas and was placed in my own group. We were fed praise and propaganda. We were trained as soldiers, as specialized weapons. Assets. I became the Black Butterfly, a top spy."

There's nothing but chatter out of the ear piece, but I know I don't have much more time. I need to get Zhang and Al to Luca. I skip the details of my first mission and the ones to follow.

"Zhang," I make eye contact with him, "my job was to get the right documents on your computer to frame the Chinese government. I never knew the details. I followed orders without question."

"You did your job well," Zhang says in a calculated voice.

"I was a damn good spy. But I failed my last mission. I was to make sure you got out of New York City alive with the incriminating evidence on you."

"You didn't fail."

I slam the wall above his head. "What?"

I don't want to believe him. My memories of the attack haven't fully materialized, but I was sure I wasn't the reason Zhang made it out alive. I thought I was the reason he almost *didn't* make it out. He saved me that day.

"You held me up with your damsel-in-distress act. I came back for you." He shakes his head, like he can't believe he did that. "I carried you and my briefcase through the tunnel. Should have left the briefcase," he says to himself. It contained the falsified documents. "I got picked up as soon as we got into New Jersey. I thought they arrested you, too. It wasn't until I was interrogated and," his voice turns low, his eyes wild, "tortured, that I knew you had set me up."

I'm stuck on the fact that I didn't fail my mission. All along I thought the Agency had been after me because I had failed, that's what Luca told me. It turns out, I didn't. What do they want from me then?

"Miss Winters?" Zhang says.

When I don't answer, he stares at me quizzically.

Al gently squeezes my arm. "Blondie?"

I snap out of it. Failed mission or not, we have to get moving.

"I did set you up," I admit to Zhang. "That doesn't matter right now. Do you want to get out of here?"

"I do."

I trust Zhang's desire to escape enough to finally lower the gun. "Al, I'm getting you out, too."

He clasps my hands. "And you're coming with us." His voice is hopeful, and I hate to cause him more pain, but I silently shake my head. "Please, Blondie...Raine," he corrects himself, "leave with us."

"I can't." Again, I wish I could explain. Even if I had

the time, I couldn't do it; he wouldn't understand. I check my watch. "We need to go."

I explain what's going to happen and what they need to do. Wishing for more time to go over the plan a second time, I have to trust they'll both remember.

Then I hug Al. He squeezes me tight, tears wetting the top of my head.

Back in the staircase, we ascend the last few flights. On the other side of this door is the Gray Mile.

"I'm going to create a diversion. Get to the surface. Follow the driveway out of the complex and take a right to a circle driveway. There will be a helicopter waiting for you there." I hope Luca has come through for me, and Legend. "Zhang, tell the pilot to take you to the place where I saved her. She'll know where that is." I give him a verification question, so Legend knows the instructions are truly coming from me.

My plan is as delicate as a butterfly's wing and constantly needs adjusting as the butterfly flies around and the scenery changes around her.

"Al." I grasp his hands. "Luca will have a manila envelope. You can take that. It's just some personal things of mine that I want you to have."

I scribble a note on his hand and discreetly slip a flash drive into it, closing his hand before Zhang can see that I've given him something.

"Further instructions," I whisper in his ear as I hug him again. "Read them as soon as you get out of headquarters and then erase them. Use your own spit if you have to. Make sure no one else sees."

I let go of Al and turn to Zhang. "Once you're out, keep a low profile. You can't let anyone know who you are because everyone thinks you're dead, and you will end up dead if your identity is revealed."

He snorts in response. I ignore the fact that I deserve every ounce of his hatred, but we're too short on time for me to bother with guilt, even if I am misleading him by not telling him what I think is going to happen. A hypothetical lie that may come to pass. "You both know what to do, right?"

"Yes," Zhang snaps. "I can remember simple enough instructions."

I put Al's hat back on my head, get a firm grip on Zhang's free arm, and hold the gun to his head. Zhang warily glances at the gun, and I shrug. He's supposed to be a prisoner. Al walks ahead of both of us under the guise of being an agent who is leading the way.

"I'm going to get you two as close to the elevator as I can, but once I'm recognized, which probably won't take long, it's up to you to get out. Here we go." The last part I say more to myself than to them.

I elbow open the door and let Al pass through first, then I shove Zhang through. Six heavily armed agents are placed along the Gray Mile. Every single one points a rifle at us.

"Stand down!" Al barks, perfectly in character. "Orders from Wolfson. I'm to take these two up to surface level."

The agent all the way by the elevator steps into the middle of the hallway, which is a lucky break because that'll put us close to where we need to go. I subtly nudge Al towards him, and let him lead us down the hallway, all the while listening in with the ear piece to see what is being reported.

"We're in lockdown," the agent says.

Al hesitates, and I fear this part of the mission is

headed south.

"Did your orders come direct from Wolfson?" Al says, recovering his brusque tone. "I want to speak with your superior."

The agent reaches for his mouthpiece, and that's all the opening I need.

"Push me," I whisper to Zhang, who obliges with no further prompting.

The momentum knocks me into Al, who in turn bangs into the agent. They both fall to the ground. Al rolls to the side, and I take that as the right moment to teeter over on top of the agent.

I catch Al's eye and mouth, "Go!"

He's on his feet faster than I've ever seen him move. Then again, this is the same man who got the jump on me when he pushed me out of the gate at the parking garage. I should stop underestimating him. I look away from Al.

The agent and I are now face-to-face. His eyes widen in recognition. He flips me over on my back and pins me down.

"It's her!" he shouts.

I catch his brief smile before checking on Al and Zhang. The agent's cheek brushes mine as his head turns towards the elevator doors, which are closing, Zhang and Al safely behind them.

"Shit! You and you go after them." He instructs, jutting his chin out at two other agents.

As the agent cuffs me, I hope that Zhang makes it to the helicopter and that Luca is there. If Al reads his hand properly, he won't be on that helicopter and he'll be out of this mess once and for all.

I can't say the same of Luca. In fact, I need the exact opposite for her.

38

The agent unceremoniously tosses me into a holding room not much bigger than a closet. There's just enough space for a tiny table and two folding chairs. Fluorescent lights buzz from the ceiling and wash the room in too-bright light. The noise reminds me of the headache I've had since entering headquarters. It's still there, drilling away at my skull.

With my hands cuffed behind my back, I have to pull one of the chairs out with my foot in order to sit. I'm uncomfortable, but that's the point.

Ten minutes go by and the door opens. A middle-aged man—5'10", 160 pounds, very fit—saunters into the room. A crisp white shirt stands out underneath his navy blue suit. A tablet is tucked underneath his arm, and he holds a disposable coffee cup.

He's masquerading as a lawyer or detective type, but I know him for a fellow agent. It's his posture, how every movement is smooth on the surface but measured and deliberate when you look a little closer. It's also in his eyes, the way they quickly dart around the room before landing on me, sizing me up as I did him.

He sits across from me, sets down his cup, and scans through a few screens on the tablet. Then he pointedly clears his throat. "Well, you have quite the file here, Agent 5891208."

I'm as still as a snake waiting to strike its prey.

"Top of your recruiting class," he continues, reading off the tablet screen. "A string of successful missions. An increase in your security clearance. More successful missions, top secret ones. Not a single infraction..."

Finally he looks up at me, a smirk splayed across his pretty face. "Until the day of the attacks. Then it's been nothing but infractions." He shoots a judging glare at me. "You know, it's agents like you why our country was attacked in the first place."

He's a hundred percent right, but in the wrong way. I stare, unable to hide my shock. They sent a not-in-the-know agent to interrogate me. What are they playing at?

He's already moved onto my latest list of infractions. "Failed mission. Claims of amnesia."

I bristle on the inside at his insinuation that I faked the amnesia but remain stoic on the outside. At least his holier-than-thou attitude has muted the shock, and I can feel my face again.

He goes on, "Removal of your tracking chip. Injuring three agents while resisting being brought in. Coercing another agent to breach protocol. Breaking prisoners out of custody." He shows off his perfect teeth in a predatory smile. "Does that sound about right?"

He knew all that before coming in here, probably had the details memorized. I would have. Reading off the tablet was for show. As a fellow agent familiar with my record, he should know the grandstanding is unnecessary because I know exactly what he is after.

I lean in over the table, careful to keep my expression neutral. "Yes, all except the last two. Luca required no coercing to breach protocol, and it was also Luca who orchestrated Zhang's release. I'm afraid I was only a pawn in that."

His eyes dilate for a split second, a reaction he can't control, and it shows I've piqued his interest. I calculate how much time has passed since Al and Zhang left and decide it's time to put the next phase of my plan into action.

This guy isn't important enough to gather any real information for the Agency. He doesn't even know the truth of the attacks. It's a test. Now that I've had a minute to think about it, I've determined someone higher up is seeing what I'll reveal to this guy.

I lean back into my chair casually, careful not to squish my cuffed hands too much. "I can tell you where Luca is." At least where I hope she is, if I've correctly predicted that she would wait for me after Al and Zhang were gone.

The agent shuts the cover on his tablet and stands. He tries to cover his excitement with brusqueness. "I'll be right back."

I shrug as he turns to the door. Who does he think I am? Some new recruit. He won't be back; someone more important will be.

He's gone barely a minute before a female agent comes in—mid 50s, 5'6", 150 pounds. She's slightly gone to seed, so no field work for her, but her gaze is sharp. No tablet for her, so she's dropped that pretext. I don't recognize her from my training or missions. She's probably an interrogator. Given my history with an abusive mother, they're probably hoping a woman will strike fear in me.

Too bad for them, the only fear I have left isn't reserved for me.

She casually paces the room on her side of the table,

biding her time before getting close. "Let's not waste time. I'm Agent Tanner. You're Raine Hickson, a.k.a. the Black Butterfly. The Agency has an interest in the whereabouts of Agent Luciana Serrurier, and you claim to know where she is. Let's just say, it's in your best interest to share that information with me."

Straightforward of her, something I can respect. More importantly, her desires are in line with what I want to tell her. First, I have to find out how much she knows of the attacks.

"I'll tell you…if you tell me something first."

She raises an eyebrow as if to say "I'm listening."

"Who was the thirteenth president?"

"Franklin Pierce," she says without hesitation.

Historically it's the wrong answer—Millard Fillmore was the thirteenth president—but for my purposes, it's the right answer.

"So you know." I let the non-question hang there without explanation.

Tanner stops pacing and faces me, a small smile playing at her lips. "I do. And I know that you know as well."

Her answer means she's in-the-know about the U.S. government being behind the attacks and would have access to my full file, which says that I was part of it.

"So we can both move on now." She folds her arms across her chest. "Where is Luca?"

"Last I knew, she was in the outskirts of Arlington National Cemetery. Are you familiar with the area known as the General's Circle?" Tanner raises her eyebrows, like she knows the place well.

When I first joined the Agency, the General's Circle was where young recruits often met to let off steam. It is, of course, the place where I kissed Luca, knowing full well she would look for me the night before our big missions. I once believed General's Circle was a secret our superiors weren't aware of, but that was naive of me. Of course, they know where we are at all times.

"At least that's where she was supposed to be about fifteen minutes ago." I throw the comment off nonchalantly, but we both know that's plenty of time for Luca to have disappeared.

Tanner speaks into her mouthpiece. "You get all that?"

She pauses, presumably listening in, before turning her attention back on me.

"If it's true that Agent Serrurier is the one who planned Zhang's breakout, you know it's in your best interest for us to bring her in, right?"

She's standing next to me now, so close I can detect the sharp scent of the dry-cleaning solvent used on her black pants suit.

I look her right in the eyes and nod once.

She leans down and a strand of her brown hair brushes my cheek, tickling it. "Regardless of what happens with Agent Serrurier, you're in a lot of trouble, Agent Hickson." Her breath smells like tuna.

I nod again, my empty stomach twisting, but my face stays impassive. I knew what I was walking into, and I must be ready to face the consequences if I'm to get what I want.

As she grabs the door handle and is about to leave, she turns back to me. "You better not be fucking with us."

The door slams, leaving me in the holding cell where it's just me and a splitting headache that's getting worse by the minute.

39

I try not to fidget as I wait. Surely, someone is watching. But the damn handcuffs are digging into my wrists...and I don't know if they'll find Luca. Things will be so much easier if they do.

My brain churns with ideas on what my next move will be if they don't pick her up. It's a pointless exercise because no more than ten minutes later, Luca is pushed into the room, hands also cuffed. She stands in the corner farthest from the door. The same spot I would have chosen had I decided to stand. I have to turn in my chair to face her.

"Funny meeting you here." She smiles, but I see worry in the way the skin around her eyes crinkles.

"It's in your best interest not to talk to me," I warn, not because she doesn't already know this but to goad her. I'm betting on the fact that she's going to talk.

"I know. I don't care about that anymore." Luca has never been able to help herself. "They're out, Zhang and your friend."

My pulse bumps up a notch, but my breathing remains calm, my face as placid as a lake on a wind-free day. I'm grateful not to be hooked up to any monitoring devices, as my accelerated heartbeat would surely give away my poker face.

To Luca and anyone watching all they see is me shrugging, uncomfortably as the motion wrenches my wrists against the metal binding them. "Good for them."

"Good for them? Good for us." She leans over the table and peers into my face, her eyes a sickly yellow in the fluorescent light. "You should be happy. You don't look happy."

"I'm ecstatic." I smile, exaggerating the expression so it's mocking. "You helped me prove a very important point." Uncertainty plays across Luca's face as her expression falters. "You helped two prisoners of the Agency escape. You gave one of them unauthorized documents."

I don't mention the flash drive I gave to Al.

She leans back against the wall in a casual way, but it's clearly feigned with the way her eyes rapidly blink. "Yeah. And you helped. This is what we wanted. To expose what really happened with the attacks."

I stand a take a step towards her, very deliberate in my actions and tone. "It's what you wanted. There is no *we* here. You were there when I turned myself in and I did what you demanded of me, thinking it was the Agency's wishes. But it wasn't their wishes, was it?"

"What are you talking about, Raine?" Her voice is a pitch higher than normal. "We both wanted this. It was your idea for me to get those documents. You broke Zhang out, and the other guy, too. It was your idea to send them to —"

"It was a test," I interrupt.

"A test? What the hell are you talking about?"

"You're the one who gave me the idea. That day we met outside the store when you followed me." I walk right up to her and fully face her and those unnerving eyes, so she'll believe I'm finally telling the truth. "I was in a dark bathroom, lit only by a flashlight, waiting for my hair dye to set in. I was sleep deprived, having fought off those agents hours before that, the ones you helped me escape from."

Luca has shrunken into the corner. Her face is a mask of indifference, dead of its usual animation. That's how I know she's beginning to process the enormity of what I've done, of what I've manipulated her into doing.

Fully into my story now, I pace the tiny length of the room as if I'm caught up in the telling. Three steps one way, turn, three steps the other way, turn.

"Maybe it was the quiet or the lack of light. Maybe it was staring at my eerie reflection for those long thirty minutes. Maybe it was unleashing my fighting skills against the agents." I pause and cock my head to the side thoughtfully. "Or maybe it was just my brain was finally ready, healed enough..."

With wide eyes, I still my pacing and make eye contact once again with Luca. Her mouth is slightly open in surprise. My face is warm with excitement and I don't care who can tell.

"Luca, I finally remembered. Everything." Almost everything, I amend to myself. The day of the attacks in New York City is the one thing I'm not a hundred percent clear on, but no one needs to know that.

"The attacks. My mission to plant evidence with Zhang. Training with the Agency. Kissing you." The blush snakes down my neck as I recall our intimate moment in the General's Circle. "My past, Luca. My shitty, miserable childhood. The Agency saved me. I owe them everything. In the moment, I remembered that. And I wanted back in. My memory loss had made me weak. Gaining back my mind empowered me in the same way joining the Agency had. But I had screwed up so badly. I needed to make amends. That's where you came in."

Luca continues to shrink into her corner, away from me, but there's nowhere for her to go. The snake trapped by the butterfly.

I could stop there, save her the misery of hearing how I did it, but I want her and everyone listening to know.

"You had already shown your reluctance to follow the Agency's orders by not taking me down after they ordered you to. Then you furthered your disobedience by helping me escape. I thought I would have to track you down, but you followed me and made it so easy. Taking your chip out, trying to make a new life. What were you thinking, Luca? I told you they'd find us, they always do. They always will."

She's breathing heavily. Her eyebrows draw in on themselves, and her mouth contorts into an expression of pain, not a physical hurt but an emotional one, doled out by me.

I continue to twist the knife. "I used your new sense of righteousness, predicted correctly that you'd try to do the noble thing and save me." I brush an errant piece of hair out of her face. "When I came here to turn myself in and was greeted by you, it was all I could do not to throw my arms around you and thank you. Then you offered up your help on a silver platter. You stole those documents from the computer, you let Zhang out of his cell. It was all your idea, Luca."

She slides to the floor, shakes her head. "No. No, no, no." Her voice turns to a whisper. "It was you, too. We did it together. You're the one who got Zhang out."

I'm pleased she doesn't mention Al this time.

"No." The denial is loud and clear, and I let it sit there

a minute before continuing, "I played along so the Agency could know the depths of your deception. And now Zhang trusts me again, and I know where he's going. I'll be able to bring him back in."

Tears fall from Luca's cat eyes. They slide down her face and off her chin. "Raine, how could you? We were friends, more than friends. We were gonna do what it took to make things right. I risked my life for that, so that even if I died, it would be for something good."

I belt out a single "ha" that echoes off the walls. In one elegant motion, Luca stands and lunges at me—an impressive move considering her hands are cuffed behind her back. I stumble and fall on my ass, whacking the back of my head on the table.

My vision blurs, but I'm able to see the hurt, the seething anger, emanating off Luca as she towers above me. She looks about to jump me when Tanner and two male agents rush in and grab a hold of her. Luca killing me isn't part of my plan, so I breathe a sigh of relief when they drag her away.

Maniacal laughter bounces off the walls. The sound spins around me, making me dizzy. It's a minute before I realize the laughter is coming from me. My mouth feels oddly detached, and I blame my agitated head injury for the sensation. Or maybe I'm finally becoming fully unhinged.

40

Some time later, who can say how long really—certainly not me in my current state—Tanner returns with the two male agents. I'm lying on the floor, cheek pressed to the cool tiles. My face is wet, from drool or tears, maybe both.

My cheek rests against my unicorn pillowcase that is soaked in tears. Aside from my stuffed bunny, the pillowcase is my favorite thing in the whole world. It's so much prettier than the stained sheets that were once white but are now a dingy gray.

My friend Rachel got new sheets for her birthday and was going to throw out her old set, but I asked her if I could have the pillowcase. I was afraid to ask for the sheets, too. She might have called me greedy, like Mommy calls me when I ask for pudding cups at the store.

I snuggle into the pillow, filling my nose with a hint of freshness leftover from when the pillowcase was clean. Mommy's boyfriend made me cry again. I went into her bedroom, and Seth was in there. He yelled at me and grabbed me. His fingernails hurt me when they dug into my arm.

Mommy was lying on the bed, smoking her cigarettes, the ones that make me cough. She didn't say a single word.

"Agent Hickson!" Tanner is down on the floor, yelling in my face. "Black Butterfly," she tries in a softer voice.

"What?" I croak.

My throat is dry from all the laughing, but I think my cracking voice is from the rush of memory. I've learned these flashes of remembering take their toll on my body. One reason I was so glad my memories returned and the flashes stopped, or so I thought. This one must have been buried deep, repressed long before my bout of amnesia.

"Are you okay?" Behind Tanner's Agency-prescribed mask of indifference, I see what comes off as genuine concern.

She helps me sit as I can't manage it with my hands shackled behind my back. She squats at eye level. Her face and the room spin but not as badly as before. Crow's feet mark her pinched face, and I wonder if she's older than I originally pegged her for. She probably doesn't have kids of her own, but maybe a niece or nephew, probably around my age.

"I'm okay," I say. Though it's a lie; it's always been a lie.

"Good." She turns to the other agents. "Bring her to interrogation room 2-B."

Of course, it's room 2-B. BB. Black Butterfly. That damn moniker will haunt me for the rest of my life.

The maniacal laugh starts again as the agents haul me up. My legs don't seem to be working correctly, so they pull me down the hallway, my feet dragging behind. We head down, down, down an elevator back to the bowels of the Agency.

Interrogation room 2-B could fit about four of the holding cells in it. The ceiling is a good 15 feet above our heads. Three of the walls are white-painted concrete. The fourth one, opposite the door, sports a large two-way mirror. The floor is a shiny gray tile with a drain in the middle—to wash away the blood. In the middle of the room, a metal table full of torture tools glints in the harsh fluorescent light.

It's a scare tactic. They probably won't use these tools on me, not right away anyway. Besides, there are better ways to torture a prisoner for information than flashy tools.

And that's what I am right now: a prisoner. I've been one all along, ever since the Agency recruited me. But now I'm one who acted in an unpredictable way. I'm a prisoner with secrets to spill.

The agents drop me on the floor remove the handcuffs, and tie ropes around my wrists. A system of pulleys is set up so that a simple yank on the rope will haul me off the ground and dangle me by the arms. I've only seen the strappado used in a training demonstration. I don't need personal experience with it to know it hurts like hell.

My mind is oddly detached from the whole situation, but that doesn't stop my body from reacting. Cramps wrack my empty stomach. A sheen of sweat covers my skin. And that damn headache that won't go away pounds away at my skull.

The horrible laughter won't stop, a waterfall of absurdity pouring from my mouth. I clamp my lips shut, and silence falls over the room.

The agents left me sitting on the floor, ready to be strung up. A few deep breaths restore my calm.

It's amazing what a person can learn to do through breathing. It's one of the first techniques agents learn. I continue the breathing exercises, steadying my heart rate, taking my mind to a tranquil place.

I know what I need to do, and it will require all of my faculties to pull it off.

A fleeting thought and twist of guilt over Luca possesses me, but I push it away. I can't feel that pain right now. I have to fortify myself for much worse pain to come.

41

Agent Tanner comes in, her low heels loud in the space. Click, clack. Click, clack.

My head droops, chin tucked to my chest. Let her think I'm tired and on my way to submission. My breathing is calm and measured.

In my peripheral vision, I observe her every move. She sets a gray plastic case on the table. Then she pulls a metal stool over.

She nudges me with her foot. "Up you go."

I allow her to help me to my feet. She pushes the stool to the back of my legs and forces me to sit. Ever the obedient dog, I allow the manipulation.

"This is so much harder when they know what's coming." She says it quietly but I hear it, and the speakers in the room probably pick it up, too. They don't miss much.

Back at the table full of torture tools, she opens the case and selects a large pair of scissors. They are larger than they need to be, meant to intimidate.

She runs the tip of them very gently across my collarbone. It tickles, but I remain motionless. Slicing into my hunting vest, she cuts it at one shoulder and then moves to the other one. The two halves slip down. The front pools in my lap and the back falls with a thud to the floor. I'm left with only a tight tank top on my upper half.

A vent kicks on, pushing cold air through the already cool room. As the sweat evaporates off my skin, goose bumps rise all over my body and my nipples harden. No amount of breathing is going to control my body's reaction to the cold, so I ignore it.

I briefly think of Elijah's hoodie tucked into my backpack but quickly banish any thoughts of him.

Tanner wheels over a cart with a monitoring machine on it. She applies electrodes to my chest, upper back, and temples. The wires coil out from the machine, snakes clamping onto my skin, just waiting to poison me with their venom. I shake away the image. No room for imaginative thoughts in my brain right now. I must stay focused.

When she clicks on the machine, a steady beep, beep, beep establishes my base level and indicates I'm calm. On the other side of the mirror, there is someone—maybe a team of people—observing, monitoring, recording everything that goes on in this room and my every reaction.

She pulls a chair in front of me and settles in cozily, like we're here for afternoon tea.

Clicking through her tablet, she fires off a series of questions. "Name?"

"Raine Hickson."

"Age?"

"Eighteen."

"Agent number?"

"Five-eight-nine-one-two-zero-eight."

All the while, the monitor beeps steadily away, my body betraying nothing of my nervousness or intentions. The mundane questions seem to go on and on and on, designed to lull me into a false sense of security. Tanner and everyone observing me know I'm aware of the protocols.

It's hard not to be impatient for the real questions to start. Namely, when is she going to ask me about Zhang and his whereabouts? It could be considered a timely question, so it's noteworthy they didn't lead with it.

Tanner is quiet all of a sudden and looking directly at me as if waiting for an answer, but I never heard her last question.

I blankly stare back until she says, "Aliases?"

"Oh right. Black Butterfly." I start with the obvious. "Cynthia Ford." That was an alias I used for my first couple of missions, one that was retired when I moved onto top secret ones. "Shauna Piermont. Jackie White."

Though technically aliases, I leave out the fact that Elijah and Imah called me B and that Al called me Blondie. Those are my personal nicknames, not Agency business, and they have no right to know them. And I shouldn't even be thinking about them right now.

Finally, I share the one I used with Zhang. "Felicity Winters."

I wait for her to ask about Zhang, but she doesn't take the bait.

"What happened during the final phase of your last mission?"

A good question. This is one of the few parts of my memory that still hasn't solidified. Aside from a few impressions—the smell of burning, the crashing noise of a city falling, the weight of a beam on my chest—and what Zhang told me, I have no idea what I did after New York City was attacked. He said I didn't fail the mission, that he got both of us out.

But Luca made me think the Agency logged it as a

failure, and the fake-lawyer agent listed a failed mission right before my amnesia. The inconsistency is certainly curious.

The memory loss and subsequent confusion give me some room to play with. I'll have to go with my gut on this one.

Subtly, so Tanner and the others who are watching won't know I'm doing it on purpose, I increase my breathing, hear the rate of the beeps accelerate ever so slightly.

"I failed." My voice breaks over the second word, as if it's hard for me to admit my failure. "I was supposed to personally escort Zhang out of New York City. I underestimated how chaotic it would be and lost Zhang in the mess and confusion..." I hang my head, ashamed of my lack of discipline in a dire moment.

Staring intently, Tanner purses her lips, glances down at her tablet, and then makes eye contact with me again. "Agent Hickson, you know I need more details than that. Consider this your debriefing. Now, what happened in the final phase of your last mission?"

"I don't know." The truth—layered with a small noise, more of a hiccup than a true sob. "We're trained to deal with stress under any conditions. To always keep our cool. Succeed in the mission at all costs. I had always done that, almost easily. I'm a soldier, a good one." No sense being modest. "Better than good. I was the best in my class."

A tear leaks from my eye and slides down my face. I wipe it away with my shoulder. A blushing warmth spreads across my chest, up my neck, and to my cheeks.

"I had no idea what it would be like." I dip my voice low, gear up for a confession. "I was scared. There was fire everywhere. And the smoke blocked out all the sunlight.

People screaming. People dying. So many dying...”

A real sob escapes my throat, even as I prepare to improvise my way through the next part. I don't have to fake the emotions. It was terrifying being in the city during the attacks.

“Zhang was with me. We were near the Holland Tunnel, our escape point. He had his briefcase with the flash drive. I made sure he took it. Out of nowhere, a large piece of wood crashed down on me, knocked me out for a minute.”

The machine blares at us now. I'm treading a careful line between real and fake emotion, so I pull myself together a little. Deep breath in and then out.

“I saw Zhang slip into the darkness of the tunnel. I blacked out again. The next thing I knew, I was waking up on the Jersey side of the tunnel. Some good Samaritan must have carried me out of the city. I was in bad shape, couldn't remember a damn thing, but I was alive.”

No mention of Imah and Elijah, and I try not to think of them. The beeps grow erratic, and I hope Tanner thinks it's because of my emotions over the attacks and failing the mission. Her dark brown eyes betray no emotion, but in them, I see thoughts swirling, her brain working almost as hard as mine.

She clears her throat. “So you don't know exactly how Zhang got out?”

“No. I assume he made his way through the tunnel on his own and got picked up on the other side. That's where my final rendezvous point was, where I was supposed to deliver Zhang with the evidence. He just would've arrived without me.”

“Then you didn't really fail your mission.” Tanner smiles like this is the best news she's heard all year, showing off yellowed teeth.

"I *did* fail the mission." Didn't I? What would the Agency count as a failure? If only I could remember exactly what happened. "I didn't hand-deliver Zhang and the evidence to the Agency. That was my mission. I got lucky he ended up where he needed to be."

"So the end result was a success."

I fidget on the stool, noticing how cramped my arms and shoulders are becoming. Luca said the Agency was pissed I failed my mission. But Tanner is using semantics to say I didn't fail, and I don't like not being able to foresee where she is going with this line of questioning.

I trust my instincts and above all must be consistent here, or the whole plan falls apart.

"I consider it a failure," I say with resolve.

"That brings us to your memory loss." Tanner taps the tablet, thankfully moving on.

I swallow, exaggerating the neck movement.

"What can you tell me about that?"

"I lost it all, everything. My name, my childhood, my training. I could read, write, use a fork. I knew what year it was. All the presidents' names." I make sure to include that detail, to remind her of my status as an agent in-the-know. "But any detail about my life, I just couldn't remember."

"Did you have any other symptoms?"

"Headaches. Nausea at first, but that went away pretty quickly. I would get visions of memories, like I was reliving them. But I could only process what was going on in the specific moment, everything else was still a blank. The memories didn't really fit together. They were from all different points of my life."

"Mmm hmmm." She nods slowly, taps on the tablet again. She asks me a few more questions and I sense she's winding down.

The beeping has steadied into a calm rhythm again. The sound is unnecessary. Tanner and the agents behind the mirror can read all my vitals on their tablets. In fact, the beeping is probably something of a distraction to them. This whole room and everything in it is a big show. And all of it is meant to rattle me into telling the truth.

What is the truth anyway? If enough people believe something, does that make it true?

For a while there, my brain was telling me I had no past—that was its truth.

The Agency has the country, and many of their agents, believing the Chinese government was behind the attacks. That's their brand of truth.

All I'm doing is fabricating my own brand, one that's not too far a deviation from the real truth.

42

Tanner finishes her interview—definitely not an interrogation—and makes one final note in her tablet before signaling to the mirrored wall.

After a minute, a male agent enters the room, one I haven't encountered since reentering the Agency. His white-blond hair and big tan muscles make him look like some kind of Swedish masseuse, as if I'm here for a relaxing spa day. He carries a black bag, and I'm guessing there's not massage oil in there.

Tanner gives me a pitying look. I knit my eyebrows for a brief moment before plastering the stoic face back on. She nods as if to say "you can make it through this" and leaves me alone with the masseuse. It's a small bit of solidarity between two agents who know what's coming.

With his back to me, busy arranging his tools on the shiny table, the masseuse has caught none of this exchange. He takes his time before he approaches me. Rubbing his smooth chin, he flashes a grin, his perfectly white teeth gleaming.

Without warning, he grabs the rope and pulls. Behind me, my arms shoot up, pulling my butt off the stool. It falls with a loud clang as my legs bang into it. The tips of my boots just barely make contact with the tiled floor.

I gasp as sharp pain shoots out from my shoulders. It radiates from all directions right to the tip of my head, fingertips, and toes. The machine goes crazy with beeps until I can center myself, remember the breathing techniques, and focus once again on the masseuse's face.

The smile remains. He's a sadistic son of a bitch, all right.

I swallow down the panicked thought that I won't be able to handle him. I'm the Little Engine that Could—one of the few storybooks my mother read to me as a child. Instead of a chant of "I think I can," I silently plead "I know I can" in my head.

I replace the masseuse's face with Elijah's. I feel Imah's soft hands on my back, slowly rubbing calm circles. Her whispered voice comes to me, "You're okay."

It's drowned out by the masseuse's soft growl, right in my ear. "That's a nice story you told Agent Tanner about your memory loss. Too bad I don't believe a word of it."

He runs a fingernail along my cheek. "We can avoid this whole thing...if you just tell me the truth."

"What I told Agent Tanner is the truth." I struggle to make my voice less breathy and push down my memories of Elijah and Imah. No matter how much comfort they could provide me, they have no place here. I can't think of them. I have to be strong without them.

He nudges me with his elbow. The slight swinging motion is enough to send a fresh wave of pain through my shoulders.

"Just as well," he says. "I'll have to extract the truth from you. I like it better this way."

He unlaces my boots, doing his best to jostle me as much as possible. With each jolt of pain, I force myself to remember every moment of my childhood in Florida, my short-lived stint running a gambling ring, and all the training and missions with the Agency—everything in my life but the brief time I spent with Imah and Elijah.

They were a means to an end until I could regain my memories. That is all they were. They were there to take care of me until I remembered myself and who I was. Mere acquaintances, not worth remembering.

The dark space in my mind that swallowed all of my memories is still there. I access it and put my misguided feelings for Elijah and Imah there, out of reach.

The masseuse yanks off one boot, then the other. Next come my socks. My feet struggle for purchase on the floor, but my toes don't reach. I'm swaying, and nothing I do can stop the momentum.

The pain, the pain. It's all pain. And it's only going to get worse, so much worse.

Pain is only physical, I remind myself. I am in control. I'm a machine, the way the Agency trained me to be. I'm that stupid engine chugging up the hill. I know I can, I know I can, I know I can.

I'm the Black Butterfly!

"Where is Zhang now?" the masseuse asks. The million-dollar question, but it's come too late to be worth much.

"Don't you want to know more about my past?" I say, proving I have some fight left in me.

He punches me in the ribs, which crunch under his fist. My body swings wildly. My arms have begun to go numb, but that doesn't stop the pain from penetrating through. I focus on the worst of it: my shoulders and his fist's point of impact. It's hard to breathe. He might have broken a rib.

I dig deep into my head and put the pain in the dark spot, too. Breathe in, breathe out. If I can get through this part, I will be rewarded. I'll be back in good with the Agency. They'll trust me again. I need them to trust me.

I gasp. "Okay, I'll tell you."

He releases the rope. The hard floor rushes to greet me with a bone-jarring crunch. I manage to prop myself up in a slouched position and assess the damage. The rib's not broken after all. There will be bruises but nothing worse... yet.

"I'm waiting." He raises a foot as if to strike my ribs with his boot.

"Give me a minute," I wheeze.

Coughing shakes me to my very bones. The never-ending headache drones on, a dull background to my sharper pains.

The masseuse crouches down to my level, so I can look him in the eye when I tell him, "Zhang's here at the Agency."

43

I'd love to hear what the machine sounds like hooked up to the masseuse when he's torturing someone, morbid curiosity getting the better of me. I have to settle for watching his eyes bulge and his tan face pale in response to my answer about Zhang being here at the Agency.

"How do you know that?" He schools his face once more, but we both know I surprised him.

"It's like with Luca," I explain. "The Agency had to know of her deception so I set her up. I set Zhang up, too. I couldn't let him escape with the documents incriminating the U.S. government. I trusted that the Agency wouldn't let him blow the whole operation. And from your reaction, I'm guessing I'm right."

The agent stands and stomps to the door. He taps the tablet, and the door slides open.

He turns and points a finger at me, sneering. "I'm not done with you, Butterfly."

The door zips shut behind him.

I slump on my side and rest on the cold floor. My bare feet are already frigid and the rest of my body temperature follows, except for my burning cheeks.

I don't allow myself to think about how heavy my eyelids are with fatigue or about the ache in my side where the masseuse punched me. I brush off the burn of my shoulders and wrists and the persistent headache.

The emotional part of my mission, the betrayals of Luca and Zhang—poor Zhang, twice burned by the Butterfly—is complete. I believe the physical challenge has only begun. They'll torture me until they can be certain I am a trusted member of the Agency.

I shake from the cold, but oddly not from fear. I'm too focused on the end game to be frightened of what becomes of my body. Pain is only physical. There are more important things.

I know I can, I know I can, I know I can.

The machine continues to beep the slow, steady tempo of my resting heart rate. It's freezing on the floor, but the coolness helps to ease my pain. I close my eyes and stop fighting the exhaustion. I should rest and build up energy for what's to come.

"Wake up!" The loud cry of the masseuse does just that.

The machine beeps erratically as I gain my bearings. He kicks me in the tender spot on my ribs. I wince but reveal no other signs of discomfort, and the beeps settle back into their monotonous tone.

Drool has pooled on the floor next to my mouth. My cheek is soaked, but my mouth feels like someone stuck a wad of gauze in it and sopped up all the moisture. I have no idea how long I've been out, but it feels like hours. My body is stone cold. My muscles have seized up. It's like I ran a marathon in arctic weather and passed out in the snow.

With hands still bound behind me in the strappado rope, I force my numb arms awake. I maneuver into a sitting position and wipe my damp mouth on my shoulder.

A second metal table had been wheeled into the room,

leather shackles ominously hanging off its edge.

A shiver runs through me, and I can't stop shaking.

The masseuse suddenly appears right in front of my face. "I'm going to untie you. Try anything, and I'll slice open your gut and let you die slowly...painfully."

His perfect teeth show in an evil smile, and I don't doubt that he would do as he promises. Not that I have any reason to try anything. I've committed myself to seeing this through to the end.

He leans behind me and undoes the rope, releasing my wrists. I rub them more for something to do than for relief. Quietly, so the masseuse won't notice, I practice my breathing routine to help me focus.

I have a mission to complete. No ambiguous failure this time.

With a rough motion, the masseuse pulls me to standing. My feet are so cold they can't feel the tile underneath, and I stumble. He grabs my shoulder, steadies me, and then shoves me toward the table with the shackles.

"Bring the monitor," he orders.

The wheels of the cart squeak as I push it along, the sound like the piercing squeal of feedback from a speaker, filling the room right up to the high ceilings. I realize my screams will fill this space soon, and suddenly it feels like the air has been sucked out of the room.

Breathe, I remind myself.

"Get on the table," the masseuse commands.

Once again, I comply with the order, carefully arranging the wires attaching me to the machine. The hard metal is colder than the floor.

The masseuse grabs one wrist and straps it down tight enough so there's not a single wisp of wiggle room. Then he does the same with my other wrist and both my ankles.

He rolls up his sleeve to show me a red spider tattooed on the inside of his forearm.

He notices me looking at the tattoo. "The butterfly caught by the spider."

I don't remind him I turned myself in. His arrogance is a trait I can use to my advantage.

Let's get this over with, I think.

From my vantage point on the table, I can turn my head just enough to watch him reach into his bag. The ping of metal-on-metal sounds as he removes each torture device and sets it on the table.

Pliers. Ping!

Forceps. Ping!

Scalpel. Ping!

The barbed cat o' nine tales sounds more like rapidly tapping fingernails as each of the whipping thongs hits the table.

I don't care to see any more. Instead, I focus on the high, white ceiling. My empty stomach twists and my mouth waters. I swallow down the nausea. A wave of fatigue hits like a tsunami, and my eyelids flutter shut.

Despite my nap, the exhaustion is already making it hard for me to concentrate. The fatigue will be the hardest part for me to overcome. I must have all my synapses firing in order to pass the torture test.

A slap to the face brings me back to harsh reality. The masseuse's features swim before me.

"No sleeping, Butterfly." Spittle hits me as he speaks.

He asks a similar series of questions as Agent Tanner about my last mission with Zhang and my memory loss. I answer each one as I did hers. The words aren't exactly the same—they can't sound rehearsed—but the details are.

Then he switches gears on me. "Let's talk about Luca."

My eyelashes flutter as I force myself to stay focused.

He smiles. "You two were lovers, right?"

"No."

He answers my reply with another slap. "Wrong answer."

"We were close, but we never slept together."

"So you're a prude in real life and will only have sex with people for the job?"

It's rhetorical, designed to rile me up. A bitter laugh erupts from my lips, earning me another smack, this one a backhand to the cheek. The copper taste of blood fills my mouth.

"I see I'm going to need to up the ante with you," the masseuse snarls.

A deeply sardonic glint shines in his eyes. Of course, the Agency would assign the most sadistic interrogator to me. He brandishes a scalpel and waves it in front of my face.

"I think we'll start with the big toe. Most bang for the buck."

If I thought for a minute my feet were numb from the cold, I was dead wrong. Agonizing pain shoots up my leg as the scalpel cuts through my nail into the tender flesh beneath. I clench my teeth and clamp my jaw shut, staying silent except for heavy breathing.

"Simmons, get in here!" he yells at the two-way mirror.

Another agent enters. I don't bother sizing him up; it doesn't matter. They can do anything they want to me, regardless of how well I assess them.

"Hold her head so she can see what I'm doing," the

masseuse instructs.

Simmons follows the order without a word, yanking me as far into a sitting position as the shackles on my wrists allow. He pins my head in between his hands so I can't look away.

The masseuse selects the pliers from his torture tools, brings them to my big toe, and clamps down on the tip of the nail. I squirm and try to turn my head.

I can't watch. I have to watch. They're making me watch.

Remember your mission, my brain screams.

But despite my training, I'm still human. All I want to do right now is get away.

44

I shut my eyes against the world, which right now is this one room full of agony.

"Open those big brown eyes, Butterfly," says the masseuse in a falsely sweet, mocking voice that turns nasty. "Or I'll prop them open with one of my fun gadgets."

"Okay!" I gasp as I force them to stay open.

"Now watch." He adjusts his grip on the pliers that secure my toenail, and then he yanks.

The stabbing pain sends a shock of energy through my body. My limbs shake, my mouth waters. Agent Simmons clamps my head tighter between his hands.

Tears flow freely down my cheeks. Screams rend the air. I don't realize that they're mine until I scream my throat raw. My vision blurs from tears and dizziness from the pain, but I keep my eyes open.

Eventually a throbbing, stinging sensation replaces the sharp needles of pain. I can breathe again.

"What about Elijah Aarons?" the masseuse asks. "Ever sleep with him?"

My heart skips a beat, but it barely registers on the machine as it blares with my reaction to the torture.

"That simpleton." The answer is raspy. "Never."

The masseuse's eyes narrow, and I'm afraid I've taken it too far. I should've stuck with a simple no. He moves on without further comment and asks me about my time with the off-gridders, referring to Imah as Dr. Crawford. I keep my answers simple, unemotional, devoid of personal details.

"Why wasn't Dr. Crawford in New York City the day of the attacks?"

"I don't know," I respond quickly, maybe too quickly. My breath hitches.

He reaches for the scalpel. "You don't know?"

"That's what I said." There's steel in my voice. I want to slice through him with it.

The scalpel digs into the tender flesh of my toe. The pain pierces me all the way to my chest. It hurts to breathe, but my body heaves in sobs anyway.

I want to forget my mission, retreat into the pain, tell him everything. My whole stupid plan. But I can't.

A snatch of a chant sings in my head, my refrain. I know I can, I know I can, I know I can. I latch onto the saying like an alligator's sharp teeth seizing on a turtle.

"Why wasn't Dr. Crawford in New York City the day of the attacks?" he repeats.

"I don't know."

He goes to work on my other big toe. There are no more screams, my throat is too raw, my breath too scarce. I can only manage a rough grunting moan.

Simmons is still there, holding me propped up, my head squeezed between his hands, but it's as if the masseuse and I are the only ones in the room.

"Why wasn't Dr. Crawford in New York City the day of the attacks?" he asks a third time.

"I don't know!" My shout echoes through the room.

He stares at me, takes in my pathetic whimper.

Through the tears in my eyes, I can barely make out the way his head is slightly cocked in an appraising way.

"Why did you stay with them so long?"

It takes a moment to block the pain enough to answer. "I was injured. I had no memory. They had medical supplies and food. They were headed to D.C., and I felt compelled to go there. So I stayed with them until I could strike out on my own."

"Do you have feelings for Zhang?"

I'm caught off-guard, as I'm supposed to be, by the abrupt change in questioning.

"Yes, a little." The truth, though the feelings aren't the ones the masseuse is thinking of. "He's sweet in his own way." A warmth creeps up my cheeks. "But nothing that ever got in the way of my work."

"This little plan of yours, to show Luca's deception and set Zhang free, how did you come up with it?"

I lick my lips, but my tongue is so dry it's like rubbing a cat's tongue on sandpaper. "I used every bit of training I've ever had. To read the situations as they presented themselves. To read people. I sized up Luca and Zhang, manipulated them, and hoped they'd do what I wanted them to do. I came here—turned myself in—not knowing if it was going to work. But I knew I had to make it work in order to regain my status at the Agency."

It's the most I've said at one time since the interrogation started.

"Why come back? Your tracking device was out. You could have disappeared. Why come back to the Agency?"

"I am a soldier. I serve the Agency. It is my purpose." I recite the mantra from training, the saying recruits would chant at the end of every lesson, every training session, every debrief.

The masseuse's tablet vibrates on the table with all the tools. He has barely grabbed it before the door slides open and Director Wolfson, the head of the Agency himself, strides in. His brown hair is graying at the edges and his forehead is lined with wrinkles. He appears older than I remember him.

He dismisses the two agents with a flick of the wrist. Simmons shoots out from under me so fast, I smack the back of my head on the hard metal. The masseuse takes his time gathering up his things.

With a final a smirk, he tells Wolfson, "She's all yours."

I face the man who recruited me into the Agency, who noticed my talents to read and manipulate people. The man who used those traits and all the Agency had to offer to train me to be the best spy in my class. The man whose orders I always followed.

I face him, and a hatred burns me more than any physical pain could.

He releases me from my shackles, so I can sit on my own. I pluck off the pads attaching me to the machine without asking for permission.

Wolfson holds out his hand for me to shake. "Welcome back, Raine."

He dares to use my first name because this is a man who can do whatever he wants. He can use young, vulnerable people like me to attack his own nation and blame it on a rival one. But maybe this one time, I can use him to get what I want.

I reach out hesitantly to let him think I've been browbeaten back into submission. Because as much as I hate this man and the Agency, I think I'm finally back in their trust.

45

Director Wolfson hands me my boots and keeps a sharp eye trained on me while I carefully pull them on. It's agony for my big toes, but I'm still careful about showing how much pain I'm in. The situation could change at any moment, and I must put up a brave front.

All I really want is to sit in a hot shower and wash the last few days down the drain. But this was only part of my mission. A success, yes, but there's more to come.

I'm unable to suppress the shudder that rips through me as I pass by the table that held the masseuse's torture devices. He took all the tools, but there is a small smear of blood on the table. It'll be cleaned and disinfected, leaving no signs behind of what occurred here, but the wounds inflicted upon me will be harder to erase.

I press on, doing my best to minimize the limp as I follow Wolfson to the door. Outside, Agent Tanner waits. She's casually leaning up against the wall, eyes on her tablet, but her whole body in tune to us—to me. Her lip twitches, I think holding back a smile, when she sets her sights on me.

Wolfson leaves us by saying, "I'll see you soon."

He fails to indicate who he means, but I'm left with a

pit in my queasy stomach

"Can you walk?" Tanner asks.

Not mustering the energy to talk, I nod.

She leads me down several shiny marble hallways, their prettiness working well to hide the dirty little secrets of what really goes on at the Agency.

We're well away from my torture chamber when she says in a quiet voice, "I knew you'd make it through. I could tell you were genuine in our interview. I think you'd be a good match for my team. It's all internal work, no field missions."

She takes in my shuffling gait and the agony I'm trying very hard to keep off my face.

"Once you're healed up that is. I've already put in a request to be your handler. I'm sure there will be other requests, but I hope you consider my team when you think of your future here."

I almost laugh. My future here is for one purpose, and her team isn't going to help me with that.

When she holds out a business card, I take it and mumble, "Thanks," playing my role.

She drones on about how internal work isn't any less important than field work. It turns to background noise because I'm having trouble not crying out in pain. Each labored breath sends a sharp stabbing sensation through my midsection, and I'm back to thinking I have a broken rib. The headache still throbs at my temples, though I've grown used to it after having suffered from them so often lately. The worst, by far, is the excruciating burn of my toes. Every step is like having the nails ripped off again.

Tanner finally stops talking and notices I've fallen several feet behind. She offers me an encouraging smile. "Almost there."

I suck in a shuttering breath and continue walking.

"You know, I've been following your track since before you became a full agent. Top in your class, of course, you know that. You've accomplished quite a lot for such a young agent."

The chattering is not only annoying, but out of sync with the confident, no-nonsense woman Tanner was when she interviewed me. As I pay a little more attention, I notice the way she keeps switching her tablet from one hand to the other and how she avoids eye contact. She's nervous, maybe a little star-struck. Is she trying to poach me out from under someone else? I wonder what other team leaders are interested in me.

I suppose in another situation it would be flattering, but right now all I feel is pain and exhaustion. And worry, but that is an emotion I have no room for here. I need to recharge.

After an elevator ride and several more hallways, we reach the infirmary at last. The door is marked with a sign bearing a bright red caduceus. The entwined snakes remind me of Luca, and then of Imah before I push her back into that deep part of my mind.

I hesitate before opening the door.

"Do you need something?" Tanner asks.

"It's just..."

My gaze darts around, looking up and down the hallway to find it empty except for us.

I lower my voice and lean in toward Tanner conspiratorially. "I can't help but wonder about Luca. I know I shouldn't, but I feel bad about having been the one to betray her." I glance around again and raise my timbre. "Of course, she's a traitor and deserves what she gets."

"I see." Tanner's face is a mask, her eager demeanor

of a moment ago locked away.

A little groan escapes my throat, and I hold my side. It's not an exaggeration of my pain, but it's an expression of it I'd normally hold in. I'm purposefully showing it to Tanner.

"Sorry," I gasp out. "I'm overstepping."

"I understand." Sympathetic Tanner is back. "You were friends." Her voice is barely a whisper. "I'll see what I can find out."

"Thank you...for this." I hold up the business card as if it's a promise—I'll give you what you want if you give me what I want. It's also a lie.

46

The infirmary is as pristine as the rest of headquarters with the same overly bright fluorescent lights, only there's an almost overwhelming smell of antiseptic here. It reminds me of helping out the injured with Imah, and Elijah telling stories to the kids. It shows just how tired I am that I've, once again, let them leak out of that closed space in my brain.

There are ten beds—cots really—made up with crisp white linens, lined up in two rows. All are empty save one.

"You!" Breanne sits up in her cot, springs squeaking in protest, and points a slim finger at me, rage in her dark eyes. A sheen of sweat coats her forehead, probably from the pain and exertion of sitting. I messed her up pretty badly.

I heave out a long sigh. I thought I would have a moment to rest and have no energy for a fight.

Luckily, a nurse bustles in from a glass-enclosed office area. He dons baby blue scrubs and a name tag that says Agent Coate—everyone who works in the Agency has been trained as an agent. He's short, maybe 5'6", but thick, his neck almost as wide as my waist.

"Lay down, Agent Holmes," he says with enough

authority that Breanne listens. "Don't any of you field agents get along?"

Without waiting for an answer, he points to a bed as far away from Breanne as possible.

"Sit there and wait," he says to me.

He gives Breanne a paper cup and instructs her to take her medicine.

To both of us, he says, "If either of you takes a step off your respective beds, I'm sending you downstairs."

Downstairs is the general term for where I just came from: the torture rooms. Most of the time it's an idle threat, but I'm not risking going back there just yet.

"You're lucky Coate ordered us not to move." Breanne's speech is labored, her words clipped. "I should kill you for what you did to me. I had to have a blood transfusion, and I need surgery on my shoulder. Bitch!"

She shuffles on her cot and swears again, this time at the pain, instead of at me. "Luca said you were all right." The acid in my empty stomach does a flip. "Never should have listened to her. Stupid girl." She's mumbling now, her medication starting to kick in.

Her head flops down on the pillow, and she's out. Good, now I can rest in peace. Or so I think, until I actually try lying down. My head pounds in protest, almost bad enough to make me forget about my toes. But nothing can drown out the pain of having my toenails ripped from my feet.

I unlace my boots and as gently as possible, pull them off. It hurts like hell when the tender nail beds brush against the leather. I knew better than to put socks on, the fabric would've gotten stuck to the wounds. I inspect my toes, but it's hard to tell how bad the damage is underneath the caked-on blood. My rib injury won't let me bend well enough to get a good angle.

"Looks pretty bad."

The voice jars me, and my body sings in pain with the sudden movement.

"Hello, Dr. Bauman," I say to the tiny, mousey creature in front of me.

"I've received my orders regarding you," she says slowly, carefully.

I resist the urge to hold my breath and force slow, steady inhalations. She surprises me a second time by holding out a hand. I take it and she shakes mine hard enough to send another wave of pain through my side, most likely done on purpose.

"Welcome back, Agent Hickson. Shall we get you all healed up and back in the fold?"

There's a challenge in her eyes, like she knows what I've done. I think—hope—that it's just hard feelings from when Al and I fled from her at the rest stop. It would have been a nice notch on her belt to have been responsible for bringing in the rogue Black Butterfly. I took away that boon to her career. It wasn't personal; I had to come in on my own terms.

She consults her tablet, apparently moving on from the bad blood between us. With fingertips to my chin, she tilts my face up to check out the injuries from my fight with Breanne.

"Some bruising. Nothing major there. Let's check out that rib." Dr. Bauman sets down the tablet and doesn't hesitate to dig into my tender side. I stifle the yelp that rises to my lips and settle for a groan. "Probably not broken, but most likely cracked. I'll order an x-ray to confirm."

She says all this as if it wasn't the government

Agency we both work for that was responsible for my injuries.

"Let's see those feet," she orders.

I lift them up onto the cot and lie on my back, head throbbing as I stare at the ceiling.

Hot, white fire shoots up my body when she touches my feet. I wince and pull them in toward me, instinct yelling at me to curl up in a protective fetal position. Several deep breaths later, I'm able to tolerate the contact.

"It's a clean denailing," she declares. "We'll get these bandaged, and the nails should grow back eventually. Agent Kilian does nice work, doesn't he?"

The masseuse has a name.

I prop myself up on my elbows. From her perch on the stool at the end of my cot, Dr. Bauman gazes at my face, not my feet. Ever stoic, I don't rise to the bait of her trying to get a rise from me, and maintain eye contact. Though I do hate the masseuse, and he did seem to garner a particular pleasure from torturing me, he was ultimately doing his job. Following orders. Like I've done. Like Dr. Bauman has done. Like we all have done.

She breaks the eye contact first, her gaze going back to her tablet. "I'll send Agent Coate in to clean you up. Any other areas of concern?"

I hesitate, but finally admit, "My head. It's killing me."

She exposes her big, shiny top teeth in a smug smile. "I'll have him give you something for that."

Hopefully it will help with all the other pains as well. My stomach grumbles loud enough for her to hear, an unnecessary reminder of how hungry I am. But I don't request food, even as Dr. Bauman stands and waits for me to do it. I've shown enough weakness in front of her by asking for something for my headache. I'll ask Coate for food.

"Feel better, Agent Hickson."

The whole conversation has been laced with malice, and her well wishes are no exception. I offer an insincere "thanks" and pretend I don't notice her tone.

Once the good doctor is gone, I risk Coate's wrath and hobble around to steal a couple of pillows from the other cots. One I use to prop up my feet, and the others I place under my head. The elevation helps with the headache.

Agent Coate brings in a portable x-ray machine and pain medication. I eagerly accept the meds and the water that comes with them. A scan shows that two of my ribs are cracked but none are broken.

Next, he has a whole new torture device for me: supplies for my toes. It's only after he's disinfected my wounds, slathered my toes with a numbing ointment, and bandaged them up that I feel like I can breathe again. The medication has left me drowsy and a little loopy.

Once Coate is gone, I'm alone except for the slumbering Breanne. I forgot to ask him for food. Aside from my recent amnesia, I never forget anything. I'm off my form and need to get back on it.

After all my scheming, the taste of success is bitter on my tongue with a job unfinished. I'm left wondering what comes next and how it will all fit together.

47

I drift off, my semi-sleep state plagued by nightmares of fire and pain.

I'm pinned down, blinded by smoke, and flailing. Smooth hands touch my face. The weight is lifted from my chest, and I can breathe again. But smoke fills my lungs. I cough uncontrollably.

With a jolt, I wake. The crisp white sheet is soaked in sweat. A shiver travels down my spine right to my aching toes. The training kicks in like instinct, calming my beating heart and erratic breathing.

It's second nature to assess the room. Breanne is gone, recovered or moved, I suppose. She's not my concern.

I am alone and hurting, but nothing I can't handle. My ribs smart when I inhale too sharply, which might make it tricky to control my biofeedback should I need to, and it's likely that I'll need to. My toes are an agonizing mess, but I remind myself pain is only pain. I'll continue to bear it.

That dream wasn't just a dream. It was a memory. The last one playing hard to get. Though I'm sure there are other things I don't remember I forgot.

If it's true that Zhang really did carry me out of New

York City, it's a debt I'll never be able to repay. In fact, I've done just the opposite by orchestrating his capture a second time.

I can't help but wonder if everyone would have been better off if I'd died in the attacks. Imah and Elijah never would have met me. Al wouldn't have either. Luca might still have disagreed with the Agency's plans, but maybe she would have been able to break free if it weren't for me.

The what-ifs are pointless. I didn't die in the attacks, so there's no sense in speculating over what could have been. I must move forward.

With my feet elevated on pillows, I lie back and close my eyes. It looks like I'm resting, but my mind is scanning through the possible scenarios like songs on a music player. The pain medication has made me a touch loopy, but I force myself to concentrate through the haze.

The distinct sound of the door sliding open and someone walking into the room disrupts my thoughts. A subtle peek tells me it's Agent Tanner. I ignore her, even as I sense her presence near my cot. Her breathing gives her away, and I get why she's not a field agent.

Not to be disregarded, she clears her throat. "Agent Hickson."

I crack open one eye and hold up a finger. "Just a minute."

I finish the scenario I'm contemplating before both eyes flutter open and I maneuver into a sitting position. "Yes?"

"Director Wolfson will meet with you."

Not what I was expecting, and new scenarios run through my mind. "Now?"

Tanner purses her lips, a signal that she's not pleased about it either. "Yes, now. He insists."

I hesitate and glance down at my feet, mummified in bandages. Boots won't fit over them.

Tanner notices me eyeing my boots and gives me a motherly pat on the shoulder. "I'll be right back." She slips into the office area of the infirmary.

What I wouldn't give for another few hours of quiet rest before having to face Wolfson...but that's not the situation, so I must press on with my mission. The soothing benefits of the medication have started to wear off, while the mind haze remains. I grab the refilled glass of water at my bedside and down it in one shot. It begins to clear my head instantly, and I say a silent thanks to whoever left it for me, probably Coate. If only he'd left some food.

Before I can lament too long over the sad state of my stomach, Tanner returns with a pair of slippers. They're baby blue and fuzzy. I examine them with disdain, while Tanner shoots me a beseeching look. As absurd as they are, they fit my swathed feet just fine. They even have non-skid bottoms, so I don't fall on my ass as I rise on my unsteady limbs. How far the Black Butterfly has fallen.

I better get my shit together if I'm to be ready for whatever Wolfson has in store for me. He can't possibly want me to go on a mission. Hopefully, he only wants to corroborate my story himself. Maybe I can wheedle information out of Tanner...if she knows anything. At least my brain finally seems to be waking up.

"Dr. Bauman says it will be good for you to walk a little," Tanner says in a pointed, slightly loud tone. "Shall we take the stairs?"

Her lack of subtlety is disturbing. She must be very good at internal work to have a high enough clearance to be in-the-know.

I agree to the stairs, though my feet may fall off in

protest. I wish Tanner would stop staring at me like I'm headed to the gallows. I was already tortured. Am I to be executed for my crimes, too?

I grab my boots, hold them to my chest, and nod to let Tanner know I'm ready to go. Out in the hallway, she grabs a familiar looking backpack off the floor and hands it to me.

"They took the weapons, but I got the rest of your stuff back."

Pulling open the main compartment, I see my provisions, the expensive watch, and the map I stole. The hunting vest, which I recall with a slight shiver being cut off, and the weapons are unfortunate losses.

Way down in the bottom, though, the gray of Elijah's sweatshirt peeks up at me, and squished next to it is Al's hat. I press my lips together to hide a smile and resist the temptation to pull the sweatshirt out and sniff it. As I fit my boots into the backpack, my heart flutters in my chest in a pleasant way, but I push those dangerous feelings deep, deep down.

Grabbing a granola bar, I scarf it down as we walk to the stairs. The food is sweet fuel for my brain and clears out the last of the cobwebs from the medication. We make it up one flight, and I pause on the landing, the upper railing blocking us from the camera's view.

I gulp in air, feigning being out of breath, and it sends spikes of pain through my ribs. "I need a minute."

Tanner leans in close and whispers, "They're holding Luca downstairs. Interrogation starts tomorrow."

Nodding thanks, I say out loud, "I'm ready."

I hope Luca is ready, too. Will Agent Kilian interrogate her? For her sake, I hope not. There are other, less sadistic interrogators in the Agency.

When I notice my thumb tapping a nervous beat

against my thigh, I repress the movement. Luca's fate isn't up to me anymore. I've pretty much sealed her demise.

Three more flights up, and I'm not sure if I can go any farther. The weight of each step is an elephant crushing my toes.

"One more flight." Tanner grips my arm, her touch telling me I can make it.

Once out of the stairway, she walks and I shuffle into a small foyer. A single door sits directly in front of us with a tinted window that blocks our view from inside. The white and black marble of the floors appears impossibly shiny, like someone just came through and buffed it.

I catch a glimpse of my reflection in the window. It's only a silhouette, but that's all I need to tell me that I look beaten, broken. My shoulders are hunched over, and my hair is randomly sticking out in all directions. I don't need a reflection to tell me my knees are bowed as I try to keep pressure off my big toes

I straighten up and try to smooth out my hair. Not much I can do about the bowed legs as the pain is too intense for me to fake it and walk properly.

Tanner punches a code into the keypad next to the door. It slides open, and I follow her in. The office is spacious. If we were aboveground, it's the kind of office that would have floor-to-ceiling windows with a grand view. The back wall is a giant mirror—a regular one, not like the two-way one in the torture room. It's easy to tell the difference if you know what to look for. The recessed lighting is softer than most of the other lighting at headquarters. It bathes the room in a yellow hue, giving it the feel of an old-fashioned movie.

I avoid my full reflection by staring at the man sitting at the large wooden desk that takes up a good portion of the room. Wolfson. He appears as casual as he always does. His nostrils flare once, so quickly I almost miss it. He's excited...or nervous.

"Thank you, Agent Tanner," he offers as a dismissal.

She tosses a tight-lipped expression my way, for once unreadable. Then, I'm alone with the most powerful man in the Agency, which probably makes him the most powerful man in the country, maybe even the world.

"Sit, Raine." His voice is quiet, serious. There's no need for him to bark orders; he's used to being obeyed.

I leave my backpack on and perch on the edge of the seat in front of the desk, the wood creaking under my weight. Not that I expect to be able to escape this office if something should happen, but it's in my nature to be prepared.

He steeples his hands, and I notice how the skin is red and cracked. It's a reminder that this man is only human, flesh and blood like me.

"As you know, we have apprehended Zhang and the documents Luca stole from the database." He falls silent, so I nod. "Did you know those documents were meaningless and would never have incriminated the Agency?"

"Yes."

"Raine, there's no need to be coy. It's just you and me." He moves his arm in a sweeping motion, inviting me to look around the room. "No cameras, no one watching. Relax."

I shuffle out of my backpack and set it on the ground next to my chair, within easy reach. Then I relax back into my seat and put it all out there. "What do you really want from me?"

"One simple thing." He opens his lips in a full-teeth predatory smile. "The truth."

I smile back to cover a gulp, my throat thick with emotion.

The truth is never simple.

48

Avoiding the secret spaces of my mind, I remind myself that I have been telling the truth. If I believe it to be true, then it is. I have nothing to hide.

I know I can, I know I can, I know I can.

Wolfson and I are two predators locked in a death stare. The falsely delicate butterfly—thought to be able to kill many with one flap of the wing. And the sharp-toothed wolf—master of the close kill. Who will strike first? Who will deliver the death blow?

"I told Luca what documents to download," I explain. "That's how I know they were meaningless. She trusts me— well, she trusted me then—so she never bothered to check if the documents actually contained evidence against the Agency. She only knew they were difficult to access."

"Seems like a very complicated way to come back to the Agency. Did you ever think about just turning yourself in and explaining what happened?"

"Of course." My voice wavers a tiny bit, and I bite my lip on the inside to catch it. "My mistakes felt too big. I needed something equally as big to make up for it."

"So that's why you decided to set up Luca?" His eyes soften as well as his tone. The wolf has decided to take a fatherly approach.

I play my role of meek daughter. "Yes." I whisper it, ashamed to have betrayed a friend.

"Let's start from the beginning. The day of the attacks, what happened?"

We go over the whole story again. His questions are pointed, insightful, never intimidating. He's trying to put me at ease so I'll fess up. It's a test. It's always a test. My answers are detailed, consistent, never dishonest, though not always truthful.

Wolves can sense fear, through body language and their superior sense of smell. They do this through instinct. As agents, we are trained to read emotions and to suppress emotions within ourselves. Eventually it becomes instinct. Some of us, like both Wolfson and I, have better instincts to begin with than others.

My limbic system remains under my control the entire time. The Agency has taught me well.

Wolfson leans back in his chair, tipping the front legs up in a vulnerable position. "It truly is a remarkable story, Raine."

Story. A fiction.

I maintain eye contact, an act of aggression among canines, but one of truthfulness in humans. "I'm relieved to be moving on from that chapter of my life."

He stands, makes his way to my side of the desk, and sits down on the desktop in front of me. "Tell me, do you still have your necklace?"

My insides freeze. I quickly kick-start my body, but the damage has been done. My heartbeat is a whisper in my chest. The metal butterfly necklace adorned with a black oval sits in my backpack. All agents have a similar trinket. Wolfson, of course, knows this.

I reach into my bag and hold the metal butterfly out as an offering.

He holds up a hand. "Ah, ah, ah. No need. As a courtesy, I'm going to let you keep it. You'll probably want it soon." My skin prickles with fear. "What I'd like to know from you, as a courtesy, is when you really got your memory back?"

My heart thuds, thuds, thuds loudly in my ears. "I told you it happened when I was in the store, dyeing my hair."

I caress the strands of uneven blond hair, as if doing so will convince him I'm telling the truth.

The pretense of calm crashes down faster than a helicopter with a busted rotor. Sweat trickles down my back, and my hands are slick. I try to swallow but find my mouth cotton dry. Even as I fear that Wolfson is about to come in for the kill, I hold a small hope in my heart that he's buying my story.

"Sticking with that story. You're persistent, I'll give you that." He rubs his chin, and his eyes have a faraway look. "Before that, I saw you fight three agents with impressive skill and beat all but one." An abrupt change of topic, which makes it all the more unnerving. "According to you, you didn't have your memory back yet."

He was the leader of those fighters, the one who told me it was time to come home, the one I escaped from with Luca's help.

I remind myself if I believe it to be true, then it is.

"I didn't remember my past, but all my skills were beginning to come back right from the start." I attempt a cocky laugh. "Maybe if I'd had my full memory, I would have beaten the third fighter as well."

He maintains an unnerving silence, one I'm unable to

match. Maybe it's best if I go on the offensive.

"Will you tell me something?" I ask. "As a courtesy." I offer him a falsely sweet smile. "Why attack our own country?"

Wolfson isn't caught off-guard with my question, rather he looks eager. "I serve at the president's will. His wish is my command. He wants to go to war with China." I note the conspiracy theorist on Cheryl Dare's radio program had the correct motive for the attacks. "They are becoming too powerful as they move further into capitalism. They are a cyber force to be reckoned with, and so we, as a country, are reckoning with them."

I can't help myself and ask, "Did we have to kill so many people?"

"I like to be thorough. The president asked that certain other targets be taken out, people who didn't agree with the direction in which he was taking the country. That required a lot of collateral damage. As I said, I'm here at the will of the president."

Thorough and sadistic. Like Agent Killian, Wolfson is a man who likes to hurt people, only he has the power to do it on a terrifyingly large scale. All the same, his explanation reeks of bullshit. Does he have political aspirations? Does he hope setting all this up will propel him into office? It doesn't matter. I'm not here to know the why; I'm here to make my own why.

"Is that all you want to know, Raine?"

I nod, playing the meek card again.

"Good, but I'm not done asking you questions yet."

I prepare myself.

"Where were we?" he asks, though neither of us believes he lost track of his train of thought. "Oh right. You had fought off two agents and were beaten by the third. All without having regained your memories."

He puts his white teeth on display in a cruel smile, full on predator again.

"Here's my problem," he says, and my stomach drops. "I don't believe you. When you looked at me, you knew me, through the mask and all." The smile is wiped from his face, but his teeth are still showing. "I'll ask you one more time. When did you really get your memory back?"

My heart stops.

He knows. The truth, the real truth. He has known it the whole time. I don't know how, but I see it in the self-satisfied smirk of his lips, the narrow set of his evil eyes. And he's going to make me pay for it, but not just me, anyone and anything I've ever cared for. Because he can, because he likes to make people suffer.

49

Paralyzed by fear for the few I love, it's only now that I can finally admit that what I feel for them is love. A maddening buzzing drones on in my head. I really thought I could save Elijah and Imah, divert the Agency's attention to everything else I've done. It was a fool's dream.

It's time to come clean, for my friends' sakes. Resolve breaks through the buzzing noise, and silence paints the room a muted shade of death.

"I got my memory back in a hospital outside of Philadelphia, while I was traveling with the off-gridders. I left them that night to find Luca." That night, I remembered everything else about my life, except for the specifics of my escape from New York.

Wolfson, ever inscrutable, asks, "Why didn't you come back with me and the fighters? I offered to bring you home."

"I was scared and confused. My memories came rushing back, but there were still gaps. And seeing all those people hurt, hearing the numbers of how many died. Knowing the Agency—knowing I—was responsible for that." A sob breaks through, but I hiccup it down. "I had to figure some things out before I returned."

"Why come back at all then?" The tilt of his head

makes him look genuinely curious, but he's very good at coming off sincere when he's not.

Not that it matters; I'm done with all the over-analyzing bullshit. All my planning and scheming has failed to get me what I so desperately wanted.

"To keep them safe." Even now their names are too precious to say to Wolfson. "I remembered seeing her name, her real name—Amelia Crawford—on the terminate list."

It was a list I had come across before the attacks. A list of names that were meaningless to me...until one wasn't.

When my memory came back in the hospital, I remembered Amelia Crawford—doctor, environmentalist, candidate for Congress—being on that list. She was somehow a threat to Wolfson and the president. Her connection to me made her a bigger target.

"And that meant *he* was at risk, too." I press a finger to my lips, keeping his precious name and my feelings for him inside. "All I wanted was to keep them safe."

I sag into the uncomfortable wooden chair. My feet ache so badly, but it doesn't compare to the pain of a breaking heart. The truth is that when I lost my memories and was forced into a new life, I found something my old life never had.

Love. Hope.

Imah and Elijah gave me those gifts. Once I had those things in my life, I could never recover from them. Even when my wicked past came rushing back like a freight train without any brakes, those things stayed with me. My past life was filled with misery, abuse and neglect, bad choices and terrible deeds. Then, I was tossed in with people who believe in second chances, and they gave me permission to remake myself.

But as soon as I remembered who I was, I knew I would have to make amends for my past before I could become anything else. I had to protect the ones who gave me that second chance, as ill-conceived as it was.

Maybe all things being equal, the Agency would have let Imah live post attack, maybe not. It doesn't matter because I unwittingly put Elijah and Imah at risk the moment they met me. I further jeopardized them by becoming their friend. That erased any chance they had at a free pass from the Agency.

With a defeated sigh, I place my forehead in my hands, no longer able to hold up the weight of my transgressions. Did I really think my actions of these last few days could atone for a lifetime of wickedness? Had I really thought that if I could see Elijah and Imah to safety that I could be saved, too?

No.

But I had believed that I could save them, and I was willing to sacrifice my own life for theirs. Finally, through my relationships with Elijah and Imah, I understood what it was to have a meaningful life. I never cared much for my own life, but theirs were precious. All I wanted was to save them.

"You came back to keep them safe," Wolfson says, startling me to look up. His lips are cocked in a slight frown. Any trace of amusement is gone, the cold smirk replaced by lines of curiosity. "After all your training. You, one of my best soldiers, my Black Butterfly, came back to defy me. All to save a couple of worthless civilians. How is that possible?"

How do I explain a purposeful life to a man like Wolfson? A man who is probably contemplating how to best break me for daring to defy him. I contemplate telling him how a meaningful life is measured in Imah's gentle touch, and in her capable hands hard at work to heal a complete stranger. In Elijah's soft words about the stars, and in his voice telling a story to scared children. In Al's tears over his daughter, and in his booming laughter that is able to cut through grief.

But there is no way to explain that to a man like Wolfson.

Tears slide down my cheeks, and I clutch the butterfly necklace so tightly it breaks the rough skin of my hands. Wolfson has already broken me, but he's not finished. He needs to destroy all that I care about, when all I've wanted to do since waking up after the attacks was to be a good person, a decent human being like my friends.

Every single action I've taken since regaining my memory has been about keeping them safe. Infiltrating the Agency, working my way back into their trust, and finding out what they planned to do, was all about saving them. I used whoever I had to along the way. Zhang and Luca and Al—though I hope my most recent actions with Al have allowed him to escape. All so I could do everything I could to get Imah and Elijah off the Agency's radar.

Even if that meant sacrificing my own life. If I could keep them safe, that would have been the measure of my life.

I shake uncontrollably as I realize there's no language to explain these things to Wolfson. I had to experience them to understand, and he's so much further gone than I was. There is no saving my friends.

50

As I break down in sobs, Wolfson remains stuck on my act of defiance.

"Tell me, Raine." He clutches the sides of my heads in a vice grip. "How is it possible that my best soldier dares to defy my orders?"

"I don't know," I whisper. I'm so tired I could close my eyes right there and never wake up. I suspect soon enough a permanent sleep will come, but not before a torture worse than death befalls me.

"Tell me what really happened the day of the attacks," Wolfson barks. "I need to know how this happened."

I flinch away from his angry spittle, but he holds my head firmly in place.

"I don't know." My eyes scrunch close. Snot drips from my nose, but what would be the point of wiping it away.

He leans closer to my face, his breath hot on my nose. "Wrong answer."

I yank my head out of his grip. "I'm telling the truth! I don't remember!"

He leans back away from me, and I can breathe again.

"Let me tell you what *I* remember from that day. The Agency feed was abuzz with news of the attacks, all of which I ignored. We had to keep the reports going for those who weren't in-the-know. Things were starting to quiet down when an agent radios in that she's picked up two suspects. She was purposely assigned the pickup point, not knowing Zhang was going to be placed there by you. That was all part of the plan. What wasn't part of the plan was when she told me that Zhang wasn't alone. He was carrying a young woman. The agent immediately pegged you as a fellow agent."

Dread starts in my belly and stretches out its tendrils, suffocating me from the inside. Wolfson's version is a bad movie that I have to keep watching to see how it turns out.

He continues, "From her description, I immediately knew it was you, my Butterfly. And I was crushed with disappointment. How could my top recruit in her first big mission leave a link between the Agency and the worst terrorist attack in the history of the United States?"

He lets the question linger in the air, though I know he's not looking for an answer, not yet.

The cold calculation with which he speaks is shocking. Was I once so unfeeling as to speak that way about human lives? Of course, the answer is yes. I was trained to be that way, and I was very good at my job.

"My agent said you were in bad shape. Unconscious, bloody, and covered in soot. I ordered her to apprehend Zhang, remove your chip, and terminate you on the spot. She secured Zhang and removed your chip, but before she could complete the task, local authorities showed up. She fled the scene, hoping you'd perish from your wounds." Wolfson lets out a throaty laugh. "I think the attacks must have made everyone a little undisciplined. An agent abandoning a mission before it was complete, and my best agent left for dead because of her foolish actions."

His diatribe ends in quiet rage that makes his chest heave.

"No," I say. "I removed my tracking chip. I remember *I* did that."

Or did I. Imah said she found me with it, clutched in a bloody hand. She said nothing about how it was removed. I think back to what I actually remember and what was maybe filled in by my imagination.

"You removed it," Wolfson says incredulously. "How can you have done that yourself when my agent said she removed it? She didn't lie about that, I made sure of it."

I think hard about when Imah gave me the chip. I assumed I had been the one to do it. I wrack my brain, searching every memory, and there is none of me removing the chip.

My voice is a hoarse whisper when I say, "You're right. It wasn't me."

"Good. We're finally getting somewhere. Now tell me, Raine, what the hell happened the day of the attacks?"

I open my mouth, about to tell him once again that I don't remember, when a memory surfaces. It's so strong all my senses are engaged, paralyzing me in the recollection.

Out the window of Zhang's swanky hotel room, the eastern sky is ablaze with an orange sunrise that gives way to blue sky above. The color reflects off the Chrysler Building, shinier than I've ever seen it. A promise of a beautiful day.

Only, I know there will be nothing beautiful about today. In a few hours, the skyline of New York City will be unrecognizable.

I shower, using Zhang's toiletries as if they're my own, and dress in my Agent outfit: black pants, black tank top, and black long sleeve t-shirt, all made of top-of-the-line moisture wicking and temperature controlled material. He thinks it's my workout clothes, but they're my work clothes.

Before waking Zhang, I stare at his form lying prone on the bed. The sheet covers his bottom half, the smooth pale skin of his back perfect, free of any blemishes. I snake a finger down his spine and tickle him awake. He offers a small smile once the grogginess of sleep has worn off, the expression reserved but genuine.

In our own fucked up way, we've come to care for each other. At first, I preyed on his sense of righteousness, his savior complex.

I staged an assault and made sure he would witness it, counting on him to come to my rescue. And he played his part exactly as I needed him to do. Punching the guy right in the nose. Comforting me. Listening when I tearfully begged him not to call the cops.

He made sure I got home safe that night and found excuses to meet up with me after that. It was almost too easy to get close to him.

Somewhere along the way, though, I'd begun to admire him. Fierce in his business dealings but always calm. I'd never heard him yell, not once, in all of his intense meetings with his colleagues and opponents—meetings I pretended not to overhear once I was practically living with him in his hotel room. I'd also seen him video chat with his sister and nephew, his whole face lit up with joy.

With all this heavy in my mind, I kiss Zhang's cheek and take a good look at his kind face. "I'll see you in an hour for breakfast. You know the place, right?"

He touches my cheek tenderly. "I'll be there."

"Don't forget your briefcase. You have your big meeting right after."

He playfully pokes my nose. "I won't forget. Now go

before you run out of time for your workout."

I leave quickly before he sees the blush creeping up my neck. Out in the hallway, I take a few deep breaths. I wipe my face and marvel at the wetness of tears leaking from my eyes.

I crack my neck and mouth the Agency's mantra, "I am a soldier, I serve the Agency, it is my purpose."

It's like a switch has been turned, and I no longer care for Zhang, for anyone. I have a mission to complete.

I gasp as I realize that I'm actually in Wolfson's office, not Zhang's hotel room.

"Did you remember something important?" Wolfson's eyes are wide, his face expectant.

I give a full recount of my latest memory, further proof that I was committed to doing my job. Despite my brief feelings for Zhang, I left his room caring nothing for him or for the lives about to be destroyed. I was single-mindedly focused on the mission. The Black Butterfly, through and through, ice in her chest instead of a heart.

My vision glazes over as Wolfson peppers me with questions, asking for details about what happened after I left Zhang's apartment and what happened when the bombs started going off in the city. I keep telling him I don't know, that I can't remember that part. He hammers me with questions, like he can bang the memories out of my brain.

The only thing that allows me to keep repeating that I don't know is that this is distracting Wolfson from thinking of Elijah and Imah. I'm trying to figure out a way to use his obsession over what happened as a way to save them when the final memories hit me like an out of control 18-wheeler ready to pulverize anything in its path, which right now is me.

51

The first blast is louder than I expect. A trembling follows the boom and fades to stillness. Similar, small disturbances are happening throughout the city. The word "earthquake" echoes through the cafe where Zhang and I are having breakfast. No one wants to think it's terrorism, but the memory of 9/11 paints fear on the faces of the older patrons.

It's New York, not L.A., so no one knows what to do in the event of an earthquake, but instinct sends people ducking under tables and crouching in doorways. It doesn't matter what they do because this is not an earthquake. It's their worst fears come true.

A glance at my watch tells me I have 9 minutes, 24 seconds before the next, bigger set of bombs will hit. Shouts can be heard from the street, and sirens have already begun blaring. I tug on Zhang's arm and pull him out from his refuge under our small table.

"We have to go." I grab his briefcase off the floor and shove it at his chest. "Take this."

"That was just a tremor," he says. "There's probably a bigger one coming. We should stay inside and take cover."

"It's not an earthquake." I check my watch again. Thirty-four seconds have passed.

"How do you know that?" He's staring at me, head tilted sideways, like he's never seen me before.

And he's right; he's never seen the real me. So far, I've been playing the role of damsel in distress, so this take-charge woman must come as a surprise. I don't have the time or the need to explain my inconsistency in character.

"Doesn't matter." I guide him to the exit. "Trust me, you don't want to stay here."

Thankfully, he follows without question—he must trust me at least a little. I break into a jog as we head west, never letting go of Zhang's hand. I check to make sure he has his briefcase.

"Where are we going?" he gasps.

He's out of breath, while I'm not even sweating, and I'm wearing an armored vest, which is a lot heavier than it looks.

"Out of the city through the Holland Tunnel."

"What do you know that I don't?"

Instead of answering, I look at my watch. I should have another 2 minutes, 16 seconds before the next bomb, but a deafening explosion throws me off my feet. Losing my grip on Zhang, I land hard, hitting my head on the pavement. Debris and fire fall like snow.

I manage to get in a sitting position. My vision spins, and my ears ring. It takes me a minute to sift through the disorientation and remember why I'm here.

My mission: Get Zhang into the Holland Tunnel and out of N.Y.C. with the evidence in his briefcase. I must complete this mission.

I am a soldier.

I serve the Agency.

It is my purpose.

As I return to the present, the motto I recalled so

many times throughout my training and the day of my fatal mission sticks with me.

Wolfson's hand presses against my shoulder, propping me up against the back in the chair. Wolfson. His office. That's where I am. Not in New York City on the day of the attacks.

The final pieces of the puzzle are coming back, and I don't know if I'm ready for them. I barely suck in a breath before more memories come to me in terrifyingly vivid detail.

The world is falling apart around me, but all I care about is keeping sight of a Chinese businessman and his briefcase.

I must complete this mission.

Nothing else matters.

Not the smoke stinging my eyes, or the coughs shaking my body, or the sharp pounding in my head from a blow by...what? Pieces of crumbling concrete, an errant steel beam, or a chunk of flying wood? Who the hell knows? The head wound could be from anything. The city's in ruins. It's chaos, pure madness.

It certainly doesn't matter that my guilty conscience has kicked in. I'm not the one who remotely detonated the bombs, but I played my part, and I played it well.

I'm doing a shit job of it now. I've lost Zhang and his briefcase in this mess.

The head wound has knocked me on my ass, but it hasn't knocked the training instincts out of me. I shake my head, push down the guilt—tucking it deep into my gut—and blink away the dizziness.

I must complete my mission. I recite the Agency's motto in my head.

I am a soldier.

I serve the Agency.

It is my purpose.

Through the smoke, Zhang's pale face shines from across the street. He leaps over debris and dodges falling objects, his slim body gracefully navigating the terrain. His briefcase waggles up and down as he moves.

I sigh with relief, the act squeezing my lungs. It's like the time I squeezed a fellow recruit's windpipe the first week of training, earning me a "good work" from my trainer.

Only this time, I'm on the receiving end. Phlegm lodges in my throat and I cough it out with a bitter laugh. No time for such pleasant memories, not with Zhang back in my sight.

I push off from the dirty ground and chase after him. A fresh, screaming pain shoots through my skull with each step. My legs nearly give out, but I stay upright and scan the scene to find he's increased his distance from me.

Catching up with him is my only option.

Failure doesn't exist, because then I won't exist. Not that the Agency explicitly tells you that. But all through training, the implied threat of termination due to failure hangs over trainees like a storm cloud about to burst with acid rain.

A temporary break in the explosions exposes a snatch of brilliant blue sky. A beautiful day to ruin a country.

That's when I catch sight of the Empire State Building. Sparks shoot out of it, kaleidoscoping into fireworks of devastation. Slowly at first the top levels collapse, and then with alarming speed, the whole building comes down. The avalanche of debris plumes through the streets. The world shakes, and my whole body shakes along with it.

I cry out, but it's swallowed by the thunder of the

approaching cloud. Nothing in my training could prepare me for the sound of a city screaming and the silence as the plume envelopes it. My heart beats the rhythm of panic.

I hold my breath until I'm about to burst. With a deep inhale, ash coats the inside of my nose and mouth with a suffocating film. Covering my face with my sleeve, I stumble in the endless gray haze. Fear grips me like a second skin, one I thought I permanently shed when I left my mother's shitty trailer for the last time at the age of 16.

While waiting for the wave of dust to settle, I find a telephone pole and hug it close. It's like I'm a kid again and hiding under the bed from my mother's latest boyfriend, and the pole is my stuffed bunny. Has it only been two years since I left?

My neck snaps back with another explosion, this one below the city streets. Chaos. Confusion. Head spinning. Vision blurred. Nose and throat stinging.

I'm not a helpless kid anymore. I left the fear behind when I joined the Agency. They gave me purpose, focus, steel in my veins.

Fight past the panic. Remember the motto.

The ash and debris settle enough for me to see across the street, at least I think it is—or was—a street. A nearby subway station has blown up. Fire shoots up to street level and blocks my path. I sprint in the other direction.

My armored vest sits heavy on my body, weighing me down. I pull one arm loose, but the other side gets stuck on my hand, spinning me around. I lose all sense of direction. I can barely breathe, let alone think.

Where is Zhang?

The distinct red storefront of a bakery I know in SoHo infiltrates the snowing ash. The Holland Tunnel is tantalizingly close.

My legs pump fast with adrenaline, propelling me through the streets. It does nothing for my lungs, though, and I gasp for oxygen in the inferno that used to be a thriving metropolis.

A crash sounds behind me, but I keep moving toward the tunnel. A beam catches the back of my ankle, and I go down. Hot asphalt singes my skin as I hit the ground. I'm rewarded with a brief glimpse of Zhang, who promptly disappears into the gaping maw of the tunnel.

I barely register the thunk as a second beam smacks me in the head, the heavy weight pinning me down. The world, once ablaze in red, mottles black and gray. An effort to buck off the beam earns me another blow to the head.

My butterfly necklace, which might give me the escape I seek, presses into the crook of my neck, but I can't reach the sanctuary within.

As I fight to stay conscious, I scream, "Zhang!"

If he hears me, he'll come. He likes me far more than he should, and he's loyal to a fault. Doesn't matter now. I don't think he hears me.

I hope for a quick death. More than what I deserve, but better than what would happen if I survive. The Agency gave me a new life, remade me. They turned me from trailer-park trash into a soldier. It's my mission above all to serve the country, no matter if that means destroying a good part of it along the way.

They don't care about old fears or new ones. They care about results. The Agency doesn't deal in second chances.

And I've failed my most important mission.

My last gasps are of burning air. A butterfly, of all things, floats by. I twist to try and see it better, but there's only ash. I close my eyes, ready to succumb to the darkness.

But before I do, the crushing weight is lifted. Thin

arms wrap around me. As Zhang holds me, he offers me a strained smile, his perfect complexion stained with ash.

He places the briefcase on my chest. "Hold this, please."

Always polite, even as the world falls apart. He lifts me—20 pounds his superior—with little effort. Heat sears my exposed face, and the world's an orange fireball ready to burn us to bits. The intensity of the heat dissipates, and our surroundings darken to an all-encompassing black. We're in the tunnel.

Zhang's cries of "you're okay, you're okay" echo off the walls as he carried me through the darkness. Then the inside of my head goes as black as the tunnel.

After that, I woke up on the Jersey side of the Holland Tunnel, under the watchful eye of Elijah.

Hands—my own—clutch a face soaked with tears as I return to the present. The sting of fire lingers in my nose. Phantom ash coats my mouth.

That's it. That's everything. My life.

A sob rushes up my throat and comes out in an animal-like moan. I double over and let it all out. The pain of remembering. The guilt of what I've done. The fear of who will further suffer for my actions. My stupid life.

It's many minutes before the sobs quiet and I right myself. I wipe my eyes and take in my reflection in the mirror behind Wolfson's desk. Bruises color my face purple. My eyes are red and swollen. The physical manifestations of the pain are a mosquito bite compared to the sorrow in my heart.

Wolfson's gaze at my sorry self is part repulsed, part predatory.

"Tell me," he demands. "Tell me what you remember."

I do, reliving the terrible moment all over again, my voice a dull monotone.

When I'm done, Wolfson finally seems satisfied. The burning desire of needing to know what happened has left his eyes.

He pats my shoulder. "I'm sorry it has come to this. You were my bright star, the future of the Agency."

His back straightens, and he touches his ear piece. He's silent for a minute, listening intently.

"I'll be right there," he says to whoever is on the other end. To me he says, "I trust you'll keep while I'm gone."

"Wait," I say, though my throat is almost too dry for me to speak. "What happens now, to them?"

I dare not hope for myself, but a spark remains for Elijah and Imah.

"They die."

The two words almost defeat me, but I have one more last-ditch effort.

"What if we make a deal?" Wolfson raises his eyebrows, allowing me to continue. "Reinstate me. I'll be the most loyal agent you have, doing whatever you say, whenever you say it. Just allow Elijah and Imah to live a free life. As long as they are alive and safe, you have my undying allegiance to you and the Agency."

He steeples his hands as if considering my proposal. But I see in his cold, dark eyes that he's already decided. There is no hope.

"The simple truth is you can't be trusted." He pats my head in a condescending way. "I'll give you the courtesy of letting you choose."

I must have a blank look because Wolfson sighs and reaches for me. I shrink away, but he only pries the necklace from my grip. He points to the black oval that makes up the body of the butterfly. It's not a jewel as I first mistook it for when Imah gave it to me. It's a pill, a one-dose-will-take-away-all-your-pain kind of pill.

"It's this...or if you're perverse enough and want to watch your friends die, we can do it for you after they're gone. As I said, your choice."

He tucks the necklace back into my hands and cups them in his. A small sigh hisses from his lips. It might be mistaken for sadness, but I know it for what it is. He's lamenting the loss of a promising Agent, one who could have been very useful. To him, my life is lost potential, a resource to be abused until it's no longer useful.

I'm no longer useful.

He lets go of me and heads for the door. Without a backward glance—I'm already dead as far as he's concerned—he hits a button for the door to open. It slides shut behind him with barely a noise, but it feels like the world closing in on me.

I'm left alone with the butterfly of death. I run a finger along the sharp wings.

It would be so easy to pry the pill from the metal, touch it to my tongue, and swallow.

No more pain, no more regret, no more guilt.

The end.

But the spark of hope for my friends flares again in my chest. What if I escape? Maybe I can get Tanner to help. She'd never do it wittingly, but I might be able to trick her into something.

My brain is so tired and foggy, I can't think of a single scenario where I end up helping Elijah and Imah. The Agency is too powerful. My friends are as good as dead.

I touch the smooth pill to my mouth, feel the cool metal of the butterfly wings on my lips. The promise of oblivion is one swallow away.

Then, I realize Wolfson never asked me about Al. An oversight perhaps. Or maybe they don't know.

I gave Al the real evidence. In addition to the terminate list, the flash drive contained proof that the U.S.

government was behind the attacks. My instructions to him —written on his hand—kept him off the helicopter. I told him to drop the drive in Cheryl Dare's D.C. help box, the one where I also left a note for her, alerting her that proof would be coming. Proof that the conspiracy theorist she interviewed was, in fact, right.

I hope he heeded my final written words. "Run. Hide." I hope that no one realizes how important Al was to me, or if they do, it's already too late to find him.

And then I contemplate the pill.

53

I pop the pill out of the metal, leaving the necklace bodiless. A butterfly without a head or heart, only wings. Will those wings still be able to fly away? Or will they simply fall?

I set the pill and the necklace on Wolfson's desk. It's almost time.

Refusing to die as anything but my best self, I take off the fuzzy blue slippers and remove all but one layer of bandaging on my feet. I painfully pull on my boots. There's more pain as I lift my arms to pull on Elijah's sweatshirt over my sweaty and blood-stained tank top. Lastly, I position Al's hat on my head, adjust the rim just so.

I leave the necklace on the desk. I am no longer the Black Butterfly. The Agency no longer owns me.

Standing, I take the pill in hand, roll it between my fingertips.

I take one last look at myself in the mirror. Aside from the bruises, the person looking back at me could be any teenage girl. She looks ready to go to a ballgame or ready to head out on a hike with friends.

She looks ready to die.

I press the pill to my mouth. My lips part.

But before I swallow, a scraping sound from above startles me. The pill rolls of my tongue, falls to the floor, and rolls under the desk.

I brace myself and crouch, though my toes are on fire and pain stabs my ribs. A ceiling panel slides open and a head pops out of the opening.

My brain doesn't believe what my eyes take in. I must be hallucinating. I can't possibly be seeing this face. Boyish despite the strong jaw. Eyes the deep brown of the chocolate he shared with me. Hair dulled with dust but distinctly his.

"Raine," he says in a loud whisper.

I don't know how it's possible that Elijah has appeared before me in the ceiling. It's a magic trick of the highest order. Surely, Wolfson would have told me, rubbed it in my face, if the Agency already had Elijah and Imah in custody. And Elijah wouldn't be popping out of ceilings if they had caught him.

"I don't..." Words, my training, my brain, all logic fail me. "How?"

"Luca," Elijah says with a smile, and I want to slap his silly face. He's in the depths of Agency headquarters, where he's destined to be sentenced to death, and he's grinning like a school boy on picture day.

Wait? He said Luca. I'll kill that bitch myself for bringing Elijah here.

Heat rises all over my body, and I ball my hands into fists.

"Don't be mad," Elijah says. "She gave me schematics of the building. We can get out through the duct work."

I stare up at him. His head bobbing in the darkness is an untethered helium balloon.

"What are you talking about?" Then my senses kick

in, maybe I can warn him in time. "You have to get out of here. Go to Imah, get into hiding. The Agency—" There isn't time for a long explanation, and there is so much Elijah doesn't know. "The people I work for, they want you and Imah dead. She was supposed to die in the attacks. It was the government, the U.S. government who are behind the attacks, not China. You're in danger."

"I know the truth about the attacks." This turns me for a spin. "Luca told me and Imah everything. Who you really are, what you both did, what the government secretly did."

Luca lied to me as much as I did to her. I can't believe she told them the whole thing. We deserve each other and everything we've gotten. But Elijah and Imah don't deserve that same kind of treatment. I have to make Elijah understand the danger he's in.

"Then you know what the Agency is capable of. Please leave," I plead. "Find somewhere safe, far away from here."

He reaches his hand down to me. "Not without you."

"No! If I disappear that will only make the Agency go after you...me...us even harder."

"I'm not leaving without you." His mouth is set in a firm line.

He stretches his hand out more towards me. My gaze darts to the door. How long before Wolfson comes back?

"Elijah, I'm not coming with you. I'm not worth it." I look away from him to the floor where my pill is somewhere under the desk. "I'm no good for you, for anyone. I've done terrible things, killed people." My voice breaks, but I continue, "I'm not a butterfly. I'm a virus-infected rat. I destroy everything I touch."

"Listen, I know you've done bad things in the past. But the girl I know, she's not like that. She has a confident hand that never wavers when helping the injured. She closes her eyes and smiles for real when she tastes chocolate. Her lips are warm and sweet. She makes me laugh and think and feel things I've never felt before."

A tear drops from above and hits me in the face to mix with my own tears.

His hand is steady, reaching out to me. "The girl I know only knew one constellation before I showed her more. She sees serpents in the stars but looks for butterflies. Let me show you more, Raine. Let's find a butterfly in the sky together."

I choke on a sob and look up at him, the tears flowing freely. This must be a dream. But the pain of my many, many injuries tells me it's not.

The fear building in my chest tells me that Wolfson will be back any minute, and Elijah is here, ripe for the taking. I'm too weak to force him to go away. Just like I was weak with Al.

Elijah's bravery, his loyalty, his love is all I've ever wanted in life. I'm lucky to have had it for the briefest of moments. But what I had or what I want isn't important. His life has always been the most important thing.

"I'm not those things," I say. "You only thought I was."

"No, you are. And so much more, if you'd give yourself a chance. Besides, Imah and I have a much better chance of keeping safe from the Agency with your super spy skills on our side."

I laugh through my tears because he might be right.

When I came back to the Agency, I tucked away all hope for myself in an attempt to save those I love. Now that I've failed, maybe it's best for all of us if I stick with Elijah and Imah. And it will immediately get Elijah away from the wolf's den. It's the only argument that could ever make me consider going with him.

At least I think so until Elijah says, "I'll jump right out of here and turn myself in to that abomination of a human Wolfson if you don't come. You can knock me unconscious and hide me away. But the minute I wake up, I'll turn myself in. That's my promise to you, no matter what. Unless you come with me right now."

The quietest person in the room has spoken. Surely, that must count for something.

I have to do what I can to make sure he survives. Even if that means doing the one thing I really want to do for myself, which is to be with Elijah.

I stare at his earnest face, his hand—an offering of a second chance—hanging down, reaching for me. Ignoring the pain of my injuries, I step up onto the chair and grasp his hand. And I dare to feel it again.

Hope.

Also by Katie L. Carroll

Young Adult
Only Dark Edges
Elixir Bound
Elixir Saved

Middle Grade
Witch Test
Pirate Island

Picture Books
The Bedtime Knight
Mommy's Night Before Christmas
Daddy's 12 Days of Christmas
Grammy's Halloween Scare

Nonfiction
*Selfies From Mars: The True Story of
Mars Rover Opportunity*

About the Author

Award-winning author Katie L. Carroll always says she began writing at a very sad time in her life after her sister Kylene unexpectedly passed away. The truth is Katie has been writing her whole life, and it was only after Kylene's death that she realized she wanted to pursue writing for kids and teens as a career. Since then writing has taken her to many wonderful places—both real and imagined.

She has had many jobs in her lifetime, including newspaper deliverer, hardware store cashier, physical therapy assistant, and puzzle magazine editor. She works in Connecticut from her home that is filled with the love and laughter of her sons and husband. If you enjoyed *Black Butterfly*, be sure to write a review on your favorite book retail sites. For more about Katie and her books, including the second book in the Spy Agents series, visit her website at katielcarroll.com and subscribe to her author newsletter.

Find Katie L. Carroll online

Website: https://katielcarroll.com/
TikTok: @katielcarrollauthor
Twitter: @katielcarroll
Instagram: @katielcarrollauthor
Facebook: www.facebook.com/katielcarrollauthor/